D0115877

THE HOUND OF EARTH

By Vance Bourjaily

*

THE HOUND OF EARTH

Vance Bourjaily

The Dial Press New York

1964

Copyright © 1955 by Vance Bourjaily
All rights reserved.
Library of Congress Catalog Card Number: 54–13161

MANUFACTURED IN THE UNITED STATES OF AMERICA

813.54
B774h

THE HOUND OF EARTH

1-11-78 Baker & Taylor 5.21

PART ONE

1 In August, 1945, in a small Southern town which still cannot be named, a First Lieutenant Allerd Pennington, a young scientist, disappeared from an inconspicuous Army installation. This post, even now, is represented to the local public as a plant for overhauling aircraft instruments.

Pennington's disappearance, which took place on the same day that the explosion of the first atomic bomb at Hiroshima was announced, caused instant alarm at very high levels. Within minutes of the first report, a Federal investigation was begun; operatives, borrowing the uniforms of military policemen, used for a cover-story the Army's purported treatment of the matter as a routine AWOL case. At first Pennington was traced only as far as Birmingham, Alabama, where he had abandoned his car. A close watch was kept on the house where his wife and children still lived, however, and after several months a letter, addressed to the wife, was intercepted and examined before resealing and delivery. This letter was largely of a personal nature, revealing nothing of Pennington's connections if he had any, and was mostly concerned with urging the wife, in tender but restrained language, to try to proceed with her life as if Pennington were dead. The examiner, a somewhat overthoughtful man named Casper Usez, found it a moving letter; having had it transcribed and photographed, however, he felt it sound to note, in adding it to the file, that, since the reasons Pennington gave for his desertion were "mystical or pseudo-mystical," it was possible that "they

11

might have been designed to mislead an anticipated interception of this document."

Now that Pennington was known to be alive and not kidnapped, the full field investigation materials, gathered on the man before his assignment to the atomic energy project, were reassembled and completely rechecked; Usez did much of the re-interviewing himself. He concluded that he could rule out both ordinary desertion of family and ordinary desertion from the Army as credible explanations: Pennington had been remarkably well adjusted for a man of his temperament, fond of his wife and children who seemed wildly loyal to him; known in college as quiet, and in graduate school for a somewhat misanthropic turn of humor which, a friend of those days remarked, seemed entertaining for two reasons:

"First because what he said was often funny in itself; second because the character of bogey man which Al liked to assume was so completely at odds with the gentleness of his real character. You laughed out of affection; I never knew a man with less bogey in him."

His life, just prior to the disappearance, had been comfortable, his work record on the project brilliant; he had been due for separation from the Service in four more months, and there had been talk of offering him either a double promotion, if it could be obtained, or re-employment as a civilian at a salary increase of close to a hundred percent. Finally, the case was given a possibility of ominous importance by the careful judgment of the Manhattan Project Security Office, that Pennington could not have known the nature of what he was working on unless there were a hitherto unsuspected system of information linkage to which Pennington would then be the first and only clue. His function had been to design and supervise the construction of certain sorts of new laboratory devices which might, for all the men occupied with this part could tell, have been useful in any of several fields of physical research.

"It would, of course, be far easier for you," Pennington had written in the letter to his wife, "if I were actually dead. But I am not, and I do not want to cause you to wait, wondering, for seven years to have me legally declared so. Can you think of me

12

as a living suicide, spared the inelegant fuss of real dying, and of this as the final note? It is written with tremendous reluctance for the pain it will cause, in the hope that it will provide whatever power of attorney, grounds for divorce, and exoneration of yourself from complicity or foreknowledge may be necessary for you to work out a life for yourself and the children. This I know you have the courage to do. You will have recovered the car by now; we've something like $3000 in war bonds in the safety deposit box which will help, and a lawyer will tell you how to cash in or convert the insurance. Believe it if you can: I love you all. It is myself with whom I can no longer live."

Acting on information gathered from the postmark of this letter, from scrutiny of the paper and envelope, the investigators were able to find, in Cœur d'Alene, Idaho, a cigar store clerk who actually recalled selling Pennington the writing tablet from which the sheet was torn.

"Queer sort of fellow," the clerk said, insisting that there could be no mistaking the photograph. "Nice. Don't sell a tablet like that once a month after school starts. Joked with me. Wanted to know about cigars, what made a good one. Funny way of talking. Soft. Had to lean across the counter to hear good."

The investigation stopped with this clerk for a space of several years; later there was a lead in San Antonio, Texas, which was established as part of the case; but it did not develop beyond that city. Meanwhile, Usez scrutinized the connections of all the witnesses in the various atomic espionage cases which developed after the war, but neither Pennington nor even the installation at which he had worked were ever mentioned. The Bureau, having no way to determine the importance of the matter, directed Usez to keep it on Active classification; but after the San Antonio lead, there was nothing new for several more years. All that showed in the file were the date stamps which demonstrated that it had been withdrawn, reviewed, and replaced, at regular three month intervals. After five full years it was placed on Inactive, with the notation:

> Presumed deceased, or may have left US via Mexico. Circulars on this man have been distributed to agents in South and Central America.

On Christmas Eve, 195—, acting on new information, and with the cooperation of local authorities, the Bureau was able to effect the arrest of Pennington who was found, living under the name Al Barker, in a cavelike room in the Italian section of San Francisco. There was some confusion over the extent of his criminality, though most of this was not of Federal concern; two deaths, which occurred the same evening, were somehow related to him, as well as an assault, subornations to perjury, larceny, and other acts of misdemeanor, felony, and disturbance. The rather considerable publicity must have tended to obscure, in the minds of both the civilian jury and the court-martial which successively tried him, the precise kind of enmity for society which Pennington embodied. The connection between him and the deaths, for example, was made to appear much closer in newspaper accounts than could conceivably have been established legally. At neither proceeding did he take the stand, but seemed content to let his court-appointed attorneys plead him guilty to whatever indictments had been returned.

Perhaps he could not himself have fully described the events of the four weeks preceding the Christmas Eve arrest; certainly they could not have been properly set forth in legal terms, nor could any investigator's report, Usez would have agreed, correctly have named the haphazard apparatus of detection and discovery which had finally located this man.

Pennington's former wife, who had remarried, was notified of the arrest and presumably followed the case in the papers. Her interests were represented in court, but she took no personal action beyond applying to change the children's surname to that of her second husband (Bowie), and writing to Pennington, in prison, what the subwarden who censored it described as a scathing letter, after her ex-husband's confinement, on a variety of concurrent and consecutive sentences, in the Federal Penitentiary at Leavenworth, Kansas, on March 11, 195—.

Pennington is a well behaved, if uncommunicative, prisoner, who calls little attention to himself except that, once or twice a year, when an occasion permits, he applies for a transfer to the Federal Penitentiary at Alcatraz in San Francisco Bay. Since his reasons for requesting so disadvantageous a transfer seem too

14

bizarre to be taken seriously, and since he is extremely useful in the prison machine shop, the requests are regularly refused. "When you've done your time here, you'll get to California all right," the Warden tells him, a reminder that his several prison terms in that state have not yet even begun.

2 The fifth floor of Mainways Department Store, in San Francisco, November, 195—: with 31 more shopping days left before Christmas, the workmen had finished building Santaland. The store architect was back in his office, having won his last subtle quarrel with the display chief by finding a triumphantly-incomprehensible technical reason for refusing to alter the reflectors on certain colored lights; the display chief had marched his crew away, with staple guns and crepe paper, to do a window, but not without scoring a final, shrill point in his eternal wrangle with the traffic expert over the arrangement of merchandise. Now the traffic expert tried to unload the whole bitter accumulation of defeats on the buyer, Mr. Finn, who lost his temper and shouted the expert off the floor. The yearly expansion of the toy department, from two counters adjoining Boys' and Girls' Clothing to an entire half floor of its own, was physically complete.

Even during the days of construction, a little selling had gone on, beginning almost as soon as the stock was transferred upstairs. It had been done by a single clerk from the flying squad, by Dolly Klamath the service manager, by Mr. M'nerney the assistant buyer, and by Finn himself.

Mr. Finn, now finally in charge, was the store's gadget man, the buyer and seller of small, fast-turnover items, arranger of pitchman demonstrations in the Housewares Basement, of special purchase sales on the street floor; and, when one came along, he

16

had charge of temporary seasonal departments, presiding in yearly turn over Gifts for the June Bride, Mainways' Beach Club, Back to School supplies, and, climactically, Santaland. He was big, energetic and, on a superficial level, persuasive; his superiors did not think him very bright.

Perhaps he was not essentially Mainways' kind of man; Mainways was dedicated to solid, middle class, family goods and a steadily controlled volume. It did enormous business with low advertising, moderate charge accounts and heavy time payments. Mr. Finn might have been better suited by the heartier policies of one of the big Market Street bargain stores, uneasily booming now.

Finn's assistant, Ralph M'nerney, earnest graduate of the store's Executive Training Program and holder of an M.B.A. from Harvard, was more Mainways' type, and perhaps even more the sort who ought to have been working at a smooth-running luxury store like Perrini-Vetcho, across the street. The two had, in fact, been put together on the toy project this year in the hope, as expressed by the vice president in charge of personnel, that "between the two they'd make one competent sales executive."

So far, the experiment could not have been said to be working. M'nerney, a worrier and smoother-out, openly disliked selling. Finn, who loved to sell, was consequently a little contemptuous of his assistant, and had been leaving most of the pre-season customer dealings to M'nerney, insisting that he'd soon get a taste for it. This had been going on for almost two weeks, and the younger man's normally cautious temper was irritated to a point where he was beginning to criticize his superior at every petty opening.

"I wouldn't have yelled at Traffic that way, Hub," he said, standing just inside the tiny buyer's office which opened off in one corner.

"Oh, you wouldn't?" Finn said, at the door but not inside. He disliked the office; his business, he felt, was on the floor. "Well, now, tell me, Mac, what would you have done? Let the sonofabitch hang around from now till Christmas, moving doll potties from counter eight to counter seven and back again?"

"He might take it upstairs," M'nerney said. "He may be right on some of that stuff, you know."

17

"What's the difference?" Finn asked. "If we sell hard, they'll buy, if they have to climb on one another's backs to get it. Let's go out and look around."

"But suppose he complains?" Still M'nerney did not come out.

"For Christ's sake, Mac," Finn took a breath and finally stepped inside the office. "I'm a crude bastard. No college degree tatooed on my ass. I started as a pitchman fourteen years ago, and pitched my way up, and there've been complaints on me since the day I got my first promotion. But I'm still here, boy, you know why? Because upstairs they know old Hub moves the goods. Understand? The day I stop moving goods, I'll go and deserve to. Meanwhile I don't care how often who complains." He emphasized *who,* staring into M'nerney's eyes. "Old Hub will be filling their arms and emptying their pockets." He smiled now and squeezed his subordinate's shoulder. "That's what we're here for, eh boy? Filling arms and emptying pockets?"

M'nerney lowered his shoulder away from Finn's hand, and did not smile back.

Slightly hurt, Finn stepped to the door of the tiny office and looked out to see if there might not be a customer he could send his assistant to, but except for Dolly Klamath, working at the service desk, and the electric train demonstrator, the floor was empty. Even the flying squad clerk had gone. "All right, Mac," he said, turning back. "I'm sorry I yelled at Traffic. Now come on. Let's take a walk around and see what kind of circus we're going to have here this year."

"Wait, Hub. I wanted to ask you about this." M'nerney turned away and took the one step between door and desk.

"The optional commission thing?" Finn asked, somewhat bitterly, hugging the doorway. "You've won on that. They work on straight salary this year. Sparlin backed you up."

"He did?" M'nerney smiled at last. "It wasn't that. It's this." He picked up a completed employment application form, stamped HIRED, from the desk. "I was looking at this two-one-hundred for the stockroom man. Dolly and I didn't think much of him when we interviewed him, you know."

"I liked him," Finn said.

"I know you did, Hub. But did you look at his two-one-hundred? I mean, it wouldn't be too late to tell him no, since the form hasn't gone back in to Personnel. Couldn't we maybe get a regular man?"

Finn, whose interest in the hiring was impulsive and occasional, would ordinarily have let his assistant and the service manager do what they liked about it; but now he was being frustrated and M'nerney's caution annoyed him. "No," he said. "We couldn't maybe get a regular man. No, I haven't looked at his goddamn two-one-hundred. I've looked at the situation, though; have you? They gave us Dolly for service manager, didn't they? What more do you expect? Jesus Christ with ten years' experience to run the stockroom?"

"But, Hub, it's going to be terrific in there."

Mr. Finn controlled his impatience. "I hope so," he shouted jovially. "Boy, I hope so. A little terrific is what we need. I want to see those boys in the stockroom lathered to the balls, moving goods onto the floor. I want to see us moving stuff off so fast they can't keep up. I want to hear the registers ring like fire alarms. Look, on the big days, when it starts to catch fire, I'll let you take over the stockroom if you want; Dolly and I can handle the floor."

M'nerney refused the truce offer. "If it was up to me, I'd hold out for a regular stock man, even if it meant letting some other department have Dolly."

"That's just why it isn't up to you," Finn said, more sharply. "Dolly's essential. Do you realize that we won't have more than two regular clerks in the whole department? Maybe only one? The rest of them will all be temporaries, housewives and college kids and God knows who, in here making a little extra for Christmas. They're good people, Mac; they can write slips and hand stuff over the counter, but they can't sell. Not unless you hop them up and hop on them." His voice was gradually growing pleasant again. "See, Mac? I'll hop them up, Dolly will hop on them, and you keep the stock moving. Now come on."

"No, wait, Hub," M'nerney said, stubbornly. He came to the door and lowered his voice, for stock was the next room over. "I don't want to seem out of line, but if I'm going to boss this guy, I'd hate to make a mistake about him."

"You'd hate to make a mistake?" Finn cried. "Any hiring mistake made around here will be mine. Is that all right? What the

19

hell's the matter with you, Mac? Think this Barker's too smart for you?"

"Hold it down, Hub," M'nerney hissed. "He can probably hear. I'm just not . . . easy about him."

"Well, if that ain't the whore's hind leg," Finn said. "We get a guy in, Personnel likes him, he wants the job, talks okay, catches on quick . . ."

"That's what I mean," M'nerney whispered. "He's too quick. He doesn't act like a crate handler. He talks like a well educated man . . ."

"That's red hot coming from you," Finn said. "What's wrong with education all of a sudden?"

"You don't understand," M'nerney pressed on earnestly, refusing to take offense. "If he's been to college, why doesn't he say so? Look," and he pointed to a blank on the form which said: College: . . . It was not filled in. "And look at this: *Previous Employment: Itinerant labor, agricultural, etc. Where Employed: Midwest and West Coast. . . .*"

"That's why Personnel liked him," Finn said. "He's strong. A little, wiry, inexhaustible bastard, toss crates all day long, never know he's tired, know what I mean?"

"But he's no migrant laborer," M'nerney said. "He doesn't dress that way. He doesn't talk that way."

"Maybe he's one of those veterans wandering around," Finn suggested. "Who cares? What's the difference if he can do the job?"

"No, look. *Military Service* is blank, too." M'nerney was getting excited. "Say he's thirty. Where was he during the war? 4-F? In jail? This form can't be right. He must have done something. Maybe he's one of those world-owes-me-a-living guys, Hub. I don't like it."

"And I don't give a good raw, red rubber damn what you like," Finn shouted, turning crimson. "I want to get onto my goddamn floor. I've got a hundred things to do. Listen, M'nerney, I was dealing with men while you were still sucking titty. I talked to him; he's all right. Now stop your goddamn worrying and let's get off our silly asses. We're wearing out the old diplomas."

It was a favorite invention of Mr. Finn's, who had quit high school in his second year, that going to college consisted of lying jaybird naked in bed for four years, at the end of which time the old, doddering, white-haired Prexy and the goddamn Dean of Women came around and ceremoniously tatooed half a diploma in Latin on the hairless right buttock and the other half, in Greek, on the left.

Waiting in the stockroom for them to tell him where to start in, the man who called himself Al Barker had heard quite well the final part of the conversation. He smiled to himself over M'nerney's concern for his character.

—No, Gray Flannel Man—Barker silently replied—no, he did not think the world owed him a living. Didn't even think it owed him an apology. The world was quite without debts to Barker—

He caught sight of some lettering on top of the unopened cardboard packing case on which he was sitting, and hitched back to read it. The letters looked up at him from between his legs: ONE DOZEN KID SISTER SEWING MACHINES, the printing said, and and under it, stenciled: MIXED COLORS. Under that, printed in script: *The Little Lockstitch.*

Gray Flannel Man, Little Lockstitcher—he continued formally—the two-one-hundred was correct. He was a man without experience, without qualifications, without talents, without exception. And wasn't management getting scrupulous about applicants for jobs advertised to *MEN AND BOYS, 18–50, light work indoors, now to Christmas?* They were not to be suspicious of Barker. They would not find this light, indoor worker truculent. Of course, they might not find him particularly succulent, either.—

The room was piled with cartons, like the one he sat on, of toys and games; and the shelves around the walls were already loaded with individual sets and items, unpacked by some departed crew from similar cartons, and there were bins of wrapping paper to be issued to the wrapping desk, and balls of string long enough to fly a kite to the moon.

—He need not love Al, the Gray Lockstitcher of Flannels, nor yet he, Hub Hubbub, coach of the Mainways Mainsprings, locker-room Irishman; if Al closed his eyes, let no tongue lick his face, not Flannel's, nor the Coach's, nor indoor MEN AND BOYS', nor woman's, nor dog's, nor the combined tongues of one dozen kid sisters—

There was a little corridor off the rear of the room. He got up and walked over to it. Doors opened from either side, marked *Male Employees* and *Female Employees*.

—Might we assume a *Female Employee*, or her dozen kid sisters, who were clinging vines, and the poor things became unreasonably angry over some trifle? Wouldn't they be truculent succulents, though?—

"Look around, Al," Coach Finn had growled. "You're in charge here. We're going to give them a battle for their goddam Chrismas pennies, and you're the boy who'll keep the ammunition rolling."

And now here was Finn's voice again, crying, "Come on, Al. Let's take a look around the floor."

Al turned from the corridor. Finn and M'nerney were standing in the wide stockroom doorway, the buyer grinning, the assistant looking severe.

—The gentlemen were to have their way with Al. Nothing more could touch him except, some day, if his luck held, the light, indoor-working hand of death.—

"Let's go," he said, and walked out to join them.

Finn tapped his arm. "That's my office there," he said, pointing to a door behind them. "I hope you'll never find me in it. Whenever things are good, I'll be somewhere on the floor. Front of your door here," he indicated the area in which they were standing, "I'll probably put a demonstrator. Kind of block off the view. Some small item, you know, so he can hop out of the way when you come out with a handtruck."

Finn started off down the nearest aisle, going towards the other side. "Let's start at the elevators," he said. "Let's see it the way the customer will." M'nerney and Al followed, a step or two behind.

"Say, Barker, glad we're going to work together," M'nerney said, with his tight smile.

"Thank you," Al said.

"Be pretty busy for all of us, I imagine. Hope we work together well."

"I'm sure we will."

"Where are you from, Al?"

"The East."

"New York?"

"I've been there."

"Go to college back there?"

"Excuse me?"

"I said, where'd you go to college?"

Al shrugged. "School of soft knocks, I guess," he said. Then, as M'nerney's smile disappeared, he added: "Soft but incessant, like the rain."

There was a delayed return of the smile. "That's a good one," M'nerney said. They were walking past a counter of toy guns. M'nerney picked one up. "Pretty realistic, isn't it? Looks like a carbine." He offered the toy weapon to Al.

"A little light for elephants," Al murmured, accepting it. "About the right caliber for sibling hunts."

"Ever handle a carbine, Al?"

"I don't care much for guns."

Deliberately, M'nerney took the toy out of his hands. "All right, then, I'll take it. I want to know if you were in the Army?"

"I gathered that, Mr. M'nerney?"

"Well?"

"Does it make any difference?"

"A good Service record never hurts you in business."

"I suppose not."

There was a pause.

"So. Were you in the Army?"

"I don't really plan on a business career," Al said, as gently as he could.

"You're evading me, Barker."

"That's true."

"You're not hired yet, you know," M'nerney said. "Now listen to me. I'm going to ask you three questions, and I want straight, non-evasive answers. Answers that will check when I write letters to follow them up. Is that clear?"

Al smiled. "Quite clear," he said. Apparently this job was over already, and he had left Seattle only the week before.

"Very well. Who was your last employer? Where did you go to college? And from what draft board can I obtain information about your past and present status?" He was looking intently at the stock man, not realizing that they had come to the end of the counter and that Finn was waiting there for them.

"Mac," Finn said heavily. "You're going to get me sore in a minute."

"Wait. Listen to this, Hub."

"I'll ask the questions around here, Mac." For a moment they held each other's eyes. Then M'nerney looked sullenly away. "Very well," he said. "If that's the way you want it."

"That's the way I want it," Finn said. "I'll be the buyer. You be the assistant buyer. That's exactly the way I want it."

"Mr. M'nerney," Al said, a little alarmed at the situation. He realized now that M'nerney's suspicions were a reflection of tension between the assistant and Finn. "In applying for a temporary job for which one may be a little overqualified, isn't it best to list only the qualifications which apply?"

M'nerney hesitated, then accepted the chance to save dignity. "Of course," he said. "Quite right from your point of view. From ours, there's the matter of protecting the store."

"Surely," Al said. "There's a social security number on the form. I'm certain the Agency would welcome an inquiry about the account."

"All right, Barker. Thank you. I'll do that."

Al relaxed; it seemed unlikely the man would follow up, and even if he should, such an inquiry would probably take many more weeks than Al was likely to be in San Francisco. It amused him to wonder into whose accounts the half dozen security numbers he had improvised through the years might have paid small sums of cash. He was pleased to have found a way to avert M'nerney's hostility; he wanted an indoor job just now. He had become pretty weary of the elements picking apples in the Northwest, early in the fall, and a messenger job in Seattle which followed hadn't always been warm, dry work.

Apparently satisfied, M'nerney turned away.

"Where are you going?" Finn asked.

"I'm going to speak to Dolly," M'nerney said. "We ought to be getting some clerks up here from Personnel. I want to find out what the hold-up is. Is that all right?"

24

"That's all right, Mac," Finn said. "That's just fine. That's a nice thing for the assistant buyer to do. You go right ahead."

"All right, Mr. Finn, all right," M'nerney said, in a rising voice. "All right then." And he walked away stiffly, towards the service desk, where Dolly Klamath was making out time sheets.

"That guy," Finn said. "That miserable fuss-feather." He sighed. "See the girl?"

"Yes," Al said, looking across towards Miss Klamath, whose desk was a circular counter in the center of the floor. She was a severely well turned out brunette, with a small, square, chunkily feminine body and a perfectly made up, perfectly impassive face. Even trim, middle-sized M'nerney looked tall and loose beside her organized compactness.

"That's Dolly Klamath, the service manager."

"I know. I talked to her."

"Toughest girl you ever saw," Finn said. "Strict, that is. No nonsense. Best S.M. in the store. Wait'll you see the way she makes them hustle. Know what, Al?"

"What?"

"You a Catholic?"

"No, I'm not."

"I am," Finn said. He hesitated a moment. Then he said: "She's a very holy girl. She used to be a nun. Believe it? When she was a kid. Thought they were too easy going—that's what they say. Walked out. Listen, I'm a tough boy myself, Al, but that Dolly, she scares me."

"You've got a pretty tough staff," Al said.

"You worried about fuss-feather M'nerney? Don't take anything from him. You're in here working for me, Al. You're my boy. Okay?"

"Okay."

"Come on. Let's see the damn place."

At the elevator door they turned around and looked over the whole expanse, as the customers would see it—a bright expanse, crackling with color—green stripes spinning, red spangles flashing, white points dancing, and the air above the counters hot with whirling, grinning, spotlighted representations of toys, fifty times life-size. The only inaction was on the floor itself, still void of customers.

25

"Gift wrappings and Christmas cards right in front as they get off," Finn said. "Mac buys them; they're his responsibility. None of that stuff in your stockroom, so forget about it."

"I'll give it my personal inattention," Al murmured, smiling, as the buyer strode vigorously on ahead. Finn seemed the nice kind of man who hears nothing that's said to him unless it's shouted.

"Trains next," Finn went on, leading down the center aisle. He seemed to be fighting, now, to recover his sense of joy in this place, after the wrangling with M'nerney. "Company sets them up. We hired that actor kid in there to run them."

Two huge counter tops had been built across, and on the oval surface had been laid out an intricate pattern of tracks and tunnels, hills, bridges, signals, water towers, even a loading platform from which mechanical men would move tiny model milk cans onto flat cars.

Standing at intervals, all inactive now, were the trains—freights, passengers, streamliners; and in the open center, in a sort of mock cab, sat a slim young man with glasses wearing an engineer's coverall suit of striped ticking, a matching cap, a blue work shirt, and a bandana around his throat. He was reading *Gide's Journals* and hadn't heard them come up.

"Hey," Finn cried. "Hey, Casey Jones. Hey, Harris."

The young man dropped his book out of sight and looked up, flushing.

"This is Al Barker. Going to run the stockroom. Al, Hugh Harris."

"Hi," Al said.

Harris nodded nervously.

"Hey," Finn said, genially critical. "You weren't wearing glasses when we hired you. They kind of spoil the costume."

Harris snatched the glasses off. "I'm sorry," he stammered.

"Can you see to run the trains without them?" Finn boomed.

"Oh . . . yes, sir," Harris said, and, looking at the panel of switches in front of him, blindly pulled one down. Two trains began to back up and the mechanical men pulled milk cans off the flat cars.

"I didn't mean turn it on," Finn shouted, above the clatter. "I just wanted to know if you could see all right."

26

"Yes, sir," Harris cried, desperately pulling the switch down too far, so that the trains now went forward.

"No. No. The other switch. Stop them," Finn roared. Then: "Oh, hell, never mind . . ." and walked on, Al following, leaving Harris to control the mechanism by himself.

"Jesus, Al." Finn sighed. ". . . you know, boy, they don't buy trains the way they used to." They began to walk between counters of dolls and housekeeping toys. "Takes up a hell of a lot of space; got to have them but it's more show than sales." He stopped abruptly. "What do you think of the dolls?"

"They look fine."

"They've got some wonderful ones this year," Finn said, but without conviction. "Look at this." He picked up a rubbery baby, almost life size, wearing diapers. "Doesn't say *mama*, like they used to. Look, you put it over your shoulder, pat it on the back." He did so. The doll belched. "Give it water out of a bottle, pisses all over hell. Soaks the diapers . . . do you think that's right for kids, Al? Here, want to try?"

Al took the doll, put it over his shoulder, and patted it as Finn had. Again it belched.

"And look here," Finn began, trying to sound enthusiastic. "Here's an item." He picked up a neatly finished, white panel-truck model. "Diaper service truck. Stick diapers in the back, kid brother drives it over. Exchange money. Cute, huh? Fourteen-forty-nine."

He put it down, a little distastefully. Al put the doll down beside; the little eyes clacked shut, as Finn moved ahead.

"Pretty music boxes, anyway," Finn said. "And good building toys this year. And look, Al, look." They had come to the wheel goods section—bikes, doll carriages, scooters, pedal cars, and among them, like an emerald among bits of green glass, stood a rakish, boy-size roadster, buff hood, turquoise trim, with basket-woven wicker sides and wire wheels, a tortoise shell dashboard, a real speedometer and soft red pigskin covering the seat.

"Imported from England," Finn said, reverently. "A hundred-forty-five dollars wholesale. Isn't that a piece of merchandise?" He got down beside it on his knees. "Listen, Al." He pressed a button; a discreet horn sounded. "Battery-run. The lights work,

27

too. There's even a gear shift." He touched the lever. "God, isn't this a piece of merchandise?"

"It's what a child would dream of if he knew how," Al said.

Finn got up. He was smiling now. "Fine bikes this year," he said.

He strode on through the section to the far wall; they were at the rear of the store, now, straight across from the elevators. "Look how it sparkles."

Out from this rear wall had been built a gleaming snowbank, interrupted here and there by glass covered cutaways through which one could peer to see various sections of Santa Claus' workshop in operation. "And listen." They came to a doorway in the snowbank and Finn reached in and pulled a switch; there was a hum. Then the sounds of *Jingle Bells* blasted out from concealed speakers. "That livens things up, eh? Plays all day—*Jingle Bells, White Christmas, Hark the Herald, Little Town, Santa's Coming* —better, huh? Two elfs."

"Excuse me?" Al said.

"Two girls in green suits. Cute as hell. One keeps the kids in line to see Santa. The other hands out this stuff." He indicated a bin of prettily wrapped small toys. "Get them all from the same actors' agency. These girls, they always work with Evans. He's our Santa."

"Evans."

"You've got to have stuff like elfs and Santa to keep the kids busy while their parents buy."

Al smiled. "Saints to find work for idle hands."

They walked along the bank and came, in the far left corner of the floor to Santa's throne. It was built on a dais, and the dais backed by a great shell of blue crystalline snow, cutting off the corner in an arc, through which stars twinkled. Ropes of simulated evergreen criss-crossed the shell, and pink bulbs, set in as footlights, would make it glow.

"There's a place in back for the old guy to rest," Finn said. "Dolly'll get you a kid tomorrow to work with you; one of the things you've got to do is have the kid keep the old man's water pitcher filled. He sweats like a horse in the costume, gets thirsty as hell." They walked in behind the shell, and Al saw a chair, a little table with pitcher, glass and ashtray, and a cot. In this corner, behind the shell, with dirty windows overlooking Geary Street, was the only pool of natural illumination left on the floor; it was bright and plain, full of the dust and hardness of the real world back here after the blue and white and pink-lit world created by the decorators.

"Fifteen minutes out of every hour he rests," Finn said. "Hey, look." He led the way back to the outside of the shell, to the knee-high railing which would keep the children in line, and the gate which would swing across the line when the dais was empty. "Look, while he's gone." On the gate, a placard said: "SANTA CLAUS is out FEEDING HIS REINDEER! He will be back at ———" and beneath this hung a snowy-blue clock shape, a twelve-pointed star, with delicate gold hands and numbers.

"The elf sets it for when he'll be back," Finn said. "Isn't that a pretty clock?"

"A very pretty clock," Al agreed.

Finn filled his lungs. "There used to be a clown, too. Sat on the steps here while they'd wait. Gave them balloons. Rest of the time, he'd be all over the floor."

"Making jokes?"

"Well, he was a good sales closer on big stuff," Finn explained. "You know, 'Whoopee, look who's getting a bike, bike, bike; here's a balloon to make it an airplane. Whoopee.' They won't let me have him this year."

"Too bad."

"You know what I'd like some day, Al?" Finn looked out around the floor, still quietly sparkling. "Some day I'd like to have a real circus here. The whole floor. Every clerk in costume—doll girls dressed like dolls, cowboys selling Western suits, real Indians, a band to sell toy instruments and play music; merry-go-rounds; a dozen clowns. Three Santas working in shifts. A guy in a cage, cracking a whip to sell toy animals; maybe a real lion. Nurses for babies. Hundreds of kids playing, hundreds of parents buying . . . you know? A perfect circus."

"That would be . . . quite a thing," Al said.

"Afraid it won't be like that this year, but it'll be a nice little circus. Won't it, Al? A sweet little one ringer."

"It'll be a sweet little one ringer, Mr. Finn," Al said, gravely.

There was a pause, while Mr. Finn savored his vision. Then he said: "Look, Al, who you were, what you're doing here, where you worked before and whether you want to tell—that's your business. It's not my way to ask a man questions he doesn't want to answer. A man starts clean with me, and if he pitches in and carries his share of the load, that's all that counts."

"Thanks," Al said, reluctantly touched by the old phrases of confidence. He had decided that he could risk working through here to one paycheck, which he needed, and that, as things had gone, he'd better plan to leave as soon as he had it.

"Listen, Al. I don't want to seem like I said that just so's I could ask you to trade favors, but there's something you can do for me."

"All right," Al said.

"See, I'm mostly a salesman. Upstairs, they complain on me; they don't think I handle the people right, you know? Personnel problems. I don't know, Al. Christmas is the only time this comes up—you have a bunch of inexperienced people, and there's a lot of pressure. I had some personnel problems last year, like there was this kid went home and shot himself on his lunch hour. I don't see where it was my fault. I mean, I never yelled at this kid or anything; but that's what they mean. They say . . . well, I don't know, Al. I'm not a very tactful fellow, I guess. And Dolly, she's tough, too; strict . . . I thought maybe Mac could keep things straightened out, but he's fussy . . ."

"I understand," Al said.

"What I wanted to ask: you'll get to know these people pretty well. They go in and out of the stockroom to go to the johns; take their breaks there. You tell them old Finn's a lot of bark and no bite, will you, Al? I mean, if any of them get their feelings hurt . . . the world's funny, Al. Different. I don't think I used to upset people . . ."

"These are the funny days," Al said. "I'll tell them, Mr. Finn."

Inside the circular counter called the service desk, in the center of the floor, and keeping a wary eye on Finn and Al as they made their tour, M'nerney said to Dolly Klamath:

"Going to get us some clerks?"

M'nerney believed in coming straight to points, but he tried to temper the technique with enough calculated indirection so

30

that nothing unprepared for could be brought up. He was not, as Finn thought, a coward; but he was cautious and thorough. He had, in an uncowardly, cautious and thorough manner, been an excellent weapons company commander in the infantry, directing, on one occasion, late in the second war, the annihilation of half a company of Japanese foot soldiers who believed themselves safe in a cave. Mr. M'nerney's Filipino scouts having located a rear exit to the cave, the machine guns had been set up to fire across it; the mortars had angled shells accurately into the mouth and the gunners held their own fire until about half the Japs were crowding out behind; Mr. M'nerney had received the bronze star for conceiving and executing this operation, and had gone on to use his GI Bill privileges to good advantage and returned to the store, at which he had been only a junior accountant before the war, as a young man for whom there were high expectations.

"I'll be in Personnel in the morning and see what I can pick up," Dolly said. "And I've tried to select a few of the people from training classes today. After that, we'll just have to take what they send if we need any more."

"They send some pretty weird stuff," M'nerney said.

"Awful," Dolly agreed. "You should have seen the first thing they tried to pass in this morning. A drab little duck from Winnipeg, of all places, and guess where for? Dolls, they thought. I sent that one back in a hurry."

"What do you think of the stockroom man?"

"He seems all right."

"You talked to him?"

"Just to tell him where to punch in and leave his coat. Why? What's the matter?"

"I just tried to ask him a couple of routine questions," M'nerney said. "Seems a rather nice fellow, but he absolutely won't give you a straight answer. And you ought to see his two-one-hundred. Everything blank, or so vague it might as well be blank. Personnel gets very careless this time of year."

"They do get careless," Dolly said. "Have you told Finn?"

"Finn's hypnotized himself. The great judge of men. Won't hear a word against Barker."

"You think he's hiding something?"

"I think he'll bear watching, for a while at least," M'nerney said. "Do you suppose he might be an organizer?"

"No." Dolly shook her head. "They work smoothly. I've seen organizers. He'd have a story you couldn't shake with dynamite. Maybe he's a man who ran out on his family. Or a criminal. Or a Communist—aren't they supposed to be going underground?"

"I wonder," M'nerney said.

"We'll find out, Mac. Don't you worry. Little by little he'll crack, and I'll find a nice boy to work in the stockroom and listen and tell us what he has to say. You've never been on a sales floor during the Christmas rush?"

M'nerney shook his head.

"He'll crack," Dolly repeated. "They all do."

3 At the conclusion of the Pennington-Barker case, there were hardly any effects found, either in the man's room or on his person, which were of any use to Casper Usez in making his final summaries—either the brief, official summary which simply marked the case closed, or the personal one which the investigator wrote to try to order his private thoughts.

There were, however, two documents, undated letters addressed, as Usez noted drily, to "an unidentified, plural nonrecipient." One of these had clearly been written on the night of Barker's finding a job in San Francisco.

Besides the letters there were only three things worth reproducing: two photographs and a photostat of a discharge. The photographs were: (1) an old snapshot of Pennington-Barker's wife and children, and (2) a small, studio portrait of a girl in Texas. Pennington's instructions had been to destroy them: "I am too sentimental a man to want to keep these," he had said.

The discharge photostat he admitted having bought in a bar in Saint Louis, early in his flight; it had been made from an original issued to a colored infantryman named Alvin Barker. Such documents were easily obtained just after the war, extra sets of them being made covertly, for sale on the side, by the side-street studios to which veterans took them for copying.

They were so common, in fact, that, when he was finally able to confront his man, Usez remarked that Pennington, who mentioned that the price was ten dollars, had been considerably over-

33

charged; the going rate, Usez said, had been two to three dollars. The ex-scientist replied that he had made little use of the document, but that it was nevertheless well worth almost any price to have carried, for so many years, a paper identifying him as a negro without ever having had the discrepancy discovered.

The text of the first of the two letters follows:

"My dears—

"I have been walking this week in San Francisco, have covered much of the city and talked to some of its people; I have found a room which is called an apartment, and I have found a job.

"What a strange, inverted place the United States of America is—a nation of overlings and underseers. Its business firms and manufacturers and institutions—all the regiments into which its people form themselves for the selling and production of the goods and services they live by—are like units in an endless army: within them, it often appears that those whose misfortune it is to sink upwards in the system are squeezed unconscious, between the wringers of privilege and responsibility, and that life and breath are allowed only to those who, through diligence, succeed in rising to the bottom.

"San Francisco, in this country, is a city more ordinary than it thinks. At its center, as is true of some part of many cities, there is a small area which preserves much of the flavor of the town from which the city grew; this area, bounded by the now disused Ferry Building, the shore line of the Bay as far as an Army post called the Presidio, a line drawn to the next apex of the triangle which is an eminence called Twin Peaks, and thence down Market Street and the skid-row line of Mission—this area is somewhat different in tradition and aspect from the typical. Within the triangle there are quite dramatic residential hills, some shrewdly commercialized foreign sections, civic buildings, theaters, a slum or two, and the financial and shopping districts. Only a small fraction of the population can live within this triangle, however; a somewhat larger fraction, perhaps, finds work here. Outside of it, with a few spot exceptions, are the usual American urban miles of row housing, uninteresting streets and avenues, zoos and parks of average charm, and, farther out, suburbs, and housing developments, and highways whose roadside clutter seems very

34

like that along the highways of Long Island or Illinois. But these geographical charms and similarities are not the measure of its averageness. It is, rather, San Francisco's people who are living the regular lives of Americans of this decade—their alarm clocks direct them to rise and pine; the men spend their strength to tiredness, towards death, to earn their daily beds; the women drudge wryly at their household beauties; and in the streets can be heard the voices of children at bay.

"There must be reckoned, among the costs of war, the damage to the nervous tone of a people. The fighting of two major and two minor wars in half a century has drained our national character incalculably; from expansiveness, drive, naive generosity and unquestioning warmth we have been reduced to pettiness, caution, meanness and suspicion. We live ungraciously, turn conservative; we have surrendered our bravery and freedom for what is, finally, nothing more than the right to over-eat. Somehow, as the new half-century gets underway, everything which seemed to have gone wrong temporarily because of the wars is staying wrong; we have no more resilience. Those who are not venal are a little crazy; America has become the land of the fee and the home of the rave.

"So the resistance of the people of San Francisco, like that of people all over the nation, is low, these years of nervousness and suspicion; the well-dressed man wears a cluster of nerve ends in his buttonhole, and his mate affects the ganglion corsage. Yet why do I speak of particular wars? Perhaps this depletion is produced in any people who reach that point of historical sophistication at which they realize that war is not a plural word, that there is only one war which may be resumed at any time; that this war is, simultaneously, the chief use to which our human energies are put and a great, eternally sardonic and hopelessly impractical joke of which we are somehow the helpless, self-appointed butts —an awful joke, this only war, the one fought steadily with only occasional exhausted pauses since Cain and Abel, the war between you and me."

Though it was unsigned, and apparently not even intended for mailing, there was no question in Usez' mind that, even in someone else's handwriting, he would have known it for a document of Pennington's authorship, both from the perverse mannerisms of expression and from the nihilism of its viewpoint. And Usez thought he knew, too, to whom it was addressed. It was not, he felt quite certain, something the writer had meant for his wife and children; not only would it have been out of character for the fugitive, but Usez knew the wife and children and they were not the sort for whom it might have been designed. Frances Pennington (now Frances Bowie) was an appealing young woman and, under that, a practical one, bright-natured and sound; her children were merry and unspoiled.

He remembered her particularly for the first thing she had said when he called on her at her own request: "I want to co-operate. I want to help you if I can, because I want to help Al. I love my husband, Mr. Usez; he has been under pressure, and I cannot be surprised and only a little bitter if his mind has slipped. I'll tell you all I can. Do you know that he loves music? Hates having his hair cut? Never gains weight? It may sound girlish, Mr. Usez, but I want you to bring him back because I think I can nurse him . . ."

Nor did Usez think it likely that the unidentified addressees of the San Francisco letters were among the people in Texas with whom his man had been briefly friendly; these he discarded intuitively, in favor of a theory he thought to be more adequate.

He imagined Pennington-Barker as sitting in that barren, underheated room with the two beds and no chair, sitting on one of the beds, then, with the evening silent around him, saddened but unsurprised by his reaction to a city which had been a sort of goal to reach, profoundly lonely and with the sensation of being profoundly aware—so starved, perhaps, for human warmth, for Pennington was a warm man for all the nihilism, that the starvation was precisely analogous to starvation for food, and the sensation of clear vision produced by it also analogous to a like sensation in the man who fasts. In this condition, having, as Usez considered, enough of a touch of his own peculiar kind of paranoia, Pennington-Barker might—might he not?—have been reaching out for a sort of universal communication, so that in saying "My dears . . ." he was trying to get through, somehow, to all his countrymen and countrywomen, to put himself in a general, transcendent touch which would take the place of the simple, individual touch so soberly self-denied.

This, at least, was Usez' feeling about the phrase, and he allowed it to become a certainty, for, as occasionally happened in a case involving his imagination, he felt identified with Pennington, felt that in the best moments of the investigation he could think with Pennington's mind, criticizing it simultaneously with his own. It was this faculty which made Usez a valuable investigator at times; it was also this quality which stood forever in the way of his promotion to the ranks of Bureau command.

4 The following day, temporary clerks began to come onto the floor of the toy department; there were three in the morning who had spent the previous afternoon in training classes, learning how to write sales slips and operate cash registers. By noon there were four more, graduates of the morning classes, and before the department closed in the evening the complement was nearly complete. At no time during the day, however, had the customers outnumbered them: though decorations and advertising had been out since two weeks before Thanksgiving, it was still the looking season; no one could tell when the buying season would start.

The new clerks were a fair-looking crew, ranging from a middle-aged salesman, whom Finn happily put into construction toys, to a nineteen-year-old who spent much of the day *sur les pointes* at the housekeeping toy counter, to show she was a ballet student; there was a tall, tanned, dumb girl, just smart enough to wind Swiss music boxes and show them; a bleached, intellectual-faced one who was put to demonstrating the little sewing machines; a splendid, wavy haired Armenian boy with an air of boundless enterprise, who was given charge of the wheel goods department; and half a dozen other reasonably attractive housewives and students and unexplained people. And Dolly Klamath had found her stockroom boy.

She had, in fact, managed to control the selection of something over half of the temporary personnel, by stationing herself

38

with an interviewer in the employment office to compete with other aggressive Service Managers for the better-looking applicants. This was permitted during the large scale Christmas hiring to speed things up. One was supposed, of course, to take people in turn, but the system to provide that this be handled fairly was somewhat simple-minded and easy to beat.

Spotting a pretty, self-possessed young woman, a well turned out man with the right touch of confidence, someone who looked as if he or she could sell, one simply moved alongside as the applicant filled out the first form and said:

"Don't bother to take it back to the application clerk. When you finish, come directly to booth three."

Since the application clerk's function was only to see that the forms were correctly and legibly filled out, and then to assign interviewers in order, this device avoided the hazards of rotation; it could be used with little risk, especially if the clerk was intimidated and the interviewer someone for whom you had done favors.

In this way, Dolly was able to beat Clara Fence, service manager in Home Furnishings, to a real prize—the wavy haired Armenian; she lost a stylish redhead to furs, but found a kitten faced blonde, pertly got-up, less of a kid than she looked, perhaps, but very suitable for dolls.

By now it was best to stay out in the room where applicants were received, picking off the better ones almost as they walked in; Dolly, took the blonde to the booth, and waited only long enough to hear Ellen open the interview:

"Sit down. May I have your form?" A pause while Ellen studied it. "Is it Miss Malinkrodt or Mrs.?"

"Miss. But I'm married. Is it all right to use my maiden name?"

"Of course."

The blonde's voice was all right, husky and polite; Dolly nodded her approval to Ellen over Miss Maiden Name's head, and went back to the other room. It was eleven by then, and she had begun to wonder if the right boy would ever show up.

Of the dozen who had appeared, answering the ads for messengers, stock boys and part-time clerks, none had looked suitable. Some had fuzz on their faces or pimples; others looked too weak

39

for lifting; one might have done but he wore what Dolly considered an untrustworthy haircut.

When her boy had finally appeared, he was almost like the picture in her mind—a tall, clear skinned, well knit kid with brown hair, cut short; he looked both bright and naïve. Dolly caught him before he could even get to the information desk.

"Name, please?" she said.

"Tom Vanderbeck, Miss."

"What sort of job did you wish?"

"Well, I hoped I might be able to work after school, in the afternoons. They let us out early if we have Christmas jobs."

"I see."

"In about three weeks, I could work all day."

"I think that's the usual arrangement with school boys, Tom," Dolly said. He was both deferential and eager. "Let's pick up an application form and I'll help you fill it in."

Clara Fence was making off, right in front of her, with a fine, ruddy, older man in a pin-stripe suit, but this kid was more important. Very likely, Dolly thought, the older man drank.

"Do you think I could sell sporting goods, Miss?" the boy asked.

"Miss Klamath."

"Miss Klamath. I play football and basketball."

"I'm sorry, Tom," she picked up a form from the information desk. "There are no sales jobs open for part-time workers. But we have an opening in the fifth floor stockroom." They were standing at the counter now, Dolly rapidly filling in the form for him.

"Age?"

"Eighteen."

"Address?"

He lived out in the avenues. Quickly she completed the interviewing, filling in *Stockboy* under POSITION APPLIED FOR, and wrote Ellen Palazzo's initials in the square for INTERVIEWER.

"Now sign this, Tom. It says you swear that all the answers are true."

He hesitated a moment. Then he took the pen and signed it.

"Come along." She walked him over to Ellen's booth. "Here's

40

a copy of the two-one-hundred, Ell," she said. "I've done the interview. Tom's my new stockboy."

"Okay," Ellen said. "He doesn't have to go to class."

"Good. Will there be many more coming in?"

"Not this morning," Ellen told him. "Just what's there now. They've let in all we can handle before lunch."

"Nothing I can use," Dolly said. "Think I could get away with coming back this afternoon?"

Ellen shook her head.

"Fence was bitching . . ." she tried to swallow the word; even those with whom she was friendly were inclined to watch their language around Dolly. ". . . complaining, about the Armenian. I don't think it would work. What do you need?"

"Three more demonstrators," Dolly said. "A couple of girls for the wrapping desk. Colored'll do. And I need another girl for dolls. I had to send one back yesterday. Little Canadian export. Find me a knockout, will you?"

Ellen winked.

"Come on, Tom," Dolly said. When they got to the floor she kept him by the elevator. She had no particular preference as between Finn and M'nerney, both of whom she disliked, but if there were going to be a contest, she had decided to throw in with M'nerney. "Tom," she said, seriously, and held the pause a moment. "Tom. You know the rule, don't you?"

"What Miss Klamath?"

"You know how old you're supposed to be to work in the store."

"The ad said eighteen," Tom said in a small voice.

"And how old are you really?"

"Seventeen," he admitted.

Dolly held his eyes sternly for a moment; then she nodded. "It's all right with me, Tom. You could probably go to jail for giving the wrong answer on that form and signing it, but I'm not going to tell. And I won't let anybody ask. If anybody does ask, tell them to see me. All right?"

"Thanks, Miss Klamath," Tom said. "You're swell."

"I had a reason for picking you, Tom. I let half a dozen boys go by this morning before I picked you out."

"You did?"

41

"I needed somebody smart and responsible, whatever his age."

"Well, I . . ." He blushed. "I noticed you came right over to me."

"That's right," Dolly nodded. "I'm glad you notice things. Tom, in a minute I'm going to take you to meet Mr. Finn. He's the buyer, the boss here. Then he'll take you to the stockroom, and you will meet a man named Al Barker. You'll be working with Barker. Tom, you know what a Communist is."

Tom nodded.

"We don't know whether Barker's one or not. We don't know what he is. But we've been told to watch him by . . . I'd better not tell you who by. We must find out all we can about him. Where he's from, what he's done . . . any clue may help. Do you understand?"

Tom nodded earnestly.

"Mr. M'nerney, the assistant buyer and I know about this. Mr. Finn doesn't. Mr. Finn is a very nice man, Tom, and he's under great strain this time of year. We want to protect him from this Barker business. So whatever you find out, tell me. Don't bother Mr. Finn. If I'm not around, and it's something special, tell Mr. M'nerney. The three of us will talk it over from time to time. Okay?"

"Okay, Miss Klamath," Tom said, finding this considerably more exciting than selling basketballs though, at the same time, it made him a little uneasy.

"You're not to say anything about it. Not at home. Not even to your friends at school."

"All right, Miss Klamath," Tom said. "I'll . . . help. I'll keep my eyes open, and remember everything."

Finn was in sight, over by the service desk, talking to someone. Feeling pleasantly that she had done a solid morning's work, Dolly led Tom up to him.

"Tom Vanderbeck to work in the stockroom, Mr. Finn," she announced. "Here's our buyer, Tom."

Finn wheeled around. "Fine, fine," he boomed. "Not buyer, son. Seller. Finn the seller. And here's one for you, Dolly. A little girl for dolls. Wants to make a great record with us and stay on after Christmas, don't you, dear?"

He pushed her forward. It was the plain girl from Winnipeg.

"But. But I talked to you yesterday," Dolly got out, as Finn threw an arm around the boy's shoulder and swept him away.

"I know," the girl squeaked firmly, in her shrill, British Canadian soprano. "But when I went to Personnel, they sent me back again, Miss Klamath. They said there must have been a misunderstanding."

Tom said to Mr. Finn, as they approached the stockroom: "Is this where Mr. . . . . Barker is?"

"That's right," Mr. Finn said. "Al's my boy. You're going to be my number two boy, right, Tom?"

"I guess so," Tom said. They had come to a doorway. He felt the kind of uneasy excitement he had just before the kickoff in a football game.

"Hey, Al," Finn called showing Tom in. "Got a boy here for you."

Tom was prepared for ugliness, or, perhaps, for movie-villain good looks. But the man who turned to greet them, sitting on a packing case, had neither; he was short and seemed woefully slight, with a round, beard-shadowed face, thin dark hair, and comically bushy eyebrows, the furrows deep between them. Bones showed through his clothing, and his brown eyes were sad, except that now he said, in a grave, sweetly ironic voice,

"You held out for the best boy they had, Mr. Finn. I can see," and the sadness went out of the eyes as he smiled at Tom.

It was like having the kickoff go to someone on the other side of the field.

Barker got up. He moved suddenly, not ungracefully, with a fluid abruptness, like a well managed puppet.

"He's a very fine one, Mr. Finn. What shall we call this boy?"

"Tom Vanderbeck," Finn said, laughing and poking Tom in the ribs. "An A-number one model boy. Two arms, two legs, and a good strong back."

"Fine," Al said.

They heard the phone begin to ring in the office. "Mac?" Finn called. No one answered. "Hell, he's upstairs," Finn said. "Just a sec, Al. Be right back." And he hurried out.

"What shall I do, Mr. Barker?" Tom asked, cautiously.

"Well," Al said. "First take off your jacket and get into one of

43

these nice gray cotton ones. Then, as far as I know, you lift one box from any pile back onto the box behind it, forming a sort of chair," he gestured, "and sit down." After a moment he added, "There's no such person as Mr. Barker, Tom. Better make it Al."

"All right," Tom said, eyeing him. "Isn't there really anything to do?" He went into the short corridor to change coats.

"That's the sort of question I used to raise myself," Al said. "Raised quite a number of them, but they didn't turn out awfully well when they grew up."

Mr. Finn came bustling back. "Right, Al," he said. He saw Tom changing. "That's it, son. Climb into the old shop-coat. When I was your age, all the clerks wore them, too. Good thing. Gave a man a chance to use his arms. You checked the way they set up your stockroom, Al?"

"Yes, I have," Al said.

"Seem all right? This is going to be your home, here. You boys are going to eat, drink and breathe stock."

"We could use a little more space in the center," Al said. "If it's all right to shift things."

"Sure," said Finn. "Shove 'em back. Push 'em away." And he set his big, black-shod foot against a carton of boy-sized tool kits (*The Carpenters' Mate*), and slid it off towards one wall. "Let's go."

"Well," Al said, smiling. "What I had in mind was something a little fancier. Tom and I can work it out."

"Tell me, tell me," Finn cried. "I'm the goddamndest crate smasher around. What do you want, Al?"

"I thought . . . well, just because it might give us something to do . . . we might rearrange the stuff so that it follows the floor plan of the counters. Later on, when things are needed at two or three places at once, we'd be able to load up for counters that are side by side without walking all over the stockroom."

"Great," Finn said. "That's—here I thought you were sitting on your tail, wearing off the old diploma, and all the time you were thinking that one up. It's great, Al. Listen, I'll send M'nerney in. He's got a copy of the floor plan."

"That's all right," Al said. "I think I have it pretty well in mind."

"No, no. I'll get Mac. And send you in some guys to help. It's a big job, and things are damn quiet on the floor." He went to the door. "Don't start it by yourselves," he said. "Listen, you show Tom around the floor till Mac gets back. Give him the tour."

"All right," Al said. "Come on, Tom."

"What's he mean about wearing off the diploma?" Tom said.

"It's a joke of Mr. Finn's," Al said. "You grow to love them as you get to know them."

"Well, do you . . . do you have a diploma from somewhere? I don't mean on your. But . . ."

"That seems to be everybody's favorite question this week," Al said. "Tom, I'm so old I can't remember." They were moving between the counters.

"You talk practically like a professor."

"Right on the nose, Tom. I am a professor. A professor of ignorance. I profess my ignorance of everything. But," he pointed a finger at Tom, "let him who would study ignorance learn it elsewhere; let him cool his tattooed tail in a punchbowl of his own devising." He grinned. "I have no ignorance to share, Tom; may I speak freely to you?"

"Sure," Tom said.

"A little ignorance is a dangerous thing," Al said, solemnly. "Show me a really ignorant man like Mr. Finn, I'll show you a philosopher. Show me a slightly ignorant one, like Mr. M'nerney, and I must warn you to beware."

Tom laughed. "I like Mr. Finn."

"So do I, Tom," Al said. "Look at the trains."

They finished walking around the floor, and stood before Santa's throne, looking at the empty seat.

"He starts next week," Al said. "You must water the old gentleman."

"How do I do that?" Tom asked.

Al led him to the dingy little corner behind the shell where the pitcher and table were.

"I'll take care of it in the mornings," Al said. "Until you start working full days."

A child's voice asked: "Are you Santa Claus?" They turned. A scowling little girl about six had followed them around behind the shell.

"He's not here today," Al said.

"Will he be here tomorrow?"

"Not till next week, I'm afraid."

"I got something for him," the little girl said. She opened her hand; it was a woman's hat pin. "I'm gonna see if his belly's real, or if it's just balloons."

"That should be interesting," Al said.

"Jimmy says it's just balloons."

"Jimmy's a rat," Al said.

Out in front a woman's voice called: "Joan. Joannie."

"That's my mother," the little girl said. "I'm sposed to be looking at dolls." She darted past them and out from behind the shell on the other side. Following out the same way, Tom and Al saw Joan caught by her mother, a young woman many months gone into a new pregnancy. She held the child by both wrists so that the hands were turned back and opened, her swollen stomach, protruding through the folds of her unbuttoned overcoat, getting in the way as they struggled.

"Joan. What are you doing with that pin? Where did you get the pin?" The hat-pin now lay near them on the floor where Joan had been forced to drop it.

"I only want to stick in the stomach," the little girl protested, butting at her mother's midriff. "I just want to stick the balloon."

Horror showed on the pregnant woman's face. "Joan," she gasped. "Joan. You go and see those dolls, do you hear me?" And she released the wrists and cracked her daughter across the ear. In tears, Joan ran off towards the center of the floor. The mother herself began to weep, grimly, and to walk slowly away.

"Oh, wait," Al said, and started to go after her. "It was Santa Claus' stomach . . ."

A voice interrupted them. "Hey, Barker." Around a counter came the bristling form of Mr. M'nerney, bound, today, in blue serge. "Why aren't you in the stockroom?"

"Just a moment, sir," Al said, but the woman, unhearing, turning into an aisle, went slowly out of sight. Al stopped. "Showing Tom around the floor," he said. "This is Tom Vanderbeck."

"Well, let's go," M'nerney said. "Got some work to do. I want some space cleared in the center of that stockroom, and I want those cases rearranged to follow the floor plan of the counters."

"Fine," Al said.

"Work's what they pay us for, men," M'nerney said. "Come

along. I have two of the clerks to help with the lifting. We should be able to finish by closing time."

They followed him back to the stockroom. A tall young man with a great deal of wavy black hair, heavy eyebrows, and black eyes was waiting for them. He was slim and quite conspicuously handsome.

"This is Harold Gullakian," M'nerney said. "Of wheel goods."

"That means bike salesman, fellows," Gullakian said. "Hi." He had a strong, insinuating voice.

"Let's go," M'nerney ordered.

"We'd better get the ones from behind out first," Al said, softly.

"Let's get the ones from behind out first, Gullakian," M'nerney commanded.

"Okay, Mac," Gullakian replied. M'nerney winced. "Glad to help out, Mac."

They began to move the cases; after a minute or two they were joined by Hugh Harris, the willowy boy from electric trains.

"Don't suppose one of these has a nice, collapsible bed in it, do you?" Gullakian said.

"What's the matter? Tired already?" M'nerney scoffed. Then, to Tom. "No. If you're going to clear that shelf, get the stepladder. You mustn't risk injury."

"Tired?" Gullakian cried. "No sirree, Mac. I mean for those doll babies out there. Those lovely, bedable doll babies."

There was the awkward silence which follows an unwelcome familiarity. M'nerney clearly had to force himself to answer. "I'm afraid you'll have to, uh, do that sort of thing on your own time."

Irrepressibly, Gullakian answered with a burst of song:

"My time is their time,
Let's have a good time . . ."

A few minutes later M'nerney, having seen them well started, told Al to take charge and left. The atmosphere became easier. They worked rhythmically and hard, clearing aisles, piling goods along them.

Gullakian, who was lifting with Harris, was talking to him about San Francisco.

"It's the milk and honey town," he said, as they heaved a carton

47

of plastic building toys to the top of another like it. "You take the milk, Hugh. I'll take the honeys."

"A lot of people say it's the most European city in America," Harris replied, in his slightly effeminate way, stopping to rest. "I just believe I'd take New Orleans."

"San Francisco every time," Gullakian said. "Right, Al?"

"Oh, no, you'd love New Orleans," Harris assured him. "It's so relaxed and continental."

"Nuts," Gullakian said. "What's more continental than good old right here?"

"Can you settle it, Al?" Hugh Harris asked. "Have you been to New Orleans?"

"I had a job there once as a bale of cotton," Al said, working on the shelves. "All day long they used to tote me. If you weren't careful, they'd tote you right onto a barge."

"Seriously, though, which is the most continental place in America?"

"West Virginia," Al said. They laughed. "What are you laughing at? Have you ever been to West Virginia?"

"God forbid," Harris said.

"It's a real piece of old Europe." Al began repacking some erector sets. "Agricultural and industrial peonage. Absentee ownership of bad soil and played out mines. Decadent peasantry . . ."

"Boy, Al, you're the greatest kidder alive," Gullakian cried, getting up to go to work again. "Isn't he, Hugh? Doesn't he beat them all?"

"He sure does," Hugh said, peering out the door. "Oh, oh. M'nerney's coming back."

"That's a good guy, that Mac," Gullakian said. "Right, Al?"

"He's all right if you like good guys."

"What's wrong with good guys?"

"I'll take a son of a bitch every time," Al said. "They're more continental."

Later, when they were nearly done, Gullakian began to whistle. He whistled beautifully.

—What?—Al wondered.—A theme from a violin concerto. Which one? Something modern—

"Alban Berg," he said, half-aloud.

"You know it?" Gullakian cried.

"Know what?"

"The Berg Concerto."

"No."

"Didn't you say Alban Berg?"

"No," Al said. "Like a bird. I said you whistled like a bird."

Gullakian began again.

"Stop the damn whistling," M'nerney shouted from across the room, finally exasperated; tired, perhaps, of being a good guy.

Riding home on the trolley, Tom Vanderbeck got out his pocket notebook and, when the car stopped for a traffic light, he wrote at the top of a fresh sheet:

AL BARKER

About thirty. Brown hair. Brown eyes. Five six(?). 140 pounds(?). Doesn't answer questions about self. Been to Europe, New Orleans, West Virginia (or was joking). Takes Kearney Bus from work. Likes music(?). Cannot tell when he's serious.

He studied it a moment. Then he put the notebook away in his pocket and opened his paper to the sports page.

Riding home on the bus, Al hummed the parts he could remember of the Berg concerto over to himself until he was tired of it. Then he tried to think of the day's work, but he was tired of that without starting. Finally, he gave in to recollection.

5 —He had always been all crippled up with music, he thought, and in the damp climate of Seattle the themes twinged and the chords ached and the compositions groaned in his head. —And if, in our only native phrase for wishing, he had a million dollars, he would buy a conservatory in a warm old building on a hill. He would bring to it wise teachers and brilliant students and performers on native instruments from all over the world. And all would teach each other and, patient with his shallow talent, would teach him too. And he would live in a plain room and study the instruments, one after another, with nothing required of him except that he be quiet and friendly, so that when an instrument was lacking in an orchestra, or a chamber group, or even, sometimes, a quartet, they could say: "Let's get Al. His tone is not good, and his technique mechanical, but he can play the notes correctly and he doesn't play very loud." And year after year they would play together, and students would be replaced by other students, and he would never think of anything. And would there be a girl— a violist with copper hair, or a wise and lovely Hindu dancer? He thought not.

—The room in Seattle was as plain as the room in the dream, and he had a flute and a zither and a bent trombone. There were instruction books for flute and trombone—he had never found one for the zither—and he practiced for hours every night. At first the cheap, beginners' books, the easy methods, were the wise teachers, and he was all the brilliant students; since it was the only room he had ever found where he could freely play, he had visited the pawnshops to collect his orchestra. The room was by a furnace in a business building, the building where the messenger service was, a building empty at night, and it was his, that room, for mopping the halls and keeping the antique furnace up at night.

—And one afternoon he had found Mrs. Mudarrik.

—Was it raining? Yes, it was raining as he climbed the steep hill past a dozen frame houses to 217 Saleebo. And there she was, a heavy, dark old lady with a face like stone, to answer the door and receive the remittance, sent every week by messenger, himself now, from her son in the city. Al was a bonded messenger, even, working under whose bond? How did the Service manage it, transferring bonds under the same name from one derelict to the next, because the renewal fee was less than a new application? Certainly the clients of Ace Messenger Service had not looked as if they could afford to be particular, and though he'd never tried to learn, it seemed that the errands they ran might well have had to do with numbers, sometimes, as well as with assignations, though surely most were no more than the cheap delivery of harmless parcels.

—"Mrs. Mudarrik, you were not happy, living in your wooden house and your stone pride, accepting the twenty-seven dollars every week from furtive hands, not the hands of your unvisiting son but the grimy hands of Ace Messengers, *we deliver the goods;* when you saw my hands were clean and my way unmenacing, you asked me in, lonely and proud, for a cup of harsh tea, because it was raining." Yes, it was raining; that checked out.

—And while she made the tea, he cautiously lifted the keyboard-cover of the old, old Knabe grand, as old as its owner or older, and looked at the time-burnt ivories, the color of her face, and she came up behind him unexpectedly, and said sternly, in the slow, proud, foreign voice: "Do you want to play?"

—It had been two years since the last piano; and he sat down and played, very badly, and she said: "When you play Bach, you must hold your hands at high from the keyboard to make striking hard."

—Then she said: "I have taught piano for thirty years," but·her

51

pride did not let her say that the last lessons had been given, the last squirming child released, ten years before.

—It was several weeks before he learned that she was totally deaf.

—Several weeks, for he volunteered for the trips up the hill after that, which were not popular trips, until finally, speaking to her back one day, he realized that she could not hear at all, only read lips, could not hear him play, only watched the fingers and knew, she knew so well the patterns, what he was playing and when he had made a mistake. What a repertoire her eyes must have had, all the student pieces in the world, and many more, learned as a girl for some unimaginable concert circuit in Russian Turkestan. Did she play Moscow and St. Petersburg? Her pride would not allow her to play for him, though he heard her one evening, arriving earlier than expected and standing on the porch, heard her playing Rachmaninov with a man's strength and unaware of her errors so that the rhythm was never interrupted.

—He went how often? Every night. For once he had the perfect audience, perfectly attentive, perfectly unforgiving of mechanical errors, perfectly unaware of his essential mediocrity. The flute, trombone and zither stayed in their cases. Perhaps they were still there, in near the furnace, gathering coal dust. For her son could not but suspect an Ace Messenger, grimy deliverer of furtive goods, visiting the mother's house night after night, with its flashy icons hanging against stained wallpaper, its handsome samovar on the dining-room card table, its lovely antique rugs on the warped, tongue-and-groove pine flooring. He, the son, Mudarrik, Mr. Goods, spoke to He the Deliverer, the Ace of Ace, Al's boss, who spoke to Al, who ignored the warning until it was delivered again, stony and proud, by Mrs. Mudarrik herself, in conjunction with the word police. So that he realized and she realized that no human world could permit so perverse a relationship as one involving a young man playing the piano, endlessly and badly, while a deaf old woman, still believing her infirmity a secret, watched so shrewdly she could hear the music with her eyes.

—So he didn't play the last movement of the Kreutzer sonata, though he was two thirds of the way to his only perfect performance, his only chance ever to perform perfectly, to the satisfaction of a closely discriminating and informed audience, the whole of a great work, for not once, in the first movements, had his fingers gone wrong or had she criticized his tempi; so that she was hearing, in her drumless ears, and he was playing, with his talentless hands, great music; but he did not finish it, in spite of their profound excitement, nor did he finish the cup of harsh tea she had offered while she rested, but put down the cup and, not knowing what else to do, he kissed a dark old hand; and she had amazed him. She had held the hand with which he took hers, and slowly raised his hand to her own stony lips. He had gone into the wet night and left that city.

6 On Thursday, with twenty-four more shopping days left before Christmas, there were two new temporary employees to complete the staff, and one of them was quite extraordinary. There were already goodlooking women in the department—Dolores Hughes, the tanned music box demonstrator, was big and soft and girlish; the ballet student was cute; Betty, the drawn girl operating sewing-machines, had a pinched elegance; and Sally Malinkrodt, of dolls, while neither girlish nor elegant, had an uncompromising upper-bourgeois sexiness which made her, at first, quite easily the queen *pro tem* in general appeal. But this new, unsmiling girl was beautiful.

She had been put in front of the door of the stockroom, discontentedly blowing bubbles—a tawny haired, tawny skinned, golden eyed, petulant beauty, required to stand, ceaselessly frowning, dipping a little circlet of chrome into some chemical mixture which she must then raise to her lovely, pouting lips and blow through, making the bubbles stream out into the strident air of the toy department. Though all the clerks passed her at one time or another during the morning, she spoke to no one; they commented to Al:

"Jesus," Gullakian said, but with more awe than admiration.

"Young woman makes an excellent appearance," M'nerney observed. "I do wish she'd smile."

Sally Malinkrodt summed up: "Who's Miss van Soap Bubble?" she asked.

54

"The new demonstrator?"

Sally nodded. "The one who simply must keep the bubbles blowing, daddy dear, though she's ill with boredom."

"I thought she looked a little desperate," Al said.

"In that dress? Three hundred bucks at Perrini-Vetcho, I'll bet anything."

Al shrugged.

"Look," Sally said. "I know men are stupid about clothes. But there aren't many kinds of plain black dress around this store. There's business-girl-basic-black, and you might get that confused with college-girl-grown-up; and there's whore-at-a-funeral, which you might conceivably mistake for this sort of number," she indicated her own piquante chiffon. "Of course, you'd be wrong. This is more suburban-cocktail-and-light-necking. But take a look at van Soap Bubble's dress, Al; even a man should be able to tell there's nothing else like it around here."

"Okay," Al said. "A girl can't be desperate in a three hundred dollar dress."

"If I looked like her," Sally said. "I wouldn't feel desperate in a twenty-four-dollar shroud."

The first words anybody heard the new girl say were to the kid, Tom Vanderbeck, when he arrived for his half day's work at two; he had stopped short, unthinkingly, to stare at her, and she had caught him with her rueful golden eyes.

"This stuff's going to make me sick," she said, evidently referring to the bubble mixture. "I thought I was going to sell dolls."

Feeling as if he'd been accused, Tom hurried past into the stockroom without replying and reported what she'd said to Al.

"At least she spoke," Al said. "I'd been considering the possibility that she was a beautiful and mysterious mute."

They began to open a carton of Big Chief Bow and Arrow Sets, with Animal Targets.

"Why do you suppose she talked to me?" Tom wondered.

"Maybe I've passed the Barker curse along to you," Al suggested. "You know, I believe that's it. From now on, you're doomed to walk the earth, listening to the intimate confessions of people you never saw before. Want to get the handtruck?"

As they began to pile Big Chiefs onto the frame of the handtruck, Al went on: "Men will stop you on the street and mutter that they have been irregular in their bookkeeping. Strange women sitting next to you on busses will say: 'Young man, I have never had an orgasm in all my married life.' "

"Do people really tell you stuff like that?" Tom asked.

"They won't any longer," Al said. "I've passed it on to you."

"No kidding, did any lady ever . . . ?"

"I have been a walking compendium of the hopes and anxieties of total strangers," Al said. "People have always spoken to me about themselves; it's because I have a dishonest face and am a poor listener. But no longer. You've got the old Barker curse now, boy. I can relax."

"I won't," Tom said.

"Won't what?"

"Talk about myself."

"Fine." Al grinned at him. "Good. Then neither shall I. These things are wanted at the Games counter, if you're feeling restless."

Tom wheeled the sets across the floor, and made space for them on the counter which was unattended. There seemed to be a few customers around today, but the pace of buying and selling was still lazy. As he was finishing the arrangement, Gullakian, the man who had helped in the stockroom, came over and greeted him:

"Hiya Tom."

"Hi," Tom said. "What do you think of the new girl?"

"Forget it," Gullakian said. "That stuff's too fancy. Even if you had the price and the pedigree, it'd be like trying to eat a pound of caviar all by yourself."

"I didn't mean I . . ."

"She won't even smile," Gullakian said. "And if she did, it would freeze you colder than when she doesn't."

"Did you try to talk to her?"

"I stay away from that type," Gullakian said. "Not my kind of music."

As if cued by the word, a blare of music filled the toy department. The Christmas records had been turned on.

Gullakian cowered theatrically, as if he were a dog threatened by a stick.

"We're going to get awfully tired of those records, aren't we?" Tom said.

"I'm a composer," Gullakian half-shouted, raising his voice louder than was actually necessary to make it heard above the sound of *White Christmas*. "Noises like that hurt me. Physically."

Tom nodded sympathetically.

"I write serious music," Gullakian yelled into his ear. "I'm working on a concerto."

"Really?" Tom backed off.

"It's for violin and orchestra," Gullakian said. Someone turned the volume down a little. "I've been studying violin and piano. You know what I want to study?"

Tom shook his head.

"Conducting. You can't really be a composer unless you know conducting."

"Maybe you can get transferred to a different department," Tom suggested.

"Why should I?"

"Well, I mean you could get away from hearing those records."

"I need the money," Gullakian said. "I've got to eat."

Tom didn't quite follow the logic, but he nodded.

"I'd better go back," he said.

He noticed on the way that the bubble-girl didn't seem to like the records either.

In the stockroom, Al had moved back to the sewing machine cartons, and was now sitting high on the stack. His feet were drawn up level with his bottom, and his arms were wrapped around his knees.

He smiled at Tom. "How's things?" he asked.

"Okay." Tom smiled back. "What are you doing?"

"Wishing I had a tail," Al said. "Have you ever seen a monkey rock himself? He sits about like this, with his tail pulled up between his legs for a rocker, and hangs onto it with both hands, hauling himself back and forth."

"I've never seen that," Tom said. "Is there anything else to do, Al?"

"Not a thing."

"Al?"

"What?"

57

"You know Gullakian?"

"The one who helped us yesterday? The one who wants to offer such delicious experiences to the lady clerks?"

"Yes."

"What about him?"

"Did you know he was a composer?"

"I guess I should have."

"He just told me."

"The curse is working now. By tomorrow you'll have learned that there isn't a clerk or stockroom boy among us. We're composers, executives, poets, dare-devil pilots, female explorers. Or the gay younger daughters of titled English families, masquerading as housemaids for a lark. The toy clerk masks come off long before midnight, don't they?"

"They sure do," Tom nodded. "Al, I'm going to be a doctor."

"That's a good thing to be," Al said.

"There's this girl Elaine. We're both going to Stanford, next year, and take pre-med. Maybe we'll do research together. She's even better in science than I am, except chemistry."

"Doctors study a lot of chemistry," Al said.

"I don't really know if I love her or not . . ." He cut himself short. "I'm talking about myself, aren't I?"

"Don't let it worry you," Al said.

Not thinking about Miss Klamath but really wanting to know, Tom asked: "What are you, Al? Under the mask?"

Al shrugged. "A monkey without a tail, I guess," he said, wondering what the boy would think if he could explain how precisely this was true.

As he started to get up, someone—a girl—burst in through the doorway from the department, bumped into a packing case, caught herself, started to run again towards the corridor off which the restrooms opened, stopped, and began to throw up on the floor.

It was the new girl, the beautiful one.

Bent over, with one hand holding on to the top brace of the now-empty handtruck, she gasped, straightened a little, said,

"I'm sorry . . .," leaned over, and started to retch again.

Al crossed to her quickly, put a hand on her back, and supported her shoulder with the other.

"It doesn't matter," he said, quietly. "Be as sick as you like."

At last she stopped retching, and leaned back against him, shuddering.

"It's okay," Al kept saying. "It's okay."

In another moment she had stopped shuddering and begun to cry, softly. "I couldn't make it. I couldn't . . ."

"Take it easy," Al said. "It's okay." He led her around the wetness on the floor, patting her shoulder. "Don't even think about it. Don't think about it."

He pushed her gently along to the little corridor, to the door which said *Female Employees*, opened it for her, and closed it after her as she went in. Then he returned to the stockroom; he and Tom got some newspaper and began to clean up. They found rags, and gave the floor a quick wiping; then Tom got the mop and mopped, and it was done.

They didn't say anything—looked at each other, smiled, and shook their heads. When the girl came back they were both sitting again on the sewing machine boxes. Al got up to meet her.

"Feel better?" he asked, leading her over and finding a box for her. She nodded, very tense. "I'm awfully sorry."

Al patted her shoulder. "Please forget it."

"Yes," Tom said.

"Let's look at you," Al said, studying her face. He went over to the water-cooler, wet his handkerchief, and filled a paper cup.

He sponged her temples with the handkerchief, and gave her the water to drink.

"Where's your purse?" he asked.

"In the first drawer of the counter."

"Get the lady some lipstick," he said to Tom.

Tom went out, and returned in a moment with the purse which he handed to Al. Al opened it, got out lipstick and a compact, and handed them to her.

"You'd better do this yourself," he said. "Of course, I'm very good at it, but I try to keep it secret."

She smiled, finally, and started to make up her face.

When she finished, she sighed and said, "Thank you so much . . ."

"My name is Al, and this is Tom."

"Thanks Tom. And Al. I'm Nickie Moore." She gave her head

a shake to get the hair back into place. It was gold-brown hair, heavy and shiny, and the color was beginning to come back into her skin. "I'm very grateful and very sorry."

"Don't be silly," Al said. "When did chivalry ever cost less? Look at Tom glow—he'll have a sense of noble achievement for the rest of the week. Want some more water?"

"Please."

Al filled the cup for her again.

"It was that soap bubble stuff," she said. "It smells so awful."

"And you didn't have much lunch," Al said. "And blowing all the time makes people dizzy, anyway."

"I hate to be a weakling," she said. "But I don't think I can stand it."

"What the hell," Al said. "Walk out. Don't even say goodbye."

"I don't know what to do," she said.

"There's a nurse upstairs," Al said. "And a place to lie down in her office. Why don't you go up there for a while? Maybe you'll feel more like it."

"Oh, I'd get sick again," Nickie said. "I know I would. But I've got to have the job." She started to sob.

"No crying," Al said, sharply. She looked up, startled. He smiled at her and winked. She smiled back. "Look, maybe we can fix this up. Mainways has a day's training invested in you that they don't want to lose."

She kept looking at him.

"Do you think you could stand blowing soap bubbles for just ten more minutes?"

"I think so."

"Okay. Go do it. And look happy. Look radiant. Blow the gayest soap bubbles of the season. Put a kiss in every one and blow it to the man you love. Can you do it?"

She laughed. She jumped up, beginning to look radiant already. "Sure."

As soon as she had left the stock room, Al said to Tom: "They'll probably fire her, but let's try. Go find Finn and tell him I've got to see him in the stockroom right away."

"Shouldn't we report it to Miss Klamath?"

"Tom, you're a monster. No. Let's take this right to that lovable old raftsman, Hubbleberry Finn."

"You want me to bring him here?"

"That's it, Thomas. That's it. Tell the bastard King Al has sent for him."

Tom went out, spotted Mr. Finn over at the electric train display, and caught him just as he was walking away from it.

"Al wants to see you in the stockroom, Mr. Finn," Tom said. "He says it's important."

"It is, eh?" Finn said. "What's it all about?"

"I don't know, sir," Tom said.

"Damn," said Mr. Finn. "Okay."

With Tom following, he strode towards the stockroom. As they passed her, there was Nickie, sparkling now, head thrown back, shoulders squared, waist slim and lithe, looking as if she were newly delighted with each little iridescent globe she sailed into the air around her. There wasn't a man alive, Tom thought, who could have walked by without admiring her.

They went into the stockroom; Al was standing, waiting for them, looking particularly sober.

"What's it all about, Al?" Finn asked.

"You know that girl out there blowing bubbles?"

"What about her?"

"Lovely kid, isn't she?"

"Sure, Al. So what, for Christ's sake?"

"So this," Al said. "Ten minutes ago she was retching her guts out on the floor of the stockroom." He pointed to the wet patch on the floor.

"She was?"

Al nodded. "Retching her guts out. She doesn't want anybody to know. That's why I sent for you. She'd have known I was telling you if she'd seen us together on the floor."

"I guess that's right," Finn said. "What's wrong with her?"

"There's something in that soapbubble mixture that makes her sick," Al said. "I tried to persuade her to complain, but she won't. She's a brave little girl, Mr. Finn."

Finn grunted.

"You can see her out there now, putting on the best demonstration in the whole department. Why? Because she doesn't want to let the store down. She doesn't want to let you down, Mr. Finn.

She said you were kind enough to give her the job, and by God she was going to do it for you."

Finn said: "Is that right, Al?"

"Is it right, Tom?"

Tom nodded solemnly.

"Don't guess there are any too many like that in the department," Al said.

"Damn few," Finn agreed.

"Well." Al shook his head. "I don't suppose you can take a chance she'll be sick again, maybe while customers are around. They might think that stuff would make their kids sick." Finn nodded thoughtfully. "I suppose you'll have to let her go."

"I'd hate to do it, Al."

"Maybe you could find another demonstration to put her on. Something bigger. That's an awful lot of talent going to waste on a six-bit item."

"Yeah," Finn said. "That's right, Al. Maybe I can. Say, thanks."

Al caught his arm. "Be tactful," he urged. "You know. Don't let her know I told you. Tell her you don't want to waste her on soap bubbles."

"I'll make her feel good," Finn said. "You're my boy, Al."

He went out; through the door they could see him talking to Nickie, a fatherly smile on his face. In a moment she had put down the little chrome gadget, gotten her purse out of the drawer, and was following him across the floor. Tom watched, but couldn't be sure what counter they went to.

"If I only had teats," Al sighed behind him. "I could make a million dollars as a wet nurse."

How would that look in the notebook? Tom wondered, turning to smile at him. Wishes he had teats. And a tail.

Just before closing time, Nickie returned and told them she was now to demonstrate story-telling records up near the front.

"They cost $4.98," she said. "And I have to make a little show with cardboard figures out of it while a voice tells the story. It's fun."

"Good," Al said. He and Tom were arranging Party-Girl Tea Sets (*For Dolly and You*) on the lowest shelf.

"Thank you so much, Al," the girl said. Then she asked: "Could I talk to you?"

"Of course," Al straightened up and turned to her.

"Not here. After work."

"All right. We could walk a few blocks together. Would that do it?"

She smiled at him slowly; it was a smile of marvelous intensity. "I don't suppose you'd . . . buy me a drink?"

He had to lower his eyes; he couldn't say no looking at her. "I'm sorry, Nickie." Then he added, to make it pleasant: "It's my wallet that has a previous engagement, not I."

"We'll walk, though?"

He nodded.

"All right." She got up. "Excuse me?"

And went lightly out.

"I thought you'd passed the old Barker curse along to me," Tom said, grinning.

"You slipped it back," Al said. "Was that a friendly thing to do?"

Outside, by the employees' entrance, just past the fat store detective who inspected parcels and collected passes for them, Nickie waited for Al. She was no longer so certain that she wanted to talk to him; it seemed quite impossible, standing outside on the every day street, the tension of the store gradually leaving her, that she had been so extraordinarily attracted. She told herself that it was gratitude she felt, no more than a response to his sympathy and kindness, that he was unimpressive, really, tired-looking, almost drab, a nice little stockroom man. Then why, she had to ask herself, when he had already kept her waiting for ten minutes, was she still excited rather than annoyed? And why, for here he came, smiling goodnight to Tom, squeezing the boy's arm, should she feel foolish and confused?

She made herself wait for Al to see her instead of calling out; she made herself stand still so that he came to her, instead of going to meet him. But she couldn't keep herself from smiling more broadly than she'd meant to, and it upset her that she couldn't control it. What did she want from such a man beyond a cheerful word at work, and perhaps a little help in defending her from the unfriendly clerks?

"It was nice of you to meet me," she said, and couldn't help

63

adding, with a touch of flirtatiousness: "You seemed doubtful."

"Sorry," he said, unexpressively.

She'd be careful. "I did want to tell you again how grateful I am."

They walked along Stockton street, rather slowly, staying on the outside, near the curb, to be away from the late shoppers and clerks who came streaming out of the stores to clog the sidewalks.

"I was glad we were able to help."

"Will you let me impose on you again?"

"Why not?"

"I'm a little nitwit to make so much of it, but I've got to know that someone in the store believes it's important for me to keep the job. The others don't think it could be, do they?"

"Perhaps not."

She stopped walking to face him for a moment, so that he'd have to look at her. "Will you believe it for me, Al?"

"All right."

She had wanted him, she realized, to say something warmer, perhaps to squeeze her arm reassuringly as he had Tom's, but he only repeated: "Why not?"

"Oh hell," said Nickie, in a stronger voice, beginning to move on and meaning several things. "What went wrong? I didn't mean them to know I came from a rich family."

"The lady clerks knew from your dress, I'm told," Al said. "But I don't think it's your background they envy you, so much as the way you look. Even the poor men are uncomfortable."

"Really, Al? Why?"

"Don't flirt. A beautiful girl is an ominous thing to a man, as who should know better . . ."

"Am I beautiful, Al? How nice."

He laughed at her.

She took his arm impulsively. "I hope you find me very ominous," she said, and could have bitten her lip; she released the impassive arm immediately. "What can I do?" she asked.

"I don't know," he said, a little wearily. "What about a false nose and a moustache?" Then, before she could resent it, he apologized. "I'm sorry. You don't feel like joking, do you?"

"Do you always see right through everybody?"

"Only to the bone," he said. "What's on your mind, Nickie? Is it the other clerks?"

"Partly," she said. "I do want people to know that I'm not just working for fun. . . . Al, you don't really feel uncomfortable because you think I'm beautiful?"

"No, Nickie," he said. "But I'm not in the running, so it doesn't put me at the usual disadvantage."

There was no reply that she could make aloud, but she turned a glance on him that promised he would take it back; unfortunately, he was looking away.

The crowds were thinning as they turned up Geary Street.

"What were you going to say about not working for fun?" he asked.

"I had this bet . . ." she began, and stopped; her feet were tired. He was making it hard. She wanted to sit down. She regretted ever getting into this. And suddenly there he was, making her smile again, saying:

"I didn't mean to be surly about it. Shall we have that drink?"

"Dutch." She said it firmly.

"As a wooden shoe," he agreed.

The Cocktail Lounge of the St. Francis, where she often met her dates, was across the street; but Al's hand on her arm pulled in the direction of a smaller bar, less elaborate, closer at hand.

They sat in a booth and ordered. When the drinks came, he said:

"A bet?"

She shook her head. "That was going to be a lie."

"Okay."

"I go to school in the East. To Smith . . ." she paused, wondering if he would know of it.

"Pretty place," he said.

"Do you . . . know what it's like around those colleges in the Fall?"

"A little."

"You see your friends again, you start new courses, there are games, and parties, and changing weather. It's like starting to live again. . . ."

He nodded, and said, softly: "The cheeks pink with cold, the bright fall coats, laughing and laughing and never losing your breath. The way the light, dry flakes of first snow stick to the wool of the pretty coats for a moment, and blow away before they melt. . . ."

"You went to school there, too." She was delighted. "Where, Al?"

"I've been in New England in the autumn," he said. "It's the place to be."

Now, with the drink relaxing her more than it should, and his feeling for things so like her own, she panicked a little; there was too much sympathy, too much communication. She tried to oppose it by talking fast: "I'm a Junior. Every year my father sends me four hundred dollars. It's an extra allowance. To buy Christmas presents for the family. In Boston, over Thanksgiving, you see and I can't use my charge accounts because he checks them. Well, this year, there was a friend of mine; she had to have the money, very badly. So I loaned it to her, but it would be awful if Daddy found out. Do you see? He doesn't let me lend money. It would be awful."

"I guess it would," Al said.

"So I have to earn the money for the family presents. So he won't find out. Because I don't know when the girl can pay me back."

"Okay."

She shook her head. "That's a lie, too."

"Okay."

"I had to spend it for an abortion." She couldn't look at him, and she couldn't understand why she had told him; then she added, her eyes on the shiny table top: "For myself, I mean."

She felt his hand cover hers. "That was a very good Christmas present," she heard him say without irony. "For an unborn child."

"Was it, Al?" she begged. "Do you think so?"

"Of course. You'll have children later, when the time comes. Life is a very dubious gift to any child, and no gift at all to an unwanted one. Mammals make such a fuss about the lives of their young."

"Am I all right? Can I still have children?"

"Of course, Nickie. Done by a competent man—a four hundred dollar man—with clean instruments and a knowledge of procedure, an abortion is about as safe as most operations these days."

"I took a room at a hotel," she said gratefully, willing to remember the scene now for the first time. "It was odd. Like checking in for a weekend. I had a drink while I was waiting. He came with his instruments in a suitcase. Then it was all very businesslike and matter of fact. I'd expected some sort of dramatics but you know, all I could think of after he left was that there I was in Boston for the weekend, and I didn't know what to do with the rest of it."

"The dramatics came later?" Al said.

She nodded. "Every night."

"No wonder. There's such a lot of damn fool talk about it."

"It's true about having to earn the money. I'd had a little saved. About half. I didn't want to borrow the rest; didn't want to tell any of my friends. And I wouldn't have told the man for anything. I decided to work for it. You're the only person I've been able to tell, Al. Do you mind?"

To her surprise and slight hurt, he sighed. "Only a little," he said; then he smiled to soften it. "But, Nickie, how brave of you. To do it all by yourself."

"Well," she said, thinking she must brighten up. "There's nothing to it. Everybody around the dorm knows the phone number. It's a big joke. You see a friend looking serious, and you say: 'Why be blue, Nickie-girl? Call IJ 5–6788 for prompt, friendly service. . . .'"

"Pretty good joke," Al said. "Except that you've been bluer and bluer, haven't you?"

"Until now, Al," she said. "Even if you did mind my telling you, it feels awfully good. It feels wonderful."

"I shouldn't have said that. Any time you need an ear, Nickie . . ."

"But now I need another drink," she said, with a silly laugh. "This is the first one that's tasted good in months. Couldn't I buy you one, Al, since they taste so good here?"

"I'll feel as if I'm snipping the fringe off your father's smoking jacket," Al smiled back. "Sure. Let's." And he signaled the waitress.

"What a lovely place," she said. "How lovely to feel good."

"I can imagine."

"How much would you mind if I told you how it happened?" she asked.

And the irksome man replied, with a smile of perfect ease: "I don't think it would bother me a bit."

Fresh drinks came.

"I don't really go much with undergraduates," Nickie said. "By the time you're a Junior, you know older men; you have city dates. Or you see graduate students, or law students or young faculty men. You know?" Again he smiled.

"I generally have my dates in Boston," she went on. "Or Cambridge. Weekends. I know a lot of men down there. But this fall, I don't know. I have to go back a little . . ."

"As far as you like," Al said.

"To last year. I had this kind of serious affair, with a man, Hank Gold. A very brilliant Jewish man from New York, who taught history at Harvard. A lovely man, and he tried to kill himself last spring because it wasn't me he wanted, after all. It was one of his boy students."

"Hank Gold," Al said. "That was a bad spring."

"It doesn't matter any more, but I took it pretty hard then. I just wanted to explain why, when I went back this fall, I felt like being younger. You know? I started taking dates for football weekends, things like that. Easy kind of dates, with nice kids and a lot of fun, and nothing serious, and no problems about the men. I went to a game at Dartmouth. There was a boy playing I knew. Not the one who'd asked me. He was a Senior, this boy, and co-captain. Very nice. Not my sort. He hurt his leg, in the second half, and had to leave the game. They were saying he wouldn't play any more that season. That meant he wouldn't play football, ever again . . ."

"Of course," Al said. "He was a Senior."

"They were helping him off, two other boys, the doctor going alongside. He wouldn't let them put him on the stretcher. I started having this feeling for him; I knew exactly what he was thinking. Sometime in the last quarter he came out again in street clothes, with a cane, and sat on the bench. I knew he'd wanted to because it was his last game, and he'd been the hero before he got hurt; then they won it for him. I felt about fifteen years old, and mad with adulation."

"I can understand," Al said.

"In the fraternity house, afterward, we were all mad with adulation," Nickie said. "He was marvelous. About one drink, because he was breaking training and wasn't used to it, and he got giddy and marvelous. He was spinning around the dance floor on the leg that wasn't hurt, lifting me up above his head. It seemed that he ought to have anything he wanted; I was the prettiest, so he wanted me. I don't know what happened to my date. I hadn't expected anything like that to happen that weekend, and I thought it would be all right to take a chance . . ." She grimaced.

"Why not?" Al said. "Being young is taking chances."

"This boy, this hero, oh, I could have turned him down easily enough, but I didn't want to. Probably I got him into it." She glanced at Al, to see if it might be making him just a little uncomfortable, but his smile was full of pleasure and sympathy. "It just seemed so right," she said. "After the game and the celebration."

"Of course," Al said. "Being young is going along with youth —wearing chrysanthemums, laughing the laughter, loving the heroes. Why not, Nickie?"

"I didn't want to spoil it by seeing him again. Maybe he felt the same way. He only called once; he wasn't my kind of boy. I probably wasn't his kind of girl."

"I should think you'd be anybody's kind of girl, Nickie," he said, with a sort of objective, old man's pleasantness; but a tumble of feelings immediately smothered her awareness of how he'd said it; she registered only the words, and was gone. She made a last try at sticking to the story:

"You can see that I couldn't have told him?"

"Youth should never know its consequences," Al said. "Losing it is consequence enough."

"Let's have another drink, Al. Let's have a lot more drinks."

This time he smiled at her for a second or two before replying. Then he seemed to sigh, and said: "Let's not, Nickie. You've told me all you had to, haven't you?"

"Oh, Al."

69

"Nickie, you deserve the world's biggest bouquet of long-stemmed cocktails, just for looking as you look and talking as you talk. But I'm not the man to buy them for you. And I'm sorry." He started to stand up.

"But Al," she said, confused. "Couldn't we do it again? If I get blue again?"

"Maybe after payday," he said, smiling.

7 *After payday.* That was a safe, dishonest thing to say. Payday would be leaving day for Al. But safe or not that night, after putting Nickie in a cab, and going to his room to eat, Al found a bar and began, quite deliberately, to drink. He did it to anaesthetize a sense of apprehension which often developed after he had been in a new location, a new job, for a day or two. It was a familiar of his, this apprehension, an enemy of sleep, an enemy of appetite, and he didn't understand completely what it was. He doubted, actually, that it had ever warned him correctly; he supposed that his various trails, if any had been found, must be cold indeed; it was almost immodest to act, in fact, as if anyone, any agency, were still very actively looking for him. And yet, though he told himself that it takes two to make a chase, and that never had there been any real evidence of close pursuit, the apprehension always recurred. He must, many times, have run without any cause but nervousness, a solitary quarry with only an imaginary pack behind him, a man playing desperation chess with only black pieces on part of a board, and no indication even that the white pieces existed on the part of the board he couldn't see.

For this sense of pursuit he had learned to prescribe a low, regular intake of alcohol for a week or so. After this period, it was well to stop before the habit could take hold; then if the sense of pursuit persisted, he'd give in to it and move on.

This time payday would provide a natural termination: he had

71

counted his money. If he went easy on food, there was enough for three quarts of drinkable whiskey—a pint a day for six days at work—and enough more to drink slow beer at night. It seemed unlikely that any suspicions he might have aroused in M'nerney would produce threatening action in that time; clearly he had nothing to fear from Finn. He thought for a moment of the Service Manager, Dolly Klamath; there had been no particular indication of suspicion from her.

He sat in the farthest booth, back in the shadows, of the North Beach bar, a place called Weary's down the street from his room. He knew, he realized, nothing about Dolly Klamath except the legend of her toughness and the story, repeated in the absence of any other personal information about her, that she had been a nun. He thought he saw a point of similarity between himself and Dolly; alone, among all the talkative people, they were stingy autobiographers.

Raising his fourth beer an inch or two from the dark table, he said, with quiet extravagance, to the glass: "Perhaps she too has sent description hobbling away in rags, a battered tin cup in his hand, crying for alms."

8 Dolly Klamath knew that the other employees in the store believed she had once been a nun. At one time she had thought of it as a silly story, too complexly half-true to try to correct. Then she had found that the belief added, in some way, to her stature, giving her additional forbidding color, particularly among the Catholic employees who were in the majority in the hierarchy of management.

The origin of the story lay in an interviewer's mistake, made when Dolly had first applied for work as a salesgirl four years earlier. Under the heading LAST EMPLOYER she had written: *Convent Hospital of the Good Shepherd, two years.*

"Were you a nurse?" she was asked.

"No. I did teach a little."

From this the interviewer had concluded that the square shouldered, self-contained girl must have been a nun; and, guessing that her being out, now, in the secular world, indicated some tragic failure of piety, had delicately not inquired further; had, in fact, smiled kindly at Dolly and said:

"Never mind, dear. I'm sure you'll be happy with us, here at Mainways."

To trace it out, Dolly's father, a strong Catholic layman and a widower from the time she was a little girl, had died when his daughter was in her teens and left some money to the Convent he had always prayed his daughter would enter. In accepting the bequest, the sisters had kept the girl on, for she was already there as a boarder at their school, assuming her eventual compliance with her father's hopes; she had always been a fervently dutiful daughter. But the time never came when Dolly felt called to enter formally on a novitiate; she was vain about her appearance and wanted to wear secular clothing. She had been content enough to live in the Convent dormitories, and had taught some of the classes of younger girls and coached their teams. But she was overstrict as a teacher, and flouted her superiors in a stubborn, occasionally violent way; especially on the playing field, at field hockey or basketball, she slapped her pupils freely, though it was not countenanced, and sometimes sent them crying back to the locker room. Once, finally, she had returned to the locker room herself, following one of her charges and, when the child came out of the shower, still weeping, had slapped her again and again until an older teacher, hearing the screams, came in and put a stop to it.

Called in by the Mother Superior, Dolly had said: "When my father whipped me, sometimes the blood came, but I loved him."

They had transferred her to the hospital, hoping that, as many graduates of the school elected to do, Dolly would take training as a nurse; hoping, too, that the call would come, that Dolly's religious fervor would regularize itself into the ancient, satisfying patterns which had brought rest to so many fierce young women. The fierceness lessened; the call never came. Nursing failed to interest Dolly much. When she decided to leave and find work in the world, the sisters were relieved, though they still hoped that some day she might return to them.

The legend of Dolly's severity in acting for the store had begun before she had been at work a year, shortly after her first promotion to Assistant Service Manager in Ladies' Gloves. One day a new clerk had been sent down, assigned to the department by Personnel; the girl had taken off her hat and coat and her own, black suede gloves, prepared to go to work, and had turned out to have strikingly unattractive hands. Apparently some one had stupidly allowed her to keep the gloves on during the interview.

"Wait, Miss," Dolly had said, as the girl started to come behind the counter, smiling. "Wait a moment, please. Stand there." She had picked out a pair of long, creamy-white doeskins from the tray. "You're a customer. See how I handle the gloves showing

74

them? See how they look against my hands as I display them? Now watch. Here." She had thrust the gloves into the fat mottled paws across the counter, and slid the upright counter-mirror in front of them. "See how the gloves look? Show them to yourself. Go ahead. Handle them. Handle them. Would you want to buy them?"

"But . . ."

"Keep looking at them. Look at your hands," Dolly had said. The girl had dropped the gloves and fled. That was when people had started to watch themselves around Dolly Klamath.

The first thing that Dolly did every morning was to check the Toy Department counter tops for dust.

There was a crew to use vacuum cleaners during the night, and spread dust covers over the stock, taking them off before people got to work in the morning. In addition, all clerks were expected to have dust rags with which they were to whisk each item displayed, to wipe the glass counter tops and clean the moldings of the stock cases behind them.

"There'll be no breakage and no soilage on my floor," Dolly would tell them, when they first reported for work. "I hold myself responsible for every item of stock in this department, and that means you're responsible to me. Is that clear? I will not tolerate filth."

So, in the morning, as the clerks were straightening out their sales books and arranging their counters, Dolly strode the floor, pointing out filth here and dust there, looking for dirty hands and fingernails and soiled shirts.

She came to the doll counter; she smiled approval at blonde Miss Malinkrodt who didn't want to use her married name, primping a doll's dress, neatly retying a bonnet that had come loose. Farther along the plain Canadian girl was fooling with a pencil. She had broken the point; she seemed to have no replacement pencil, indicating a five minute dawdle in the stockroom, where the sharpener was.

Then Dolly noticed:

"Winnipeg," she said, not trying to suppress the dislike in her voice.

The girl seemed almost unable to focus her pale eyes.

75

"Don't you people understand English up in Canada?" Dolly asked.

"What's the matter, Miss Klamath?" the girl quavered.

Now Miss Sally Maiden Name was listening, pretending not to; Dolly settled to her rightful work. "Do you know what B-L-A-C-K spells?" she asked.

"Yes . . . Miss Klamath. Yes." The girl was trembling slightly.

"Black, dear, black. Not blue. Blue is B-L-U-E."

"Oh, Miss Klamath." The girl clutched one hand with the other.

"Let me hear you spell it, dear. Say it."

"Which . . . which one?"

Dolly simply stared at her.

"bbB-L-cC-KkkK," the girl stammered. "B-L-U-eeeE."

"Blooey is right," Dolly said. "Or perhaps you thought B-L-A-C-K spelled navy, is that it? Anchors aweigh? Jolly old Canadian tars, what?" A nervous smile touched the girl's lips; Dolly pinched it away: "Weren't you told to wear black on the floor? At all times? Weren't you? Did your instruction book mention any exceptions? Did the Canadian edition say it was all right for Winnipeg girls to wear navy, perhaps? Special exceptions? Is that it?"

"But, oh, Miss Klamath." She was ready to weep. "Muh-my black dress . . ."

"Muh-my black dress is at the cleaner's. You only have one. You can't afford another till you get your paycheck. Things are terrible in Canada. You had to sell your little brother to the Eskimos for blubber." She hardened her voice. "Well, blubber away, dear; I've heard every lying excuse you little rainbows try to pull. What shall we see tomorrow? Purple? Now get this, Winnipeg, and get it straight." Dolly paused, poised; the girl looked as if she were going to shake to pieces. Dolly glanced at Blonde Malinkrodt to see how she was doing; Blonde looked fascinated. Dolly fixed her stare on Winnipeg's forehead, and waited for the pale eyes to raise; then she continued to hold the illogical pause until she saw the girl's mouth droop open and a syllable struggle forward in it. "Shut up," Dolly said, softly. "Keep quiet. Wait for me to tell you what to do. I'm going to tell you what to do now, dear. Are you listening?" Gradually she let her voice raise. "Walk over to the elevator. That's the thing that goes up and down. Go up to the eighth floor. Get your coat. Go home. I don't care whether you come back or not, but if you do, see that you're wearing a black dress. Is that clear? And now, get off my floor."

When she saw the tears spring out of the girl's eyes, Dolly turned and started briskly away. And nearly bumped into the stockroom man, Al Barker, who had been standing ten feet away, quietly listening. His expression was so critical that she stopped and said: "I suppose you have no interest in seeing that people do their duty?"

"On the contrary, Miss Klamath," he said, in that cheap, ironic tone. "I was very interested."

"I suggest you find interest in the problems of the stockroom," she snapped, and walked on. She wouldn't let him spoil it.

It was too bad if people didn't know that a rule was a rule. Next time she would take the girl into the office and close the door and talk to her, so that she didn't have to worry about people like Barker. Except, she'd like Sally Malinkrodt to be listening again; clearly, Sally had admired her, had realized that it took real strength not to let up. As a reward for doing it well, Dolly allowed herself to fantasize about Sally: they would be friends, eat lunches together. Sally was sick of her husband, that was why she used the maiden name; an awful man, always hitting at her with his thing which Sally hated so. Sally would come to Dolly in terror, and Dolly would get her a real job in the store; they would be room mates and live in Dolly's immaculate apartment, and Sally would obey her. . . .

"Oh, my dear." As Dolly left, Sally Malinkrodt ran to the mousy Canadian girl and put an arm around her waist. "Oh, honey, you mustn't mind." The chunky girl turned to sob against Sally's shoulder.

"Oh," she moaned. "I didn't know . . . it was . . . so serious."

"It isn't, honey," Sally soothed her. "It isn't. There are plenty of girls wearing navy on other floors. She can't talk to you that way. You go to Mr. Finn and complain. Go to Personnel. Ask for a transfer."

"Oh, I couldn't," Winnipeg sobbed. "I just couldn't. I couldn't do a thing like that."

77

"Do you want to quit?"

"No," the girl said. "Oh, no. I want to . . . work here. Even after Christmas. I wanted to do so well."

"You'll do fine, honey," Sally said. "Was she right? Do you only have one black dress? And it's at the cleaner's?"

"How did she know?" The girl pulled away a little, and took the handkerchief Sally offered to wipe her eyes.

"Have you any money?" Sally asked.

The girl shook her head.

Sally took her purse out of the belongings drawer, and opened it. "Here," she said, offering the girl a twenty. "Go down to the fourth floor and buy a dress. Get something you can wear right back. That'll show her."

"Oh, I couldn't take your money," said Winnipeg.

Sally sighed. "Look, I don't need it," she said. "I'm working here to spite my husband. Not because I need the money. You can pay it back payday if you want to."

"I just couldn't borrow money," the girl said. "It's . . . against my principles."

"It is?" Sally was a little taken aback. It was not a statement she had ever expected to hear spoken seriously.

The Canadian girl nodded.

"How about clothing?" Sally asked. "Would you be willing to wear a dress of mine?"

"I don't know."

"Of course you would."

"If you'd let me have it cleaned for you," the girl said.

Sally shrugged. "Here." She took a key out of her purse. "I live on Green Street. 401. Know where it is?"

"Yes."

"The apartment is on the first floor; the name is Rivers. You'll go in the living room, and see a hall. Go in the first door on the left. That's my room. Look in the closet. You'll find five or six black dresses; take your pick."

The girl reached hesitantly for the key.

"Make all the noise you want," Sally said. "My husband's asleep across the hall. Won't do him any harm to be waked up."

"Your husband?" The girl drew her hand back again.

"Don't worry," Sally said. "He's harmless. Completely, utterly,

78

harmless. If you hear him moving around, just say, 'Jerk, Sally says go back to sleep.' "

"Jerk?"

"Everybody calls the jerk Jerk," Sally said. "Now go on."

Hesitantly the girl took the key.

"Thanks, Mrs. Rivers," she said.

"Miss Malinkrodt," Sally muttered. "Miss by God Malinkrodt."

As the girl left, Sally caught the eye of the tall girl who demonstrated music boxes, and they traded grimaces. Then she was alone, without customers or colleagues for twenty minutes.

At the end of that time Mr. M'nerney came chugging by, stopped himself, and said:

"Were you the young lady without a black dress?"

"No, Mr. M'nerney," Sally said. "I have a black dress."

"I see." Perhaps half an hour after that Winnipeg returned wearing, as Sally felt she could have predicted, the oldest and least suitable of all the black dresses in the closet. She squeezed the girl's hand, and told her she looked fine. Mr. Finn appeared.

"Well, well," he said, solicitously, leaning across the counter to pat Winnipeg's arm. "We do look fine now, in the black dress. Yes indeed, Miss. Ready for the customers. Now when they start coming, you know . . ."

He ran on with nervous cordiality, repeating instructions on how to demonstrate the burping doll to attract customers; apparently he thought it was soothing.

According to the laws of the State of California, female employees must be given fifteen minutes off to rest in every four hour period; this, in Sally Malinkrodt's opinion, was the best damn law ever enacted, and she would gladly lead a parade of working girls up the streets of Sacramento, offering their bodies to whatever chivalrous legislator had introduced it; but right now it was still a few minutes too early to take advantage of it unless Uncle Funny left.

"You girls just keep showing them," he was saying, seizing a doll to act it out. "You know. Like circus barkers. Someone's walking by, you say: 'Here, over here, look right here.' Have the the doll all ready on your shoulder. Whack hell out of it. It burps. Give a laugh. Whack it again. Burp. Bring them over. Ask them if they want to try . . ."

79

"Yes, Mr. Finn," Sally said, finally, honey-voiced and giving him her sweetest smile. "Do you think, since there's nobody around, now would be a good time for me to take my break?"

"Is it eleven already?" Finn asked, looking at his watch.

Sally smiled even harder. "You don't want me demonstrating what the doll does after she's had her bottle, do you?" she asked. She pressed her knees together like a child who needs to go to the bathroom, kept the smile large and undulated up and down.

Finn laughed; Winnipeg blushed.

"Shall I wear my diapers tomorrow?" Sally asked, huskily.

"Boy," Finn said. "Wouldn't that sell dolls."

"Any way you want them sold," Sally said. "You're the boss." And she leaned towards him and touched him lightly on the hand. Then she whisked away, towards the stockroom, thinking that it was a little easy but rather fun.

In the stockroom, Al Barker was sitting.

"Hi," she said.

"Hi."

"Got a cigarette?" She had forgotten to bring her purse.

"Pockets full." He offered her a remarkably crushed pack.

"Such fresh ones," she said, coquettishly.

"I'm a walking humidor," Al said, without emphasis.

She didn't feel like disappearing into the Ladies Room yet. "Where's your cute helper?"

"He doesn't come in until afternoon."

"Do tell him I asked."

"Okay."

There was a pause. Then he said: "How's the kid from Winnipeg?"

"You heard all of that?"

"Most. And the balance distorted in several ways."

"Klamath was pretty vicious."

"M'nerney said Winnipeg was intolerably sassy."

"Oh my God," Sally said, and laughed. "That girl couldn't sass a one-legged rabbit."

"You looked pretty good in there," Al said, finally smiling at her.

"She picked the most unbecoming dress I own, of course. Probably in a hurry, afraid she'd wake the jerk."

"Your husband?"

"Yes. Did you think I didn't have one?"

"I hadn't thought about it."

"Look, no ring," Sally said, offering her left hand to him.

"No ring." He didn't take the hand. Suddenly he looked up at her with a curious smile: "Is Jerk his given name?"

She laughed, moving her hand back. "Damn near it. His name is Rivers—I'm Sally Rivers, but I used my maiden name when I got the job here, just to torture the poor bastard."

"You dislike him?"

"I don't know," Sally said. "He's from the East. Nice clothes. Nice manners. I'd helled around a lot, you know. Married him fast; thought . . . it might be restful." She paused. Then she added: "Believe me, it's been restful."

"About the name?"

"May I sit down?"

"Of course." But instead of moving over for her, he indicated a box across from him.

"When he was a kid in prep school, the boys called him Old Man. Old Man Rivers. Then he went to college, and the boys there were a little more sophisticated: they changed it to Onan. It's just a step from there to Jerk, and the poor guy has been busy living up to the name ever since. It was better, I guess, to be miserable and patronized than simply disliked."

"Good American decision," Al said. "Poor guy."

"I think he hoped by coming out here he'd shake that idea of himself. But one of his college mates followed along, got a job on the *Journal* where he works, and the nickname started in all over again; and the act. That was just after we were married. You know, he'd actually started to make a comeback from all that—he was threatening to turn into a man any minute. He even talked back to me one evening—I was awfully tickled. But when Robbie appeared with the name poor Jerk had a relapse; he's never recovered."

"And were you revenged on Robbie?" Al asked.

The dryness in his voice startled her; it was as if he had guessed. "I'd have run away with Robbie in a minute," she told him, not even surprised at her candor. "But he didn't ask me. After a casual night or two, in fact, he wouldn't have me at all."

81

The stockroom man's face didn't seem to register one way or another; neither disapproval, which she'd half expected, nor the interest of a man who is told that one is no stranger to adultery. "Come on," she said, finally. "Say something to Sally."

"Good luck, Sally," he said.

She shrugged and went on to the ladies' room. That pretty well completed Sally's survey of the men around the department, and left her with nothing but Finn. She thought Gullakian too obvious, M'nerney unattractive, and Tom, she regretted, a year or so too young. She sighed, looking in the mirror, not liking nor disliking her appearance but simply acknowledging it; she had thought, not altogether idly, of having an affair when she took the job. How much better than nothing might Finn be? she asked her mirror image. Perhaps he had a kind of old-fashioned virility; then again, his idea of a caress might be to hoist a girl over his shoulder and hit her on the back till she burped.

When she returned to her counter, there were customers lined along it, waiting, for the first time; within a few minutes she had rung up six sales.

She found herself saying, "Be with you in a moment, ma'am," in the same tones clerks had always used with her, and was pleased with herself. After an hour of it, though, for as lunch hour approached the trade seemed to increase, she began to feel harassed.

She got involved in a complicated discussion with a little woman in a shabby brown coat who wanted to see every doll in stock, though she was obviously going to buy the $8.95 one.

"I'll take it," the woman said, finally.

"This one?" Sally was a little surprised. It was a somewhat more expensive doll she held. "Or the little one?" She picked up the other.

"No. The first one. The sweet one."

"All right," she replied, automatically adding: "We're selling a great many of them this year." She wondered why that should be any recommendation. From the stock shelf behind her, she picked out a box marked *green,* for the dress color.

"Will you gift wrap it for me, dear?" The woman smiled. She was a short creature with a heavy layer of pale make up.

"I'll put it in a bag for you," Sally said. "And you can have it gift wrapped at counter ten."

"Do they charge for that?"

"I think it's a quarter for small packages," Sally said. "Thirty-five for larger ones."

"Really, you people," the woman complained. "Last year every store in town did gift wrapping free. This year you're all charging."

"I know," said Sally, beginning to write the sales check. "Is this cash or charge?"

"Here," the woman said, rather crossly, extending a ten dollar bill.

"Thank you," said Sally, taking it and waiting. "That's $11.95. Twelve-oh-three with the tax." She finished writing the check, looked up, and smiled; the customer snatched back the bill.

"$11.95?" she said. "Listen, Miss. You said $8.95. Very distinctly."

"That was the smaller doll we were looking at," Sally said, reasonably. "Was that the one you wanted?"

"Don't get high and mighty with me, young lady," the woman said. "I want to buy this doll here. And I want it at the price you said, $8.95."

"I'm sorry, ma'am. The price is $11.95." Sally was firm. She reached to retrieve the doll from the counter and saw it snatched away. The ten dollar bill was slapped down in its place.

Amazed, Sally raised her eyes and saw that the little woman, breathing heavily, now held the doll box against her breast.

"Are you going to take my money and sell me this doll or not?"

"I'm sorry, ma'am. I can't do that," Sally said.

"Oh . . . keep your damn doll," the woman cried, and hurled the box at Sally who threw her hand up just in time to deflect it; it fell on the counter, crushing in a corner as it landed. She was so astonished that she barely had presence of mind enough to call out, after the woman who was scuttling away, "Your money, ma'am," pointing to the ten dollar bill.

The customer stopped. She turned. Sally saw that tears were running down her face.

"Keep the money," the woman wailed. "Your chiseling store

83

will get it out of me some way," and she turned again and ran down the aisles between the counters.

First Sally was stunned. Then she seized the bill and trotted after the flapping figure; she knew she looked ridiculous, yet she was without choice. She couldn't keep the bill. She couldn't let the woman get away.

If I had it to do again, she was thinking, as she made a fast turn around Housekeeping Toys, I'd pay the difference myself. For a moment, she lost sight of the customer; then she saw the shabby coat dodging between Christmas Cards and Gift Wrapping, heading for the escalator, and ran down the aisle by the *Zoom-Spaceman, Yippee-Cowboy Suits* to cut her off.

The little woman moved quickly; there was no way to catch her except to break into an outright run. Sally found herself laughing, as she reached a clear stretch, keeping the bill in sight as if to explain to her fellow-employees what she was doing, putting on a sprint as she went by on the far side of Gift Wrappings and saw the woman tangled with other customers; they reached the escalator simultaneously, Sally's final spurt giving her just enough advantage to block the way. The little woman stopped short as Sally extended the bill, turned to run the other way, and went thudding into a man in a Chesterfield.

"Lady," Sally cried, "take your money," and she managed to stuff the bill into the woman's shopping bag, and start away.

"I'll never come into your awful store again," the woman called after her, but Sally didn't trust herself to turn around and look again; she was already half hysterical.

Making her way back, she began to calm down; there was still, of course, the damaged box to explain and the sales slip to be canceled. You were supposed to get Klamath to cancel incorrect slips, but Sally felt reluctant to give her an opening. She could get M'nerney. ("If the Service Manager is off the floor," the training lecturer had said, "the Assistant Buyer . . ."). But then, why not the Buyer? Reaching her counter, Sally smiled.

Dolly Klamath, who had followed the whole incident from the Service Desk, saw the smile and stood poised, waiting for Sally to call her. She would take care of this for Sally, straighten it out, and tell her she had handled it nicely; she would ask her to have lunch. She waited five minutes. Sally neither called nor glanced at her. Dolly was ready to go to the counter of her own accord when she saw the blonde beckon outrageously to Mr. Finn, who was passing, saw her offer the salesbook, saw Finn begin to fix the slip. Dolly was furiously hurt. He had no right; Sally was behaving like a prostitute.

Not much later, from M'nerney, Dolly learned how Sally had taken Winnipeg's side; vengefully, the Service Manager altered her fantasy of Sally: now Sally went, in terror from her husband, to Finn, instead of to her true friend. And Finn locked Sally in the office, and did it to her on the desk, mercilessly, till her legs ached. She imagined Sally after days of this, her thing hanging down flabby and exhausted, like the jowls of an old dog; and Finn, big as a baseball bat, beating at the old jowls, pounding at the aching legs. Dolly fixed her stare malevolently on Sally's back, as if she could stare through the dress, and imagined herself an omnipotent Dolly, a Dolly of wrath, reaching under the skirt to fasten an incredibly painful, eternally disciplinary pinch to the hateful jowls, not using her fingers, of course, but wearing rubber gloves and with something like a pair of pliers. At twenty-eight, Dolly Klamath was the strictest of virgins; she had stopped accepting dates with men two years before.

The day kept after her; there were checks to okay and inquiries to answer. Hugh Harris, the revolting little pansy from electric trains, tried to sneak back ten minutes late from lunch. She caught him.

"I'll expect you to shorten your lunch hour by ten minutes tomorrow, Harris," she said. "Unless you prefer to lose a half hour's pay."

He tried to protest.

"Any fraction of a half hour means a half hour's pay loss," she said. "That rule is in writing, Harris. Which shall it be?"

He promised to cut his lunch hour short.

"Don't imagine for a moment that I'll forget," Dolly said. "Not for a sneaky, little moment."

Towards the end of the afternoon, Finn stopped by the service desk.

"Uh, pretty good start today, Dolly," he said. "Got the old snowball rolling a little bit, eh?"

"Yes, Mr. Finn," she said.

"Start the old snowball rolling down the money hill, picking up the old wet dollars and packing them in, eh, Dolly?" He went on. She didn't answer him. "Nice, uh, bunch of people, here, you found this year. Couple of pretty nice little girls there on the doll counter, I think," he bumbled on, and she understood that he was preparing to reprimand her.

"Mr. Finn," she said, coldly outraged. Barker must have told him. "It's my job to protect you from any personnel problems connected with the inadequacies of the temporary help. I intend to do that job. I will not let any personal weaknesses of yours interfere with my doing that job."

"What do you mean, Dolly?"

"I mean that I am not going to let that blonde woman disrupt discipline in my department by taking you for a fat fool," Dolly said. "I have a certain reputation in this store . . ."

"Oh, hell, Dolly girl," he said. "Now, Dolly. Don't get sore. Hell, you're the best S.M. in the store. Everybody knows . . ."

"I don't care for profanity, Mr. Finn," Dolly said, and turned away. She must certainly have a minute with the boy Tom before the day ended.

She did, finding him helping to straighten out the cowboy and spaceman counter, on which there had been a heavy run that afternoon.

"Tom."

"Yes, Miss Klamath."

She beckoned him aside.

"What have you learned about Mr. Barker?"

"Well," said Tom. "Not much, Miss Klamath."

"Nothing? In four days?"

"Well," he said. He took a small notebook out of his pocket. "I know what bus he rides from work. And . . . well, I can't tell whether I really know some of the places he's been or not. He talks . . . you know, as if he were making things up all the time. Joking."

"You like Mr. Barker, don't you, Tom?"

"Yes, Miss Klamath." He looked at her eagerly, perhaps hoping to be let off.

"So do I, Tom. In some ways he seems a very brilliant man.

86

But have you considered what it means? That he talks as if he were making things up, as you said? That you can't tell what's true and what's invented? Do you think he knows what's true and what's invented?"

"I don't know, Miss Klamath."

"Tom, I told you, we aren't sure why it's important to watch Mr. Barker. But I've talked to him several times. I wonder, now, if it may be that there's something wrong with his mind. It's occurred to me that he may be a fugitive from some institution, where they were trying to help him."

"But he's very smart," Tom said.

"That's just it." She nodded. "Often brilliant and charming men need that sort of help more than we humble people. These are things for experts to judge, don't you think? If we find that he needs mental care, Tom, it's our duty and God's will to see that he gets it, if we really like him. Isn't that so?"

"I guess it is."

"Look, Tom. You'll hear stories about my being strict with the clerks. That's my job. All the Service Managers are that way. We don't really like it, but someone must be responsible for seeing that the store rules are obeyed. That's what makes things run efficiently. That's what brings us all our paychecks. But, whatever the clerks think, you know that in a special case, I can overlook a rule, don't you, Tom?"

"Yes, ma'am."

"I've prayed for Mr. Barker, Tom. He's such a brilliant man; it's really a shame. A terrible shame. If he needs help, well . . . I'm going to do whatever I can to see that he gets it. Are you still with me, Tom?"

"All right, Miss Klamath," he said, but she couldn't be certain she'd convinced him.

At almost the same moment, Al was changing into his suit coat in the stockroom. He had gotten through the day quite nicely on his pint of whiskey, but he was grateful there were only five more such days left to go.

A voice spoke his name; he turned. It was Mr. Finn.

"Just going," Al said.

"Talk to you for a minute?"

87

"Of course."

"I'm worried," Finn said. "I can't trust M'nerney with it. I wonder if you'd help."

"If I can."

"Have you heard the story about Dolly . . . sending one of the girls off the floor because of her dress?"

"Yes, I overheard part of it."

"What'd you hear?" Finn asked.

"Maybe Dolly was a little rougher than she needed to be."

Finn nodded. "That's what I was wondering. She had the girl crying?"

"Yes. She did."

"Maybe the girl was having . . . you know, a female day. Something like that. Maybe she's nervous."

"I hope that was it," Al said.

"I hope so." Finn paused. Then he went on: "Dolly's right according to the store rules. But a warning should have been enough, first time. That's what I wanted your help with, Al. I haven't worked with Dolly since last year. She seems different. Touchy. Bullying. She's really a good girl, Al, and she's supposed to keep these people on their toes, but . . . well, that's her job, but . . ."

"What can I do?" Al asked.

"They talk to you," Finn said. "They won't to me. I don't mean I want you to spy, but just this one thing—listen to what they say about Dolly. There'll be lots of plain bitching, always is. But, well, if you think it sounds like she's going too far, I'd like to think someone would tell me, so I can try to do something. But I don't want to make a fuss for nothing, Al. Dolly's nervous, too."

"I'll bet she is, Mr. Finn," Al said.

"Al, you're a kind of an executive, running the stockroom. I wish you'd call me Hub."

"All right."

"I can't trust Mac with it," Finn said again.

"I know."

"Could you do it, Al? Would it bother you?"

He hesitated. "Okay," he said. "Okay, if I hear anything really bad in the next few days I'll let you know."

As she often did, Dolly Klamath worked late. She liked to stay on after hours, particularly if there were nobody responsible to see how late, to know the secret fullness of her devotion to the store. Let the Finns and Barkers match it before they got ironic with her.

By seven, however, there was nothing left either to do or to redo; she turned off the light at the service desk. Because she had served the store well today, she yielded to a little temptation which had suggested itself to her. First she looked carefully across the floor in all directions, to make sure there was no watchman in sight.

Then she went to the doll counter. In the half light, she found a bottle, and from it fed water to the burping doll which Winnipeg demonstrated. Then she removed the diaper and squeezed it gently, watching the water first trickle, then squirt out from between the rubber legs.

Looking around again to make sure she was unobserved, she took bottle and doll to the little office, turned on the light, closed the door, and repeated the operation. But in the bright light it lacked magic; feeling empty and a trifle guilty, she returned the toys to the counter and rang for the night elevator, putting the little game out of her mind.

9 In the first year of the case, Casper Usez did not wish to consider Allerd Pennington a man motivated by nothing more than an eccentric individual conscience. There were three other hypothetical sources of motivation: the political, the criminal, and the insane.

Any of these, from the standpoint of simplifying the search, would be preferable to accepting as full and complete the reasons given in the Cœur d'Alene letter to the scientist's wife. These reasons, in summary, were simply that Pennington could not accept himself, or ask that he be accepted, as a useful human being with the knowledge of what end his work had been directed toward; that he felt he must remove his potential for such work from the world by removing himself from the training, professional circumstances and relationships within which he had been happy doing it; that he doubted it would ever be possible for him to overcome his conviction of personal guilt sufficiently to make him a decent husband and dependable father; and that, even if he could, he did not wish to exploit his family's loyalty to him by requiring, or even permitting, them to share the sort of existence to which he now condemned himself.

For Usez to accept this would be to acknowledge that the man was unlikely to establish new relationships, through the expansion of which indications of his places of hiding might come to the Bureau's attention.

If, on the other hand, his motivation were political, they might

90

expect to apprehend Pennington at any time, for the Communist and other proscribed organizations, with which a politically motivated man would be certain to make contact, were thoroughly infiltrated. If, next, his motivation were criminal—if, for example, he had deserted because he felt he had something to sell—the elaborate informer system on which American police work is based would disclose clues to the man's activities sooner or later. If, finally, one understood Pennington's motivation as insane, it could reasonably be expected that further irrational behavior would follow as the imbalance developed, and that this, too, would reach the notice of authority.

In order to think through these possibilities as thoroughly as the materials he had would permit, Usez used a technique of which the Bureau had no knowledge; he took summary sheets of the Pennington case home over a weekend, and argued it through with his wife.

Like her husband, Betty Usez had had legal training; they had, in fact, met in law school, though she had never practiced. In the discussions, Betty would become Usez, a prosecuting theorist, while Usez, using the debater's trick of preparing by arguing against himself, became the defender.

"It's clear that his college and graduate school friends were radical," she said, when she had studied the summaries.

"In the late thirties, every intelligent and sensitive young man was radical to some extent," Usez said.

"At least two of them were Communist party members."

"The group itself was not Communist," Usez said. "And the others had no knowledge of the actual membership of those two men. Further, Pennington cannot be shown to have had any contact with those two from the time of his graduation."

"But under the shock of conscience when he deserted, four years later," Betty said, "there was clearly a change in Pennington. You acknowledge there was a pre-existing emotional commitment to the left? The left in general, that is?"

"The left in general," Usez admitted.

"And you agree that a change in character is clear in the very fact of his having deserted?"

"Yes."

"Then why isn't it reasonable to suppose that the change would be in the direction of the obvious channel of protest: the formal joining of what had, in late adolescence, only engaged his sympathies?"

Usez got up and poured himself a cup of coffee from the automatic Silex. "Care for some?" he asked. She shook her head. "Why isn't it reasonable? Because his first move, under party discipline, would necessarily have been to seek re-admission to secret data; in other words, to return, attracting as little suspicion as possible, to the Project."

"And if it were judged unfeasible, because too much time had gone by, or something of the sort? Or if he had joined them, but not informed the Party of his atomic project connection, that is, wished to be assigned to other work?"

"Our recruitment information is pretty good," Usez said. "Unless he joined the Party and subsequently was completely inactive, never attended a meeting, had an assignment, there would at least be some information on a member who could conceivably be Pennington; there isn't. And if he joined but is inactive, it's as if he hadn't joined."

"Suppose he left the country? Was sent to work in a laboratory in Russia?"

"Remote possibilities," Usez said. "If so, what was he doing in Cœur d'Alene? There's no Communist cell there."

"You're not giving me a fair chance," Betty objected. "You've denied me the possibility that he was already a member at the time of his desertion."

"It denies itself," Usez said. "First, if he'd been subject to discipline, they'd never have let him leave the base, as long as he was unsuspected. Second, you yourself point out an extreme change of outlook as the impulse-motive for leaving; then if he were already a member, this change would have led him away from political convictions, not towards them."

"Aren't you going to offer me any coffee?" she asked.

"I did."

"Well, I'd like some."

"Certainly." She was sitting closer to the pot, but since he had won the point, he got up and got it for her. "Try to make him a criminal," Usez said.

"The very act of desertion from the Army is criminal," Betty said.

"Yes."

"Desertion of wife and family is criminal."

"Technically."

"Morally," she said emphatically. "To abandon a wife and two children? You contend that's only technically criminal?"

"He felt that he was unfit to live with them."

"Male rationalization. Look at the picture you can draw of this man. Complete irresponsibility in boyhood; he and his brother were the scourge of the neighborhood. A growing fascination not with ethical or social studies, but only with the coldly factual, the scientific. A resentment when, finally, the scientific work is put to social use. Friendships with the anti-social at college. Evidence of at least one extra-marital affair, and presumption of others, showing a contempt for social tradition. In an era when you yourself said 'every sensitive and intelligent man was radical,' a refusal to join and work effectively in the organizations which served these beliefs; therefore, a strong presumption that his radicalism was directed not by conscience but by a desire to outrage. A sentimentalism about music, the most socially useless of the arts. A misanthropy which his friends choose to describe as humorous; as a man jokes, so he thinks. Doesn't this background, in connection with two known acts of criminality, create a strong presumption of further criminality?"

"It can be read that way," Usez said. "But you still have something to show . . ."

"Of course. I'm not that stupid, dear. What specific criminal purpose had he in deserting? How can we know unless we know what information he took with him?"

"None," Usez said. "None that can be proved."

"But even if he were under the illusion he had such information . . ."

"His most intelligent course would have been to stay where he was, and try to gather more. You admit his intelligence?"

"Yes," Betty said, wearily. "I admit his intelligence."

"Don't be irritated with me," Usez said. "This is helping."

"I'm not irritated," she said. "I don't see how you can argue that it was moral for him to leave a wife and two children without means of support . . ."

"He left them something like five thousand dollars when everything was realized," Usez said.

"I know," his wife said. "You spent nearly a week working out that insurance deal for her."

"No more than a couple of hours."

"It's so nice when your work involves pretty little wives with no one to turn to," Betty said.

"Stop it, honey," Usez said. "Come on. Let's finish. Can you show me that the man's insane?"

"You never admit it when I win," Betty said.

"Come on. You've got your best case to make this time."

She studied the sheets. "There's nothing insane looking about his family background," she said. "He was a normal kid. Normal family. Father had a lumberyard. Prosperous until 1930. Tough time during the depression. Doing okay again by '36. Mother and father separated for a year but not divorced; back together in '35. Bother him much, do you think?"

"We don't know," Usez said. "Normal enough thing. He'd have been fifteen. Probably bothered him a normal amount."

"Father's a trifle wild-eyed," Betty said.

"Pretty strongly individual," Usez admitted. "Pennington was closer to his mother, though; took her side when they separated. So'd the brother."

"The brother. Yes." Betty read on. "Pretty close, weren't they? I don't find what happened to the brother."

"Next page," Usez said. "Killed over Italy. A flier."

"Well, there's a shock to work from," Betty said. "If we can assume that the relationship was really strong."

"I don't think it was that strong," Usez said. "They used to call themselves Dizzy and Paul, after the Dean brothers. But that was when they were little boys."

"Who in hell were the Dean brothers?" Betty said.

"Baseball players. Come on, honey. You're not working."

"There's nothing to go on," Betty said. "They were a couple of little scamps. Actually, most of the neighbors thought the mischief they got into was cute. Pennington has a couple of bad

94

years in adolescence; cheerful poverty—something like that. Some family strain. Breach healed. Gets into science; hangs out with an intellectually free-wheeling bunch at college; marries a pretty girl. Wait a minute . . ." she stopped to read. Then she smiled. "This college group of his didn't turn out too well, did it?"

"No, it didn't."

"About half of them seem to be okay, but the others have pretty odd records."

"Yes."

"Not very stable boys, then?"

"Maybe not."

"Let's get back to the brother's death, then," Betty said. "And at least one little excursion outside of marriage—the girl you talked to in New York. Talk to her alone, dear?"

"Stick to the point, honey," Usez said. "No. Chub was with me."

"We know your boy was kind of restless, then. Had been a bit wild as a kid, and ran with an unstable bunch at college. He was upset over his brother's death. Doesn't seem to have seen much of his parents . . ."

"He couldn't after he got into the Army," Usez said.

"All right. But there's a pattern of instability. Not exaggerated, but existing as potential. The word comes that he's been doing something he considers hideous; whatever complicated guilts have been showing themselves in small ways now get focussed; he's outraged with himself and the world. He feels persecuted. They didn't have any right to order him to do things like this. His wife considered he'd been under too much pressure. I see him as deserting in a kind of blackout of his responsible self . . ."

"That's got it," Usez said, suddenly.

"What?"

"That's the problem. Which is Pennington's responsible self? The man he was, or the man he is?"

"The man he is is charged with two crimes," Betty said.

"But in his own view," Usez insisted. "Are they crimes? Or leave aside the abandonment of his family; we know he isn't happy about that. But the big thing, deserting the Army. Leaving important work. Isn't it likely that he'd argue the Nuremberg precedent? Remember, it's established there that a war criminal isn't absolved of individual responsibility on the plea that he was merely carrying out orders."

"But it's insane for Pennington to think himself a war criminal."

"Not necessarily," Usez said. "It may be incorrect in our view, but it isn't necessarily insane."

"But what he elects to do about it is," Betty said. "He elects to become a kind of zombie. After all, what's more insane than to kill yourself, which he claims to have done symbolically, pleading a kind of motivation which is personal and unique? You know, there were other sensitive and intelligent guys on the project, who didn't find out until later what they'd been doing, but only little Pennington . . ."

"No," Usez said.

"No?"

He shook his head. "At least four of the young scientists who hadn't known what the project was committed suicide. Real suicide. That's very strictly classified information."

She got up from the white corduroy covered, living-room day-bed, and walked over to the window, overlooking Arlington. "You were saving that," she said. "You knew you had me beaten."

"I'm sorry, Betty." He went over to her. "I really wanted you to win. Look what having you beaten does to my case." He held her hand, and they looked out the window together, at the meaningless street. "I've had too much coffee," he said. "Have we got any seconal?"

"I was afraid it was going to be one of those nights," Betty said.

10   Saturday was the first of the big days, though it started slowly. At a quarter of ten they had been open forty-five minutes; Mr. Finn, pacing nervously up and down in the stockroom, looking out the door each time he passed it, kept saying:

"Jesus, boys. It's Saturday. What's wrong with their calendars?"

There was a new bubble demonstrator to take Nickie's place in front of the door, an erect, bosomy lady of fifty-odd, and he kept fretting about her.

"Why did they have to send her up, Al? My God, boys, what we need out there is a little more pep, a couple of classy janes to throw in with that bunch of hens. We'll never move any goods with characters like this."

Al, who was rather charmed by the serenity with which Mrs. Kelsner kept the bubbles blowing, said: "I think she gives the place a homey touch."

"Homey!" Finn cried. "Good God, Al. We're not running a living room bazaar."

Fifteen minutes later, by ten, the elevators began discharging people, first in singles and pairs, then, as the aisles filled up, by dozens. One car became a *Santaland Express*, discharging its entire load into the toy department every five minutes. More customers came streaming off the escalators. By eleven they were surging impatiently, three deep, at every counter. The crowd at

97

Nickie's record demonstration was so large it blocked the aisles. No one could get near electric trains. The noise of voices grew so loud that, for the first time, the Christmas records could not be heard in the stockroom.

At the doll counter, a masher moved in, pinched Sally on the breast and disappeared into the crowd. The plain girl from Winnipeg was hit in the eye by a little lost boy whom she tried to pick up because he was crying. In spite of these disturbances, they sold so many burping dolls that Al had to send Tom, working his first full day, to the top floor wareroom for replacements.

Clerks from the Flying Squad were sent in to bolster the force, and there was an atmosphere of under-the-breath recrimination as they stole sales and made mistakes in price. A woman beat Gullakian with her shopping bag to get his attention. The man in Zoom-Spaceman-Yippee-Cowboy Suits broke down and began making sales without taking time to write out slips; Dolly Klamath had to rush over to work with him. M'nerney hid in the office.

The confusion was so general that a very small girl was able to struggle away from the building toy counter with a thirty dollar Erector set and get all the way down to the third floor on the escalators before she was stopped.

Only Finn, moving through the jam fast and smooth, his jumpiness finally gone, closing a sale here, approving a check there, settling squabbles, getting redder and redder and jollier and jollier, a duck returned to water, seemed happy and at ease.

Al, returning from a tortuous trip to Hobbies, where he'd delivered an armload of wood burning sets, was seized by an indignant woman who shouted, pointing at Gullakian, that that man wouldn't let her son take a bike out for a road test; like a genial genie, Finn appeared to lead the woman off, shouting jovially: "Why certainly, certainly he can road test it, madam. All we need is a small deposit, just a few dollars, sign the easy payment plan, he can ride it all around the world. Bring your book, Mr. Gullakian, here's a lady wants a bike."

Finally, it was too crowded to try to keep the stock levels up; M'nerney, slipping into the stockroom from the office, agreed that they had better let the clerks sell the goods on down until some sort of break came. Al, who had unpacked all the units which the shelves could hold, was finally able to rest. M'nerney left for the office.

There was a new item on hand, a Henry Hen Radio Set with Corncob Earphones; Al took one from the shelf and sat down to examine it. It was a four-tube set, made of plastic, in the shape of a fat chicken, with a tuning knob in place of one wing and an off-on-volume switch in place of the other; a narrow celluloid grin across the beak was the dial.

When Tom came pushing back from the doll counter, Al had the thing upside down in his lap.

"Fixing it?" Tom asked.

"Nothing wrong with it." Al smiled. "Admiring it."

"Do you really?"

"They do remarkable things with injection-molded plastic now," Al said. "The wiring is molded right into this."

"It is?"

"Wonderful." Al stood and put it back in its place on the shelf. "Glamorous, low-priced."

"It is . . . kind of cute," Tom said, uncertainly.

"Science, rational man's improvement on the slave system, eh, Tom?"

"Well, I guess so," Tom said. "That is, it's cute and cheap. It's four-seventy-five, isn't it, and a kid can have his own radio?"

"What else, Tom?"

"Well, it's pretty durable."

"Yes?"

"It's pretty awful, isn't it?"

Al grinned. "Just the thing to go with little injection molded plastic brains," he said. "Why don't you go to lunch, Tom? It'll be a couple of hours before we can start getting stuff through again."

Tom took off the gray cotton jacket, hung it up, and put on his suit coat. He signed himself out, pushed his way across the floor, and took the employees' elevator to the ninth.

He got in line at the store cafeteria, thinking that after today he ought to start bringing his lunch to save money. The food looked attractive; it was all priced in amounts ending in odd pennies: eighteen cents for a small salad, forty-one cents for hot dogs and sauerkraut, three cents for two slices of bread and a pat of butter, nine cents for coffee with cream.

He took his tray over to a small table in the corner and began to eat. He had hardly started when he saw Gullakian coming across the room with a tray on which were a sandwich, a glass of milk and a piece of cake. Gullakian smiled and sat down opposite him.

"Next to the piano, Tom boy," he said.

Tom looked behind his chair; almost under his elbow was a small piano. "I hadn't even noticed," he said.

"Notice what you're eating?" Gullakian asked, taking half his sandwich in two bites. "Those hot dogs look green. God, the crap they give you here."

"I think I'll start bringing lunch tomorrow," Tom said. "That's what Al does."

"Al? He doesn't seem like the lunch-bringing type?"

"He has a thermos bottle downstairs," Tom said.

Gullakian grunted. His mouth was full. When he'd cleared it sufficiently he said: "They ought to give us a decent amount of time to go out for lunch. What can you do with half an hour? Barely get a chance to look at the quail."

Tom looked around the lunchroom. There certainly were a lot of girls in it. He recognized one or two from their own department.

"So. How about a little music?" Gullakian finished his milk and brought his chair to Tom's side of the table. The instrument and the table were so close together that Gullakian, sitting at the piano, and Tom, eating his lunch, were actually sitting side by side, faced in opposite directions, with Tom hemmed in against the wall.

"We'll give them a little schmaltz," Gullakian said, into Tom's ear. "Something to ruin their digestion."

With much ornamentation, he began to play *Night and Day*.

Some of the chatter of conversation stopped in the room, and several of the girls turned to watch Gullakian as he played. One, who had finished her lunch, came over and stood by the piano, singing the words of the song under the music. She was good looking, in a flashy way, but a little fat, Tom thought, and past thirty.

100

Gullakian finished the piece and began on *September Song.*

"Oh, that's my favorite number," the girl said, leaning towards Gullakian. "And now I've got to go back. I'm late already."

"I'll play it for you tomorrow," Gullakian promised.

"I work in lingerie," said the girl. Tom was aware simultaneously of the odor of her perfume as she leaned closer for a moment, and of Gullakian's left elbow poking him in the ribs, while the hand continued to play the bass.

"I've got to relieve Al," Tom said; he got up and squeezed his way out.

On the floor, the jam was still severe; he pushed himself through to the stockroom and signed back in.

"How's it, Athlete?" Al said.

"Fine," Tom said. "Gullakian played the piano in the cafeteria."

"Yeah? Good?"

"He's very good."

"Right," Al said. "What do you recommend?"

"In the cafeteria?"

Al was changing coats. "Yeah."

"The hot dogs are all right. I thought you brought your lunch?"

"Started to," Al smiled. "Couldn't find a thing in the icebox but ptarmigan salad." He went out.

Tom was puzzled; he was certain he had seen Al with a thermos bottle of coffee. Sure he had. Because he'd thought it strange that Al didn't offer him any. Of course, you had to be careful; you weren't supposed to bring any food downstairs.

Just to be sure that he hadn't been mistaken, Tom started to search for the thermos. It would be hidden somewhere. He checked the opened cases without finding it. He climbed to the top of the tool kit cartons and looked across the tops of the cases. Not up there, either.

He started looking on the shelves. Mr. Finn poked his head in through the doorway.

"Straightening things out?" he called.

"Sure," Tom said.

"That's the boy. Ought to be able to get some stuff out here in another half hour. They're starting to realize they're hungry." He stepped into the stockroom. "Old snowball's rolling down the dollar hill today, eh, Tom?"

101

"That's fine," Tom said nervously. His eye had just caught the shiny, red and black tube of the thermos bottle, casually camouflaged among some red and black cut-out sets.

"Al eating?"

"Yes," Tom said, turning and taking a side step so that his body would be between Mr. Finn and the bottle.

"When he gets back, go down and get me some coffee and a ham on white, will you, Tommy? Mustard."

"As soon as he gets back," Tom said.

"Right," said Finn, turning to go. "I'll be out there rolling the old ball," and he plunged back into the crowd.

After a moment, Tom went to the door to make sure Finn was out of sight. He watched Mrs. Kelsner, the new bubbler, make a sale. Then he went quickly back to the shelf and got the thermos bottle. Not really thinking, just for assurance, he unscrewed the cap from the top. He pulled the cork out. He pursed his lips so that the hot coffee would trickle in and not burn his tongue, and took a sip. Then he set the bottle down in complete astonishment. The liquid was ice-cold, and it was whiskey.

Simultaneously a girl's voice said: "Hi, Tom," and he jumped around, panicked.

It was Nickie.

"I'm sorry," she said. "I didn't know I was so frightening."

"Oh, no," Tom said. "I was just . . . I mean I didn't want anyone . . . well, I was afraid it was Miss Klamath, and I thought she'd see my thermos bottle."

Nickie laughed. "I'm so glad I'm not really a fright," she said.

"No," Tom said. "Honestly. You're not," screwing the cap hastily on, and putting the thermos back. Nickie was laughing at him again. "Well, you're not supposed to bring food down here," he said.

"I'm sorry, Tom. It's not that funny. I'm just so keyed up, the way things are out there today. Where's Al?"

"Eating."

"Oh. I was going to try to trick him into taking me to lunch," she said. "Throw a fit or something."

Tom smiled. "You like him, don't you?"

"It's a fact, Tom. You can tell him, too. Only add that a fact can't be taken as a compliment."

102

"All right," Tom said.

"What do you have in the thermos? Coffee?"

Tom nodded.

"I don't suppose you could spare a tired girl a cup?" She sat down.

"I was lying, Nickie. It's Al's."

"I didn't mean to corner you. Sorry again."

"Nickie?"

"Yes, Tom."

"Do you think Al's all right?"

"That would be kind of an understatement."

"Miss . . . somebody was saying that, well, from the way he talks sometimes. Saying just the opposite of what he means. Turning things into jokes. This person was worried he might not be sane. I mean, she said a lot of brilliant men need help . . ."

"That's nonsense, Tom. If Al's not sane, God pity those who are. Don't let Miss Whoeveritis get you upset."

"Well, I was supposed to kind of listen to him, and tell her what he said, because she was worried . . ."

"Who was this? Miss Klamath?"

"I'm not allowed to say."

"But why should she care about it, as long as he does his job?"

"I don't know," Tom said. "I mean, she doesn't really know. There's some kind of mystery . . . she said she'd been told to watch him, and asked me to help."

"Told by whom?"

"She couldn't say."

"Have you told this person anything?"

"There wasn't much to tell before."

"There's something to tell now?"

Tom hesitated. Then he nodded. "About the thermos bottle. It's got whiskey in it. I didn't think this person was right, but listen, Nickie: if Al has to drink at work, would that mean there's . . . something wrong?"

"Who knows?" Nickie said. "I could have used a drink myself this morning." She paused a moment thoughtfully. "I didn't realize that Al was an official mystery."

"He is."

103

"I wish you wouldn't tell Miss Klamath, Tom, about the whiskey. Not right away."

"I didn't say it was her. I don't want to tell about it."

"Listen, Tom. Why don't we—you and I—see what we can find out ourselves, first. We know whose side we're on. When we know enough we can decide whether it ought to be passed along."

"All right," Tom said. "All right. I'd much rather do it that way."

"Not a word to anyone unless we both agree?"

"Okay."

"I'll tell you what I know," Nickie said. "I'm pretty sure he went to college in New England. Something tells me Harvard."

"He's crazy about music," Tom said. "And he's traveled all over the country."

"That's something," Nickie said. "Where does he live?"

"I'm not sure. North Beach, I think. He takes the Kearney bus, at the corner of Post."

"I wonder if I could follow him?" Nickie suggested, dropping her voice and narrowing her eyes.

"Would you dare?"

"It would be fun," Nickie jumped up, tawny and intense. "I'll get to the corner first, Tom, turn up my coat collar and wait in Snider's Cafeteria, at a table by the window. Do you leave work together?"

"Sometimes."

"Can you arrange to tonight?" He nodded. "Okay. When you come along with him, and he goes to the bus stop, signal. I'll take a cab, and have him stay behind the bus Al's on. Then, when he gets off, I'll ride past a little way, get off, and turn back."

"I wouldn't dare ask a cab driver to do a thing like that," Tom said, full of admiration.

"Sweet boy, you would if girls drove cabs."

"I guess it ought to work," Tom said, blushing. "All right. Let's do it."

By the time Al returned, Nickie had gone, and the energies of the department were absorbed once more in the battle with the customers.

That evening, letting himself into the room with two beds and

104

no chairs, Al was tired. He felt the let-down which followed having finished the whiskey by mid-afternoon; he was even, he thought wryly, a little hungover. He lay down, thinking he might sleep for an hour or, if sleep failed, rest; then he might feel more like getting up and going, for beer and a sandwich, to Weary's down the block.

He had taken his shoes off and sleep, miraculously, was half his when the knock came on the door. He woke abruptly, and held his breath, hoping it might have occurred in a dream. The knock was repeated. A window in the rear wall opened, crazily, into a sub-hallway; he got up cautiously in his stocking feet, slipped over to it and eased it open. He had oiled this window carefully when he'd moved into the room; it was the sort of precaution he often took in his life as quarry without visible pursuit.

"Al, I heard you. Please let me in." It was Nickie's voice.

He went to the door, opened it, and said: "How could you have heard me? I couldn't hear myself."

"I heard you say something when I first came up. Were you asleep? You look exhausted."

"Why are you here?"

"Are you going to ask me in?"

"I don't know. Did you follow me from the store?"

She nodded.

"Any particular reason, or just fun?"

"Particular fun," she said, brightly.

"Come on in, Sharpy," he said. "It's darker in here, and you'll lose some of your power."

"Then I'll turn on the light," she said, stepping in and finding the light switch. She turned it. The big bulb in the ceiling came on. He closed his eyes. "I'm sorry." She flicked it off. "Do your eyes hurt?"

"No, Nickie. It's just that I'd been almost asleep. Turn the light on." He walked back towards the bed where he'd been resting. "Come in. Sit down. It's nice of you to come."

"Is it, Al?" Again she switched on the light. He sat on the bed.

"Pretty nice."

She looked around. "Al, this is awful. I was going to offer to get supper for us. But there's nothing to cook on."

"There's a hot plate in the closet," Al said. "And dishwashing goes on in the bathroom, I'm afraid, which is down the hall."

"Al. Let's go out to my house. My parents are in Sacramento, and the maids are out. We could find things to eat and drink . . ."

"Thanks, Nickie," Al said. "It's a very sweet idea. I'm afraid I've gotten to a point where it takes discomfort to make me comfortable."

"Then we'll stay here," Nickie said pertly, and sat down on the other bed, facing him.

"Nickie," he said slowly. "Maybe I should tell you how often I've lain here, waiting for sleep to come, with the Pizza sign flicking off and on across the street, lighting the room with a red glow for four seconds, every four seconds; and in the dark seconds, how I've opened my eyes, and fixed them on the place where you're sitting; and when the red came on again, closed my eyes again because there was no vision there like you."

"Al . . ."

"No. Sit still, Vision. I wanted to make you a pretty speech, because I want you to know I'm not indifferent. I'm afraid you're getting caught in a silly, accidental process; sometimes a sought-after girl's interest is caught by an appearance of indifference. It's just an appearance; I'm not indifferent. . . ."

"I see," Nickie said. "And now I'm supposed to feel that I've made some sort of conquest, and withdraw? How you underestimate yourself, Al Barker." She smiled wickedly, and pushed herself to her feet.

Quickly, he too got up. "No, wait," he said.

"I'm going to wait," she said. "I like it here."

"Nickie, I'll meet you on neutral ground. Let's go down to the corner and have supper. There's a place called Weary's." He half-turned away to pick up his jacket.

"How strange," she said, staying where she was. "You're afraid to be touched, aren't you?"

"Don't be silly."

"I've felt that way. But men don't feel that way, do they? Unless . . . you're not . . ."

"I'm not a homosexual, Snooper," Al said. "I'm not much of anything. Let's get supper."

She took a step towards him. "Al, do you mean you're . . . impotent or something?"

"I've just enough male pride left not to take the easy way, and say yes," Al said. "What do you want me to say?"

"I want you to tell me."

"Maybe it is a kind of impotence," he said. "I find it best to live pretty much as an ascetic."

"Why?"

"Beautiful asker of indecent questions," Al said, "I say to you in high school Latin, *nolo contendere.*"

"As well as *Nolo tangi?*"

"You are a sharpy."

"I'm unwilling to contend, too," Nickie said.

"I know." Al opened the door for her. "You just want to win."

She stepped in front of him. He started to follow, and she stopped short, so that his chest moved forward and met her shoulders. She leaned back against him that way for an instant, turned her face along his cheek, and murmured, "I'm going to, too." The tremor that ran through him was so violent that he knew she felt it.

"That's unfair," he said. "You don't play fair."

"Don't think I'm playing," Nickie said, so seriously that it gave him, finally, a chance to laugh at her and push her along.

At Weary's, in the farthest booth back, she whispered to ask whether it would be all right to order Scotch. "I mean, I'll pay, but would they think I was too fancy?"

"They'll think you're fancy whatever you order," Al said. "Don't worry. There's hardly any thinking goes on at Weary's, and whatever is thought is soon forgotten. That's what the place is for."

They ordered spaghetti and drinks, and Al found, to his surprise, that he was hungry; he'd expected to be too tired to eat.

"You've revived me," he said.

"Do you drink a good deal, Al?"

"Be decent, Nickie. Eat your supper. Make jokes. Flirt. Don't ask questions." She looked at him steadily. "I drink as much as I need to help me sleep," he said; he tried to appeal to her: "Nickie, I used to think I had a kind of useless gift for being gay; would it be interesting to see if I have it still?"

107

She shook her head. "I want to know why you have trouble sleeping," she said.

"You have the face of fate and the body of immortality," Al said, "and I will not answer your questions."

"Didn't you once have a profession, Al? I know you're trying to be nice, but I'd much rather be hurt than evaded."

"Then you've come to the right man, Nickie. I'm a woundlicker by profession. And where there are no wounds, it's my nature to make them. Nickie, stop asking. I'm a man who wants to be forgotten."

"Please order me another drink, Al. There's no such thing. A man who wants to be forgotten is the only thing there isn't."

"Nicholas Nimblebee," Al said. "You make it very hard for a man to be an isn't." He paused. Now he would have to do it. "Nickie, hadn't it occurred to you that I might be married?"

"Hadn't it occurred to you that I might not care? Anyway, I don't believe it."

The fresh drinks came. He nodded; he took from his coat pocket a battered wallet, and from the wallet an old photo of Frances and the children.

"Here," he said.

"Where is she?" Nickie took the photograph and looked at it.

"In the East."

"How old are your children, Al?"

"Two and four."

"Recent picture?"

"A couple of rough years old."

"Al Barker, the dress this woman is wearing is wartime length. This was forty-four or forty-five."

"I said it's an old picture." Al reached for it.

"And you said your children were two and four. Why these kids must be eight or ten by now. Al, how long since you've seen these people?"

He stood up. "Give it back, Nickie."

"But . . ."

Stiff-faced, he held out his hand. She put the photo in it. "Come on," he said. "You caught me. It's time to go now."

She stood, too. He helped her silently with her coat.

"Are you mad at me for catching you, Al?"

"I'm not very pleased," he said.

They walked to the door, and out.

"Al?" Nickie said hesitantly, when they reached the street.

"What?"

"Have you drunk enough to go to sleep?"

"I don't know."

"Couldn't we go back to your room. And talk?"

"No," Al said. "We couldn't do that."

They walked without speaking down to Union Street, and stopped on the corner. He looked away from her, scanning the street for a cab; when he looked back, she was crying silently.

"Nickie," he said, and touched her hand. "Nickie. Don't."

She put her face against him wildly for a moment, snuffled, and then threw her head back. "I'm sorry, Al. Please forgive me. That wasn't part of the game, and it isn't because you turned me down, it's just . . . Al, I'm sorry I've been a nosy little girl and spoiled things. Al, even if . . . I need you, Al; please say it's all right. You're the only one I can talk to . . ."

"You're very easy to forgive," Al said.

"I tried to be so clever, and I've been so clumsy," Nickie said. "There's some grown-up reason why you can't talk about yourself, something desperate and serious and I've been treating it like an adolescent game. Have I ruined it for myself, Al? Can we still talk when I . . . need to? About . . . if I promise not to ask questions?"

"Sure we can," Al said.

A cab, seeing them standing there, drew up. He opened the door.

"I'll bet I don't even get a goodnight kiss," she said, lifting her face towards his. "I never asked for one before."

"Nicholas Nimblebee," he said. "I'm so goddamn vulnerable, I'd better let you win that bet," and he could tell from the quick way she bit her lip and turned that, even then, at the end, she hadn't really been able to believe he meant it.

11 It was not a happy thing to have in mind, Al thought, walking slowly back through the mist, up Stockton Street: that final image of the crest of eagerness fallen from a lovely face, when she had turned away.

He was restless, now, and didn't want to go home. Nor could he return alone to the populated loneliness of Weary's, not just now. It was easy enough to admit that she'd affected him, but to know it was not enough to clear away the undeservedly offended image, to keep from feeling already a nostalgia for the exhilaration of hearing her voice, for the vibrancy of her hand as he had seized it for a moment when she cried. That was a hand one pressed and wanted to continue pressing, to hold, to bring against one's face.

No rhetoric could keep his cheek from twitching where the radiant energy of that hand hadn't touched it, as he walked through the bright and dark of Chinatown Saturday night, past the identically stocked shops, not even the rhetoric of his full and awful title: King Al No.–1, the Kiss Killer, Render of the Rendezvous, Teeter-totterer of Tete-a-Tetes, the Genghis Khan of Candlelight, Offender of the Faithful and Murderer of the Moon.

And next, as the King found himself standing in the quiet above the entrance of the Stockton tunnel, watching the car lights plunge into the black beginning, a worse thing began to happen and, at the same time, a thing which told him that surely he was

110

right to have made Nickie go: through the first, accusatory image began to show, strong and then fading, strong and then fading, a second face, not quite so lovely but more childlike, larger-eyed; with the echo of Nickie's clever, tense, educated voice mixed the echo of a soft, Texas voice; now his cheek twitched alternately for the touch of Nickie's hand and for another hand, shorter-fingered, warmer perhaps, quieter; and with the nostalgia for exhilaration intermixed another nostalgia, for a kind of tenderness which was all kinds of tenderness—one's tenderness for the defenseless and for the innocently self-reliant, one's tenderness in knowing that, whatever is said and done, another will respond only by trying to give pleasure; and the tenderness, even, which one means in saying, of a healed wound, it is still tender.

He sought, standing above the tunnel mouth, for a song, a piece of music, to drive the double-image away, and sent through his head, blatantly fighting the mood, with an imagined blare of trumpets and trombones, to the tune of *Blue Skies*, King Al's Royal Anthem:

> "(Come on an') Hate me
> All that you can.
> Pinch and deflate me,
> Mary Ann."

He danced a shuffling step in the quiet street, hit the palm of one hand with the fist of the other, and sang, anguished, aloud:

> "(Come on an') Hate me,
> Countin' on you.
> Kick and abate me,
> Mary Lou."

He stopped. Rhyme was no more use than rhetoric, less even, for now the image was insistently becoming triple. Mixing itself intolerably with Nickie's and the second face was a third, the delicately-merry face of Frances, his wife, and to prevent this third apparition from bringing with it two children, concerning whose ages he had been in loving error, and the offer of a whole life, he walked on, above the tunnel, surrendering to the second image and the recollection of San Antonio:

—At first, he recalled, when flight had had its romantic com-

111

pensations, and seemed worth the effort of imagination, he had devised a plan to avoid the possibility of someone's anticipating where, should part of the pattern of excursion become known, he might be headed next. It seemed wise to have a particular set of geographical objectives, for intuition told him that an aimless wanderer too soon begins to circle. So he had chosen towns and cities for the beauty of their names, certain that no such frivolously aesthetic design would show itself. He had carefully memorized twenty place names for a start.

—Now he did not even know for certain which of the list of beautifully named towns and cities he had passed through: Talladega, Alabama, and Valdosta, Georgia, yes. But Paragould, Arkansas? Tell City, Indiana? Pass Christian, Mississippi? He remembered Sandusky, Chagrin Falls and Massillon, Ohio. Blue Island and Rantoul in Illinois (he had never found Nokomis). Had he reached Thief River Falls, or Sleepy Eye, or Eveleth, in Minnesota? No more than one of them. But Cœur d'Alene, in Idaho, yes. Las Animas, in Colorado. Hoquiam, in Washington.

—All right, he thought. The list ends with Texas: Laredo, Corpus Christi. But he had reached neither; he had stopped in San Antonio. Wait.

—Wait. It had been in Cœur d'Alene, early in the half sardonic, half wistful quest for a town or city which could match the beauty of its name, though he had no thought of staying if he found it; it was early, in Cœur d'Alene, before his money ran out and he had to hitch-hike to Nebraska to work in the sugar beet harvest, that he had allowed himself a woman at all. For in the first weeks, perversely, perverse because before this separation he had been opportunistically unfaithful to his wife, in the first weeks he had required strict chastity of himself in Frances' honor, as if assuring her in this way that it was through no failing of hers that he had left.

—And in Cœur d'Alene, Idaho, the most beautifully named of all the beautifully named cities, he remembered feeling, once the letter was written, a truly different man now, and thinking that he had never known a whore, and that the man he now was, King Al No.–1, would be Prince Consort of Whores. And so, in a spirit of mocking himself for the fetishism about place names, he had set out to go from bar to bar to find the Whoor d'Alene; and found her, the Whoor de la Cœur, rather a sweet girl but overshrewd. And cried, afterwards, not with her but back in his room, packing up to leave, for the only time in his adult life, sober tears; for it was with the Whoor d'Alene, for whom he could feel no lust but only pity, whom he had taken, finally, in pity because she had a pride in her work one couldn't disappoint, it was then he had to accept the fact that King Al No.-1 was a Pretender, that he was and would be only Pennington, homeless.

—Could any other recollection be interposed between Les Pleurs d'Alene and San Antonio?

—The old man in the lobby who had looked at him severely, as he came down with his suitcase and said: "We're here to smile, fella." And Al had replied: "That's right. That's what we're here for."

—The strange German-Russian people in the sugar beet fields of Nebraska.

—The fantastical horse van he had ridden through the mountains in.

—He had sold records in a music shop in San Antonio. There was a girl, a model, a young one, just nineteen; she'd stop in, sometimes, when she had time to pass. She had liked to have him tell her what to play, what to listen to, sometimes what to buy when she had just been paid, and wanted to see the money turn into something she could prize. She was a glowing, overdressed little model on whom the late fashions, this week's hair style, were not only becoming, they were silly and therefore charming, and her attentiveness to them childlike and delightful.

—"I'm Dessie Chapman."

—"Dessie's not a name."

—"I know it. I was named Desiree. Isn't it funny?"

—He had walked back with her and into the record playing booth one day—could it really have been only the fourth time she came in?—to adjust the speed of the turntable, and he remembered the way the booth filled with her too grown up perfume, and he'd thought Good God, perfume was effective, after all. So he'd straightened from making the adjustment and turned to smile at her, and she was smiling back before his smile had really started; there was no choice but to kiss her, if only to teach

113

her it was risky to be so pleasant. She squirmed with pleasure, like a puppy, and kissed him back. Then, very sloemnly, she took a Kleenex out of her purse and wiped off an absurd amount of lipstick, and he laughed with delight, she had invested the task with such a marvelously disproportionate gravity.

—He had made his face grave to mock hers, and kissed her again, and at the end of it she had looked solemnly into his eyes and said:

—"I love you."

—"But you can't."

—"I don't care. I do."

—"You're a ridiculous little girl, and you mustn't ever say that terrible word again."

—"I know I am. I love you."

Her love was conceived as simply and uncritically as a pet's, and whatever one said: I'm thirty, you're nineteen. I'll be leaving; you'll stay here. You may have arms from any man in the city, fine arms, strong arms, while you can't have so much as a worthless finger, finally, from me. Don't you understand, little Dessie Chapman, I'm King Al No.-1, who banished love? You can't love me.

—She'd only have repeated, not bothering to understand, "I don't care. I do."

—Like many of the dear and silly, she was perfectly intuitive: "Poor Al," she would say, when he told her insistently ˙ that he was married. "Poor Al. He can't marry me. And he wouldn't, even if he could."

—What had Nickie said about setting out to renew her youth, through doing youthful things? But Nickie, still youthful, had been aiming at it, had been deliberately re-accepting a state she hadn't, if she chose, already gone beyond. For Al, the renewal had overtaken him by surprise. He hadn't supposed that one could feel this way again, this lovely frenzy of intensity for Dessie, a re-opening of whole canals of sentiment he had supposed were closed to the foolish, gay traffic of popular songs and close dancing; of sitting up all night to talk; of escapading in borrowed cars; of exchanging secret symbols of caress in public; and finally of the miraculously unassuagable thirst for the communion of each other's bodies, a mystery which she absolutely trusted him to teach her, so that he tenderly presided over Dessie's emergence from apprehensive sensuality, to hesitant desiring, to charming wantonness, to a full and open womanhood; all for him. It was being young again in a way one had forgotten to hope to be.

—She was part of a world, and it took him in, a world of pretty fashion models whose friends were photographers and young advertising men, graduate students, baseball players, ranchers— nice boys, bright ones, good dancers, adept at having fun; light drinkers but frequent ones; party givers, breezy, unquestioning in the Texas way, sometimes intellectual; Al liked them. One of the young photographers gave him a darkroom job and, because Al's undeclarable knowledge of theory was so thorough, he was enormously good at it, and enjoyed it—even worked out a modest research problem, destroying his records, and had an idea for a larger one. The photographer, impressed, offered him a partner- ship; Dessie was more adorable every day. He was in love all right. Except that the darkroom techniques fascinated him, he hated the time he wasn't with her, and there was very little such time once work was done—only, really, the hours when she slept at home and he, properly exhausted with work and love, slept in the apartment he could afford now, and where they made love almost every evening, unless there were a party. Could he not have stayed?

—How could he? It had been four months. He was almost happy. There was no sensation of pursuit and imminent capture. But he was happy; that was the sire of discontent. Happiness and freedom are opposite states. What was true of this life in San Antonio which had not been true of his life with Frances? Only that the responsibility, the guilt, was less apparent because less direct. He needed freedom, not happiness, because freedom was all he deserved; it had taken, finally, so reluctant was he to face it, a newspaper to tell him that—a newspaper which head- lined, blackly:

ATOMIC EXPLOSION REPORTED IN RUSSIA

—That was when the West Coast became his goal; there were only six cities left now, indifferently named, in which he could set his portable throne: Spokane, Seattle, Portland, San Fran-

115

cisco, Los Angeles, and San Diego where the fleet was. For one or all of these must be among the first places, and the King must be at the head of his inattentive troops, the first to accept the death which he had fashioned.

—He did it better in San Antonio; withdrew gradually, less abruptly, presided now, wretchedly, but knowing it was otherwise inhuman, over the transference of Dessie's incalculably precious affection from himself to the nice photographer. Love ripened into friendship, friendship into fond acquaintance, acquaintance into casualness, until one day he could say to the man, Paul, and have it seem no more than correct:

—"She prefers you. It's best if I move on."

—Only Dessie, with her animal disregard for calculation, her sure instinct for physical truth, could know the flimsiness of his performance, could have said once (only once):

—"What's happening, Al? I don't believe it."

—"Please believe it, Dessie, even if you don't."

—And he had left that city, minding terribly, but knowing that one minds a little less every day. For a while, one out of every three well groomed girls whom he saw—in a magazine, a movie, walking on the streets of unremembered towns—was Dessie, would make him catch his breath.

—But the fashions changed, he couldn't have said how, and the hair styles . . . lovely girls looked different, as the months went on; only one a week would be she, and then only one a month, and finally, the King could have seen Dessie herself without having to catch his breath. Almost.

—Almost.

—The breath starts so quickly.

PART TWO

12 Usez came closer to having had his man in San Antonio than at any other time before the actual arrest.

The break—or perhaps pseudo-break, since it had finally led nowhere—came about because a photographer named Paul Emlen had employed a man named Alvin Barker in his darkroom. He had paid him, in the course of two-and-a-half months, about $400, and had mailed, shortly after Barker's leaving, a final check to a forwarding address. At the same time, it being just after the first of the year, he had mailed in a W-2 form on Barker to the Internal Revenue Bureau, a copy of which was enclosed with the final check. These things had been returned from the forwarding address (General Delivery, Laredo) which, apparently, was spurious. Realizing then that Barker might be a fugitive, and not wanting to get his friend into trouble, Emlen, the photographer, had tried to recall his studio income tax return for amendment, meaning to add the $400 back into his year's gross profit and expunge Barker's name.

The Revenue men, however, had been suspicious of a business man who seemed to wish to pay additional tax, and began the investigation; particulars were sent to other investigative agencies for cross reference, and Usez' attention was caught by the quoted statement, made reluctantly by the photographer, that "Barker had behaved in the darkroom like a scientist." When he learned in addition that, according to Emlen's fiancée, Barker had first worked in a record shop, Usez had a strong hunch that this man

119

could be Pennington. His superiors generally indulged Usez' hunches; they allowed him to fly to Texas. By luck, there was an excellent set of fingerprints preserved on a discarded sheet of emulsion paper which was found crumpled in a corner of the darkroom; they were easily shown to be Pennington's. This was fortunate since the identification from such photographs as the Bureau had was not so certain:

"I think it's him," the girl, Desiree Chapman, had finally admitted when he had assured the child that they knew the man by his fingerprints. "But oh, his face is so thin, now, Mr. Usez."

Everybody to whom he talked in San Antonio seemed to have liked Barker, and Usez had patiently come to expect that all these brief acquaintances would try to protect the man from some fancied persecution. It had, for example, taken several consecutive talks with Emlen to get out of him the fact that the forwarding address given was Laredo; for a long while Emlen had insisted that it was Brownsville, and finally had to be confronted with a duplicate of the W–2 form which he had himself addressed. It was the conjunction of these two border towns in the man's mind, associated perhaps as tourist gateways to Mexico, which led Usez to speculate that Barker-Pennington might have left the country.

The Chapman girl talked more freely, artlessly trying to convince Usez that the fugitive was a man who deserved to be left alone. Thus, he was able to ask her fairly intimate questions and, since he found himself rather attracted by the girl, and since she was remarkably open, their final interview somewhat transcended the limits of official information gathering. He was particularly curious about why she had become interested in the man, for, by her own account, it was her initiative which had started the affair.

"He seemed so wise . . . and so helpless," she said.

"At first sight?" Usez asked, dryly.

"Well, after you'd talked to him once. It looked like he knew everything and had done everything, and it wasn't doing him any good."

"Yes?"

"He wanted you to think he didn't like people very much, but he really felt all torn up about everybody, and since he couldn't

120

make any use out of all that wiseness and . . . experience, well, he seemed like he was inviting just anyone who wanted to use him. Only he was kind of surprised if anyone wanted to. Does this make any sense, Mr. Usez?"

"Go on."

"Well, you kind of felt with Al that he could protect you, all the time, anyway you needed. And he wouldn't ever let you feel bad about yourself. But he couldn't protect himself. That's what I mean. You wanted to take from him, because he wanted you to, but you wanted to give to him, too; and he'd never let you. And that just made you love him more."

"I see."

"Mr. Usez?"

"Yes, Dessie."

"I knew he was fixing to leave."

"You did?"

She nodded. "He didn't think I did, but I knew, right away, when he started telling me how much Paul liked me, what was in his mind. And I sort of guessed—what it was about. It was something about the war, and he thought he'd done something bad, only nobody could see it was bad. Like, I used to imagine that he'd killed a lot of men, and they gave him a medal, but he wished he hadn't killed all those men. What did he really do, Mr. Usez?"

"He was one of the men who worked on the atom bomb, Dessie."

She thought about it for a moment. Then she slowly shook her head: "I don't guess I understand, Mr. Usez," she said. After a moment, she repeated: "He didn't think I knew, but I knew. That was one place I was able to protect him. I never let on I knew he was fixing to leave."

He had gotten up. "Thank you, Dessie."

"You going to find him?"

"I don't know."

"I wish you the awfulest bad luck, Mr. Usez."

13 On Monday, at ten o'clock, Santa Claus arrived.

Flanked by two elves in green, he strode out of the employees' elevator, toweringly tall, magnificently plump with padding, the face a glowing red, the whiskers laundered white as a shirt.

Though there were no unrehearsed children on the floor, there were newspaper photographers to take pictures and one of them had brought a child along, a plump little girl who cried, with quite spontaneous enthusiasm:

"Santa's here. Santa's here. Santa's here."

The clerks, a little giddy after the exhaustion of Saturday and Sunday's rest, stopped what they were doing and came as close as their counters would permit to watch; Al was called from the stockroom by Mr. Finn, beaming like a minor Santa Claus himself, and they stood by the electric train counter watching.

"Every year, isn't he great?" Finn said. "Look at him."

"He looks two stories high," Al said.

"Like a statue of Santa Claus." It was the boy called Hugh Harris, speaking behind them.

"He's more expensive than the others. Equity salary. A real actor, John Charles Evans, a star in his time," Finn said. "It's worth it. He's the one they always photograph for the papers."

"Are the elves really little girls?" Harris asked.

"Short models," Finn said. "Four and a half footers. He makes

122

them look like children, doesn't he? The old man's nearly seven feet tall."

The photographers finished, and Finn stepped forward grinning to greet his man.

"Hello, Santa Claus," he said, offering his hand.

"Hello, Hub," boomed a great, beautifully modulated voice from behind the whiskers. "Have you been a good boy?"

"Sure have, Santa."

"That's fine, that's fine," the old man said. "Glad to hear it. Same corner?"

"Same corner," Finn said. "Let's go."

"Hello, Santa. Hi, Santa Claus," the clerks called, as they moved across the floor.

"Hello there, little boy," Evans would say. And the clerk would grin happily. "Hope you've been behaving, eh? What a nice family you've got, Hub."

Not moving out from behind the service desk, Dolly Klamath watched Santa Claus' progress towards his throne, noting carefully which clerks were silliest in playing up to him. As he approached her, she had to instruct herself not to turn her back on all of them and walk away. At the same time, she knew that her face was registering a cold smile, her shoulders set straight, her eyes steady; no one could see her hands below the counter top pick up and break in half first one pencil, then another, then another.

"Hello, Dolly," shouted the old man as he came up to her. "Have you been a good girl?" And he actually reached out his great paw and patted her head.

She was appalled. All the clerks were watching. One or two giggled audibly. She stood as stiffly as she could, until he uncertainly drew the hand away; then she said:

"Good morning, Mr. Evans. Will you be coming in at ten o'clock every morning this year?"

There was a trace of offense in the old voice when he answered: "Why yes, Dolly. That is, I believe that's the arrangement."

"I only need to know to keep your time chart straight," Dolly said, looking hard at the man beneath the fake whiskers.

Then surprisingly, hatefully, the old fool laughed: "Ho, ho, ho," he went. "Oh, Dolly, you're my favorite child. The solemn little disbelievers are the cutest of all. Ho, ho, ho."

And, horridly, Finn joined in the laughter, and Barker, and Harris and Sally and the clerks behind them, laughed at her, laughed at her, face after face at the counters, working back towards the elevators until the dreadful contagion spread out of sight and the world was laughing.

Checking at eleven, Al found that Mr. Evans had already drunk a whole pitcher of water; when he returned with it full, the old man was on one of his fifteen minute breaks, sitting in the straight chair behind the shell, reading the morning paper and smoking a pipe, his red coat and trousers open, and the padding which filled them out lying next to him on the floor.

"Thank you, son," Evans said, "one does get thirsty."

It had become, gradually, a fairly busy day, and already some dozens of pre-school children had nestled in Santa's arms, sat on his lap, kneaded the stomach padding and whispered into his ear.

"I enjoy doing Santa Claus when there are plenty of kiddies," the old actor said, with a sigh. "It's a fine role." His accent was more or less British. "When there are a great crush of them, one gets excited and hasn't time to think how heavy the costume is."

"Have you been doing it long?" Al asked.

"Oh, six or seven years I should guess," Evans said. "San Francisco is no theatrical town, you know. It once was. Once one had a choice, very nearly. Shall I be a modern hero this season, or do Shakespeare, or consent to a comedy role? And now it's, will they think I'm too thin to do Santa for three weeks?"

"You don't look thin," Al said.

"I haven't removed all the padding." He sighed again. Then a wink and a twinkle passed across his face, like a spasm. "I do seem to know how to make the kiddies happy," he said. "Hub knows it well enough: I'm quite in demand."

"Of course he does," Al said. "Wouldn't New York be a better place for you?"

"Too old, my boy. And too damned big. There was never a time when the name John Stanley Evans was on every tongue, as you might say, but there could have been. Do you see, I'm nearly seven feet tall. If I'd known I was going to be, I might never have prepared for the stage, but at twenty-two I was still growing. There were damned few directors who would bother handling a man my size in groups; they'd simply hire someone else." He paused. "In my early twenties, I had fine luck with juvenile roles in London and New York, and when I was going to be very nearly a freak, I decided I must come to the provinces where experience might outweigh the awkward size. Oh, there've been times when I had to wear elevator shoes and get up over seven for circus work. And others when I wore bedroom slippers to play opposite some little lady; spent most of my time on stage sitting down.

"It was better as I got older. I started doing noble old men before I was thirty, because they didn't have to lean over and kiss people you know. I did Lear one season, long ago, at the Geary and they said it was the finest Shakespeare San Francisco ever saw. But it's gone down since then. There hasn't been a play cast out here since before the war, and there certainly won't be one with a part for a thin man past sixty, seven feet tall." He got up and began to replace the padding.

"Have you children of your own, Mr. Evans?" Al asked.

"No, sir. Mrs. Evans died a barren woman."

"You're very nice with them," Al said. The wink-twinkle flickered across Evans' face again; he bowed.

It was true that he was good with the children; one could hardly watch Evans' performance without being half convinced that there was a special saint who doted on every child in the world, spent his year making toys for them at some ice-bound Willow Run, and who, when he met them at last in the sparkly, blue-white dome in Mainways' Toy Department, actually delighted in being able to pet them, kiss their foreheads, and hear their secrets.

Later, coming through the stockroom for a smoke, one of the elves filled in the story:

"You really look like an elf," Al had said.

"Well, it's a real good thing. I'm 'most too little to act, and the only thing I can model are children's clothes. A lot of times they put me in a little girl's dress or underwear or bathing suit, and they take my picture from the back. Cause you'd look at the picture and never realize you wouldn't see a real ten-year-old with legs that nice."

125

"You and Mr. Evans make quite a pair."

"We do. We been doing Santa and the elf together six years now. We were at Landons' first, and then all the stores were trying to get us."

"What about the other elf?" Tom asked.

"Oh, she's real young. Hasn't got her growth yet. Me, I'm 'most thirty." She arranged her cap. "She doesn't know how to handle him."

"Handle him?"

"Keep him away from the liquor. That old man could have been a great actor, but he worried so about his size he started drinking, and he's a terrible man when he drinks. Did he tell you he did *King Lear* out here?"

"Yes."

"Well, he could have had his choice after that, Broadway or Hollywood. That's what they say. But the last night of the show, the cast started to drink. And Mr. Evans, he'd been on the wagon, all through it, but he started to drink, too. In the second act, he went to sleep on the stage. They got him up to finish the act, but when the curtain went down, he didn't understand why the play had to stop. He went out in front of the curtain and started shouting to the audience to stay in their seats. When he had them quiet, he said that he was sorry to announce that William Shakespeare had died, so it would be impossible to finish the play. They led him backstage, crying; he broke away and started to beat up a stagehand who was laughing at him. After that, everybody knew you couldn't tell what he'd do when he was drunk, so no one would give him a job."

"What a shame."

"Don't you worry. I take care of him, now. I watch him like a little old hawk."

"You take care of him?"

"We live in the same rooming house," she said. "We always work together Christmas. I watch him."

"Good elf," said Al.

After lunch, business fell off a little and Sally Malinkrodt found herself much relieved. She had worked hard all morning; Klamath, who seemed to watch the doll counter with special intensity, had caught Winnipeg in an error in tax calculation, and started being vile again; and Sally had, defiantly, stood by her co-worker, all through it, with her arm around the girl's waist. It seemed to help Winnipeg, but Sally knew she hadn't done herself any good with Klamath.

Accordingly, she'd been flirting assiduously with Finn when he stopped by the counter, though about all she got for it were slightly tiresome speeches about a good old snowball rolling down a money hill, packing in old wet dollar bills.

Winnipeg was off on her break when Finn showed again, shouting: "Where'd they go, Sally girl? We were having a pretty good day."

"Guess the money hill leveled off," Sally said, a little snappishly.

"You sound kind of tired out."

"I am," she said. "I'd trade my precious white flower for five minutes on a good, soft bed."

"Would you, eh?" Finn chuckled. "Well, now, Sally, you be careful. I might just take you up on that."

"Be a fair trade," Sally said. "You haven't got a bed and I haven't got a flower."

"Now, Sally. Don't talk that way. You see," his eyes danced, "I do have a bed, Sally. I wouldn't tell the other girls, but if you'd like to lie down," he looked at his watch, "the old man would be finished now. There's a nice little cot in behind Santa Claus."

"Really?" Sally straightened up; she'd been sagging against the counter. "You wouldn't mind if I took my break there, when Winnipeg gets back?"

"Why wait, Sally?" he cried. "There's no customers. Come along and I'll show you."

Sally hung back. "I don't know, Mr. Finn."

"Come along, girl. Dolly'll watch your counter." And he called to Klamath over on the service desk to watch Dolls, he was taking Miss Malinkrodt to see Santa Claus.

She followed him across the floor, towards Santa where only two or three children were left in line, and around behind the shell, where she saw the cot. Dubiously, keeping an eye on Finn, she sat on it.

"You see?" He was turning back, towards where they had en-

127

tered. "I did have a bed, Sally," and he walked to the corner, apparently about to go out. "Don't you tell, now."

"Wow," she said, relaxing and lying back. "Don't you worry." And she swung her feet up and closed her eyes. She didn't hear him recross the floor to her, but the next moment he was kissing her as hard as she'd ever been kissed, and she could feel him squeezing at the whalebone and padding of her wiry brassiere.

"Now what about that flower, eh girl?" he whispered. "Where would it be, I wonder?" And a heavy arm wrapped tightly around her.

For a moment she was too astonished to protest.

"Here, I'll bet," he was saying, roguishly, his hand at her stocking tops, before she could get to her elbow and promptly be kissed down flat again.

"Don't you think . . . it's a little public?" she gasped, trying to struggle against his considerable weight, but fearing mostly that someone would hear them.

"No, darling, no. Oh, you're a wonderful girl, Sally." One of her arms was trapped; the other was hardly strong enough to keep his prying hand away; she supposed that, if she could see the window, past his shoulders, it must be getting dark out.

"Wait," she whispered, relaxing to throw him off. Instead of responding by letting up, as she had planned, giving her a chance to get away, he held tighter; after a long moment, in which she was quite helpless to prevent what he was doing, he rocked back, grinning at her and puffing, and commanded:

"Open your clothes, girl."

Quickly, she pushed the skirt back down, shook her head, and started to sit up, saying firmly: "Now. That's enough."

"Oh, no you don't, Sally girl," he said, with a big breathless laugh, as if it were a joking kind of game and, to her renewed astonishment, fell onto her again, once more pinning her arms and mouth and beginning again with his hand.

"All right," Sally whispered, finally catching fire. "All right. Let me . . ." And, in a blurred moment, she arranged her clothing, wrapped her arms close around the thick neck, and accepted him.

It was not precisely what she'd had in mind, this boss and

128

salesgirl act, but when they were through she felt a kind of bawdy satisfaction in it, an appropriateness, and she began immediately to wonder whether it would spoil some illusion about her that, perhaps, made Finn's performance possible, if she were to take him up to the rather expensive apartment where she lived, now Jerk was working nights again.

Finn himself seemed apprehensive, eager to be away, ordering his clothes quickly, handing her her shoes in silent haste, urging her with his eyes to be quick.

She listened, wondering if he had heard something to make him anxious, and as she held her breath, a great voice suddenly filled the corner, booming,

"Well. Well. Well. And have you been a good little girl?"

For an instant she thought they were seen; then, realizing that it was only Santa Claus' voice, carrying from out front, she couldn't control herself any longer, and burst into ribald laughter which she had to muffle by burying her face against the suddenly rigid hip of the man beside her on the bed.

They emerged separately, with caution, from behind the shell, Finn going first, Sally following after a moment and hurrying to her counter. Winnipeg was there.

"Where've you been?"

"Oh, opening a Christmas present," Sally said, feeling flushed and foolish.

"What?"

"Mr. Finn got a present, too," Sally teased, sure the girl wouldn't understand.

"Well," Winnipeg said. "Miss Klamath was looking for you."

"Really? I hope she didn't get a present." Sally smiled, not much worried.

Dolly had not. She had not allowed herself to look. She had listened, however, first on one side of the shell, then on the other, rigorously forbidding her eyes to follow around the corners where her ears strained. And while her experience was not complete enough to tell her the exact degree of sin behind Santa's back, she was certain of the intention of sin, and she had heard and been deeply shocked by the loose, hastily-stifled peals of woman's laughter.

129

She had backed off to the wheel goods section, and stood, half concealed by one of the pillars, to watch them come out; as soon as she saw Sally return to her counter, Dolly followed Finn to the stockroom. She found him chatting expansively with his crony, Al Barker, and the boy Tom Vanderbeck.

"Mr. Finn," she said, "may I see you in the office?"

"Why sure, Dolly girl," he said. "What's up?"

Without replying, or even looking to see if he followed, she walked to the office, reaching into the neck of her dress as she entered to pull out the gold crucifix her father had given her at confirmation. As she turned to face Finn, coming along a few steps behind, she could feel it blazing against the black cloth of her dress.

"Close the door," she said. Finn closed it.

"What's up, Dolly girl?"

"How can you pretend not to know?" She watched the grin fade; then he forced it back.

"Why, what's the matter?" he said. "Something gone wrong?" She only looked into his eyes. "Something I've done?"

"Don't be childish, Mr. Finn," she said.

"Dolly . . ."

"I'm so sickened and disgusted I can hardly speak of it."

"You mean . . .?"

"I mean the blonde woman. What did you think I meant disgusted me? Your lying face?"

"Dolly, don't talk that way."

She laughed at him.

He turned red and began to bumble: "Dolly girl, if you mean Miss, Miss Malinkrodt . . . well, Sally. Now I was talking to her, why, just now. Yes. She's a fine girl. Fine girl. I was congratulating her. She's making a great record. Kind of like salesgirls used to be, I was telling her . . ."

"Oh, shut up," Dolly said, now certain of her ground. "For a man to use his position to force . . ."

"I didn't force her, Dolly. She . . ."

". . . another man's wife into sin . . ."

"She's not married," Finn said. "I looked on her form."

"She's married to a man named Rivers," Dolly said. "If you weren't so stupid about the people who work for you, you'd have

130

found that out. For some vile reason, she wanted to work under her maiden name. I guess the reason's perfectly clear now, though."

"Dolly, we were just . . . it was weakness. We . . ."

"Did you pay her?"

"Weakness, Dolly . . ."

"I doubt that Mr. Sparlin will take that view," Dolly said.

"You wouldn't tell Sparlin?"

"What else do you think I could do?" Dolly asked. "Tell all the clerks to go ahead and fornicate, right where they are? Maybe you think it would be nice to have the customers do it, too? Do you honestly think you should go unpunished, Mr. Finn? For a crime against the store? A crime against the woman's husband and your wife? A lewd and horrible sin against your God? Do you?"

"Dolly, he'd . . . Doll, girl. I'll lose my job if you tell Sparlin."

"Do you think you deserve to hold your job?"

"Dolly."

"Do you think you should be given power over innocent girls and other men's wives?"

"Dolly."

"Do you?"

"I was weak, Dolly," Finn said. "I was weak. I've never done a thing like that before. I swear I haven't."

"Why should I believe you?"

"Once," Finn said. "Only once with a girl from the store. Seven or eight years ago."

"What girl was that?" Dolly asked.

"You wouldn't know her."

"What girl was that?"

"She . . . she doesn't work here any more."

"What girl?"

"Connie Brooks," Finn said, in a low voice.

Dolly smiled. "Miss Brooks, of Personnel," she said. "How long ago?"

"Seven or eight years," Finn said. "Dolly, she's . . . she's Sparlin's girl now."

"Is she?" Dolly said. "I never understood how such a stupid girl . . . well, Connie Brooks."

131

"Dolly, if you tell Sparlin, I'd have to . . . talk to him about Brooks."

"Yes. That's what you'd do," Dolly said.

"You'd be taking a chance," Finn said, desperately. "He might . . . after all, you can't prove anything about me. Sparlin might see it my way, rather than . . ." he was gaining confidence. "It might go against you."

"And suppose I told Mr. Rivers?" Dolly said.

"Mr. . . . ?"

"The woman's husband."

"Oh, my God," Finn said.

"Your God is Whom you might have thought of before," Dolly said. "Doesn't your religion mean anything to you?"

"Well, now . . ."

"Well, now . . ." Dolly mimicked. "I hate a well-now Catholic. It's worse than a Protestant. What a filthy soul you have."

"Dolly, don't, please don't say anything. Dolly, if I promise not to, not to do . . ."

"What good's your promise?" Dolly asked. "You say it was weakness. Why should I believe you won't be weak again?"

"Dolly, I promise . . ."

"That's not enough," Dolly said. "You want to make me a promise?"

"Anything," Finn said.

"All right," said Dolly. "You're not to speak to her again alone. Not on the floor or off it. I don't care what about. Unless there's somebody there, whom I can see, when you talk to her. What you say to her will be entirely businesslike. I want you to be prepared to tell me your exact words to her any time I see you talking. I want you to speak to her in such a way that, if I come up behind you and listen, I will hear nothing that isn't entirely correct between employer and employee. Is that clear? And I want you to avoid even that much conversation unless it's absolutely necessary . . . wait a minute. You're willing to make me a promise, Mr. Finn?"

"Yes, Dolly."

"Promise that you will not speak to the blonde woman again, and will not go near her, without coming to me first, telling me what you intend to say, and asking my permission."

"Dolly, I can't . . ."

"Promise."

"Dolly, you've . . ."

"Promise."

"I promise," Finn said.

"And now if I were you," Dolly said, "I'd get down on my knees and ask for God's forgiveness." She waited. He looked at her not quite believing. "I mean it, Mr. Finn," she said. Slowly the big man sunk to his knees. When he was in praying position, she turned abruptly and left him alone in the office.

Standing in the doorway of the stockroom, Al and Tom watched her walk past.

"Wonder if something's wrong?" Tom said.

"Finn'll be out in a minute," Al guessed. "And we'll be told." But Finn did not come out before they left. It was nearly closing time. They transferred their attention to Mrs. Kelsner, whose presence seemed to grow, daily, rather than diminish, teaching a seven-year-old boy how to use the bubble set. As the kid dashed happily away with it, Mrs. Kelsner straightened herself up and began again steadily to fill the air around herself with little iridescent globes.

"The extremities of our magic world are in fine shape," Al said. "At one end we have Mrs. Kelsner blowing bubbles; and at the other, John Charles Evans, promising the children that they'll never break."

133

14 Usez' hunches were not invariably correct. It occurred to him, sometime after the trip to Texas, that Pennington's sense of order might have led him, at one time or another, to try to visit his father in Pennsylvania. Mrs. Pennington had died before the disappearance. The father and son, according to the interviewers who had seen the old man, had never been on particularly good terms; but it was precisely because of this history of misunderstanding between them that Usez thought his quarry might have tried to make the visit home. He was wrong.

"That spy?" the old man had said. "If young Benedict Arnold ever sticks his nose across this threshold, I'll shoot up enough flares for you, officer, to light the sky."

It was on a Saturday. It was a call Usez was making on his own time, finding himself in Philadelphia on other Bureau business which couldn't be completed until Monday. At first, arriving in the town of Norman and looking up the name, Usez thought the old man might have died since the last interview, for Louis A. Pennington appeared in the phone directory only as part of the name of the family lumberyard.

At the yard, however, a manager was able to give Usez the address, explaining that Mr. Pennington was retired and wouldn't have a telephone.

"Old man has a hate on them," the manager had said. "Wouldn't have one in his office here. After his missus passed on, he tore it

134

out himself at home. Just tore out the instrument, and tossed it into the street. Well, the phone company had to sue to recover, and the old man said . . ." Usez had thanked the man and gone on.

"Telephone? You tried to find me in the telephone book?" Mr. Pennington had shouted, when Usez introduced himself and mentioned his difficulty in finding the place. Though the house was large, and the furniture expensive if unkempt, the old man was dressed in overalls; the shirt beneath them was full-cut, fine and white, and he was ferociously clean-shaven—one could almost see the marks of scraping on his cheeks. What little hair remained on his head was still brown and curly at sixty-eight, and he wore heavy white sneakers with the toes cut away and no socks under them. "What do you mean by looking for me in that book, Captain? Whores and pimps, sir, that's what's listed in the telephone book. Would you put your name in one?"

"Why yes," Usez said. "Yes, I am in the phone book at home."

"You couldn't pay me to do it, sir. Advertise my home, my place of residence, to every cheap numbskull jack with a piece of poison pie to sell? Not I, sir. Invite them, give them a formal invitation, a written invitation in that book, to pollute my privacy? No, sir. Not I."

"Well . . ." Usez began.

"We had one of those black devices in this very house when my wife was alive, officer, ringing like a nanny-goat's bell, night and day. I would not pick it up. Never. They breathe into the other end, Mr. Usez, spit in it, and that spit is conveyed electrically along the wire, into your ear . . ."

"I came to ask whether your son Allerd had been here, or made any attempt to reach you," Usez said, formally.

That was when Mr. Pennington had called his son a spy.

"I tried to raise those boys right, in spite of their mother's interference," he said. "I tried to raise them to stand on their own feet, think with their own heads. They always took their mother's side. Ashamed of me. Wanted to be respectable. Lawyers. Scientists. Makemonies. Go to church . . . that's where you'll find him, officer. You have some of your spies hang around the churches. You'll find him there, sniveling around the altar . . ."

"I doubt that," Usez said, smiling.

135

"Traitor to his country," the old man went on, irascibly. "Makes a pretty good bomb, blow them all to hell, and then what? He's ashamed of himself. No insides."

"I suppose he feels it's a pretty terrible thing, the bomb."

"You on his side? Good God, they'll never find him that way. You don't send out kittens to hunt cats." And the old man had half-turned away.

"I simply meant there are two sides . . ."

"Two sides to nothing," the old man said fiercely, turning back. "There's one side to any matter and that's the right side and that's all there is to it. Do you or do you not agree?"

"Partly," Usez said.

"You either do or you don't," Mr. Pennington snorted. "Partly. Partly. Sending out minnows to catch sharks. Did you ever hear that the fellow who sharpened the first sword felt bad about it? Or the one invented gunpowder? Look here. The world's made up of countries. Countries have enemies. Your enemy gets a gun, you damn well better get two guns, isn't that right? Now where's the difference with that big bomb of his?"

"I suppose your son would say that that the man who invented gunpowder did an evil thing," Usez said. "Like the men who invented the thumbscrew and the rack, both useful in warfare, incidentally, for extracting information. I don't mean I agree, but I suppose he'd say that if you get two guns, your enemy will get three, and that the thing to work for is not to have enemies."

"Not have enemies? Use your brain, Captain," the old man said. "What's wrong with enemies? You know what an enemy is? He's competition. Like business competition, but bigger and more dangerous; that's what keeps the world on its toes. Enemies. Competition. I wouldn't give a damn for a world without enemies."

"But enemies lead to war."

"Exactly. And every single bit of progress ever made was made through wars."

"I wanted to ask you about something," Usez said, yielding.

"Shoot. Get out your two guns and shoot, captain," Mr. Pennington chuckled.

"In 1935, when you and Mrs. Pennington separated . . ."

"She walked out on me," the old man said, flatly. "That's all there was to it. Took the boys and kited. Want to know why she left?"

"If you don't mind telling me," Usez said, perfectly aware that he was being trapped.

"That's the most peculiar damn thing I ever heard," the old man laughed. "The Government of the United States of America wants to know, by God, why my wife left me sixteen, seventeen years ago. Sends a smart little minnow swimming all the way up from Washington, to say look here, Lou Pennington, we want to know why your wife Ruth took off back there and left you for a year. Don't guess they can go on governing till they've got the answer, eh?"

"I don't really need to know, of course . . ." Usez began.

"No, sir," Pennington said. "I'm going to tell you. Why it's my patriotic duty, seeing as they can't go on and pass any more laws, all those Senators and Representatives, they'll just be sitting on their hands, drawing taxpayers' money till you swim back with the answer, captain. But it just goes to show something I've been saying, Mr. Usez, we haven't got a good government down there and we haven't got a bad government—we've just got a peculiar government, am I right?"

"About the separation?" Usez asked, stiffly.

"Well, it goes back to a hobby of mine, you might say." Mr. Pennington was clearly enjoying himself. "I used to have a kind of hobby of running for mayor every now and then in the fall. I'd get the boys in the lumberyard and a few of the town drunks to sign me a petition, and I'd run. Had to invent a new party every time, because I'd never get enough votes to make it legal to run again on the same ticket. Ran about five times, used to like to campaign, make a few speeches, call some names: gave me a chance to speak my piece about things, you know, and every time I'd get maybe forty, fifty votes. Had some pretty good tickets back there; had the Farmer-Atheist Party. Another year it was the Ingersoll Republicans; then I ran one time on the Bachelor Tax Ticket—got about seventy votes that year—and then I had the Anarchist-Normal Party in '32. It was always a pretty nice little scandal, gave the town something to fret about.

"Well, in 1934 things were pretty tough. I'd lost a whole lot of money and I wasn't making it back. Looked for a while like

137

we might have to close up the yard. That time I had a whole lot to say. Every year we'd have the same bunch in at Town Hall, and they just weren't about to go along with what was happening in Washington or even in Altoona to try to get things going again. And that was just the time when Mrs. Pennington was pestering me not to run for mayor any more, she never did like it, said I shouldn't take time for such foolishness now, not when I'd mortgaged the house to meet my payrolls at the yard —not when I was only letting her buy meat for the family one time a week. She was kind of bitter . . . ever notice women don't understand politics, Mr. Usez?"

"Perhaps not," Usez said.

"No sir. I was bound to run again, wanted bad to make those speeches, and she wasn't stopping me. She kind of felt like she was slipping back a little bit hereabouts, I guess, what with having to let the cook go, do her own wash—thought another one of my election scandals would finish her off." Suddenly he chuckled. "I really had me some little ticket cooked up that year to run for."

"What was that?" Usez asked.

"The Star-Spangled Robin Hood Fascist Party," the old man said. "I made speeches saying we ought to put some of the out-of-work boys into black shirts and march 'em around, taking from the rich and giving to the poor. I even threw a rock through the window of Town Hall to get myself arrested one day at noon hour—don't remember just why."

"And Mrs. Pennington?"

"Left with the boys while I was making my first speech. Went over to Germantown, to her family. Scalding mad. Took me a year to get her back. I guess . . . I guess she'd had a lot to put up with, those years in there. But you know what happened?"

"What?"

"I'll tell you. We'd had a hard winter the year before, and some of the drunks and the old coots who'd used to vote for me for fun, they'd died off. So they were betting in town that I wouldn't break fifty votes that year. Know how many I got?"

"How many?"

"Six hundred and five. They recounted, and I came out six-twenty-one. Of course, that was about two thousand short of making me mayor, but I tell you, officer, I was the most surprised man in town. Next to the politicians. It scared them plenty. I mean, there were some changes around here . . ."

"How did you feel?" Usez asked.

The old man shook his head. "I didn't know what to think—except it looked like I'd made my point. Anyway, I promised Mrs. Pennington I wouldn't run any more, used to write that to her every week—tell you the truth, I didn't much feel like it. She came back with the boys . . ."

"And how did the boys take it?"

He sighed. "It was that changed them," he said. "It changed Allerd. He was fifteen when they came back. He'd been my boy when they went away—wildcat. Full of good, clean cussedness. Cross the street to spit on a preacher if I told him to. A real boy. Came back, no insides. Didn't like to hear people in town cuss me. Didn't like to be poor, work after school in the yard. A lickspittle makemoney, that's what he wanted to be, fool around with science, make everybody think he was smart, have a car, dress up slick, go on dates, go to church, go to college, be nice people." He shook his head again. "Never thought he'd be his mother's boy."

"You feel he continued to be, even after he went to college?"

"Right up to the last time I saw him. Too polite to me. Didn't want to argue. Coat and tie. Took his mother for a drive, see her friends in town. . . . Want to know something?"

Usez nodded.

"I did run for mayor once more, after Ruthie died. Just last year." His voice saddened. Usez decided not to interrupt. "Got me up a pretty good party, The Red, White and Blue Communistic Imperials. Kind of upset about things here . . . You know, they made it hard for me to hold meetings. People didn't turn out much when I did. Didn't get but three votes. One of them was my own." Abruptly he returned to the subject of his son: "Going to shoot him when you get him? You better. Where is he?"

"I'd like to know."

"Some monastery. Some do-good, Salvation Army place, hand-

139

ing out buns. Playing a tuba in the Salvation band. That's where you'll find him. He was always trying to play some kind of horn . . . he giving you fellows a pretty bad chase, is he?"

"We don't have any trace of him at all now," Usez said.

"Giving the cops some trouble, eh? He hanging out with the reds or what?"

"We don't think so," Usez said.

"Not with the reds, not with the do-goods, not with the church. Just kinda lonewolfman spy, sneaking around, spitting in your eyes and slipping off before you catch him, eh?"

"Well, something like that, but I wish you wouldn't feel badly . . ."

"Maybe got one of those bombs of his, blow up the capital of the United States one of these days, something like that."

"We have no evidence that your son is a traitor, Mr. Pennington," Usez said.

"Lonewolfman with a big damn bomb," the old man mused.

"Please," Usez said. "Please forgive me if I've seemed to imply . . ."

"Forgive you?" Suddenly he was shaking his head, trying to shake the tears out of his eyes, trying to shake a smile onto his face. "Look at that," he managed to say. "Look at that . . . sneaking around, spitting at cops . . . why, that boy's all right. Why, you're just never going to catch Allerd, captain."

"Well . . ." Usez began.

"No, sir. You're not going to catch him. Say sometime, say maybe he'll catch you. That's what, Captain, he'll catch you. And you tell him, tell him it's all right. Tell him it's all right, Captain. Tell the boy to turn you loose and come on home . . ."

Usez excused himself as gracefully as he could and left.

15 During the following week, Tom Vanderbeck felt that he was learning how to listen
to Al, how to recognize the facts and feelings on
which the fantasies and inventions were built:
As on the morning when M'nerney told Gullakian,
in the stockroom, that he'd noticed, coming to work, that
the banks were going to stay open from six to eight on
Tuesday evenings during the Christmas season.

"Hey, that's interesting, Mac," Gullakian had said. "It's Tuesday today, isn't it?"

"That's right, Gullakian," Al had said. "Tonight you can get
right over after work and bank your ass off for two glorious
hours."

M'nerney and Gullakian both had laughed.

"These people," Al had said to Tom when they left. "They seem
to think I'm some sort of little pet wasp with his stinger removed.
Jesus. Let me tell you, Athlete, my poison works slow; one of
these mornings they'll try to get out of bed and find that the
legs they stand on have dropped away during the night."

That probably meant Al hoped he hadn't hurt Gullakian's feelings.

It was a week of steadily mounting business; weekdays began
to resemble Saturdays. The clerks reacted: snappishness to customers became routine; people who would, at home, have stapled
their lips together before speaking sharply to strangers adopted
the animal snarl as automatic response; the customers themselves
were steadily, painstakingly, offensive. Dolly grew stricter and
more terrifying, and it seemed almost justified, for errors in the

141

simple sales procedure were so common that M'nerney, who checked salesbooks against cash register totals each evening, seldom found one which balanced on the first try.

One of the girls, thin Betty Connaught who demonstrated the sewing machines, came scurrying in to hide from Klamath one morning before break time; Al warned her against the ladies' room.

"Klamath will wait you out," he said. "Tom, let's build a cave." Back in the recesses of the stockroom, where an apparently blocked doorway led out past the wrapping desk, they quickly arranged a hidden nest, reached over the tops of deceptively piled boxes. When Miss Klamath came in to ask if Miss Connaught was in the ladies' room, Betty was safely smuggled away, able to leave at any time without being seen.

The Service Manager stood waiting, arms folded, disbelieving Al's denial.

"What do you think we've done, Miss Klamath?" Al asked. "Hidden her somewhere?"

When she had finally checked the ladies' room herself, and left, Al said to Tom: "Nothing in life is more fun than to lie by telling the truth."

That probably meant he disliked doing it.

On Wednesday there was a long conversation in the stockroom between Gullakian and Hugh Harris, loafing during one of the now rare lulls, about the Army. Tom and Al, slightly withdrawn from them at first, were opening each of three gross of little water color sets in tin boxes, to check whether the manufacturer had included brushes; several had been returned that morning.

"I didn't ask to be company clerk," Harris was saying. "But I don't mind saying I had a more comfortable time that way."

"Were you overseas?" Gullakian asked.

"Sure," said Hugh. "England and France. I met Gertrude Stein in Paris. You'd have liked her, Al."

"Who's she?"

Hugh started to reply but Gullakian interrupted. "Don't answer him, Hugh, he's trying to kid you."

"That's true," Al said. "Gertrude Stein is my favorite niece. I wish I had seventy-five cents for every bag of horehound candy I've given her as she trudged by on her way to school, her pudgy little bare feet kicking up the dust, her freckled bottom waggling cutely under the cotton pants, her little . . ."

"She's dead," Hugh said. "Oh, let it go. Where were you, Harold?"

"In this country mostly," Gullakian said. "But I got to make one swing through the Pacific, playing concerts."

"Violin?"

"No. Piano."

"Bach for the G.I.'s?" Hugh asked.

"You'd be surprised," Gullakian said. "I generally gave a program with the first half good popular stuff—show tunes and things like that. Then I'd do a really fast boogie-woogie number, just to show I could. And then I'd play Chopin and Bach. They loved it. People like good music; it's just that no one will play it for them."

"That's true," Hugh said.

"I don't," said Al, getting up.

"Don't what?"

"Don't like good music. It irritates the pants off me. It's as bad as good paintings and good books."

"Heavens," said Hugh. "Are you against art, Al?"

"Against it?" Al asked. "Am I against rattlesnakes? Art never made anybody happy. You want to see gloom sometime, look behind you at the faces at a concert. Look at the people at a gallery. Or watch some poor son of a bitch reading Dostoyevsky. And as for the artists, whoever heard of a happy one? Art doesn't make happiness. Art makes trouble." He peered into Gullakian's astonished face, and nodded. "You're a troublemaker, Gullakian, if you're any good. You express the things which ought to be kept to oneself, even, if possible, from oneself . . ."

"But . . ."

"Interrupt me again and I'll cut off your bowing finger. Art keeps people out of churches, marriages, and wars. Art is society's only real enemy. Popular instinct is right: what we need is more mediocrity, more saccharine, more corn; more pretty girls on calendars; more campfire scenes; more poems about mothers; more impossible romances, more songs about you, you, you. Banality for banality's sake . . ."

143

"My God," Hugh said, smiling, "you're some critic, Al."

"Mister," Al said, portentously, "I'm a critic's critic, and a poet's poet, and a Philistine's Philistine."

"What were you in the war, Al?" Tom asked, grinning. Somewhere in the ridiculous answer he expected there could be an underlay of fact.

"Oh, I had a very exciting war," Al said. "Disguises, dark alleys. Aliases. Always one step away from capture."

"What were you?" Hugh asked, playing straight man for them. "A spy or something?"

"Draft dodger," Al said. "Don't you guys have any work to do?"

Gullakian got up and walked to the door. A soap bubble floated above his head for a moment, and then broke in his wavy black hair. He turned back toward them:

"No customers in my section. Dolly's out to lunch. Finn's got a salesman in the office, and Mac doesn't give a damn," he said. "Hey, Tom?"

"Yes?"

"You know Dolores Hughes?"

"Sure."

"How'd you like to wind her music box and hear it tinkle, boy? I almost had that, Sunday night. Took her up to the apartment to hear the old concerto—guess I tried to push it a little too fast." He walked back into the room. "She'll come across. You can always tell. You know how?"

"How?" Tom asked.

"Trade secret," said Gullakian, smugly.

"Listen, Gullakian," Al cut in. "Will you stop composing sonatas for right hand and penis, and get the hell out of here?"

At noon Thursday, lunching together, Tom and Nickie compared notes. "I think he was in some kind of secret work during the war," Tom said. "And he's crazy about all kinds of art, not just music."

"I've really got something," Nickie said. "I haven't had a chance to tell you. He was married and had two children. A boy and a girl. But he hasn't seen them for years."

Tom got out his notebook and they filled in a fresh page; it was beginning to take on considerable outline.

AL BARKER (Real name?)

Thirty years old. Brown hair. Thin. Brown eyes. Heavy brows. Five-foot six (approx.). 140 pounds (approx.). No visible scars.

Generally speaks ironically. Gentle.

Lives 46 Gerke Street; frequents Weary's Bar.

Has traveled most of U. S.; may have been abroad. Graduate New England college, probably Harvard. (Technical training?) Much feeling for arts, esp. music. War work: secret (O.S.S.?).

Wife and two children, separated or divorced.

Probably a fugitive, but could not have done anything bad.

They were firmly agreed on the underlining.

Then, that afternoon, the investigative alliance of Moore and Vanderbeck was able to fill in one of its most important blanks.

Tom and Al were in the wheels goods section, checking a damaged floor model bicycle to determine whether or not it would have to be replaced. Behind them, Gullakian was showing a customer the little British pedal car.

"It's a hundred and ninety dollars, sir," they could hear him saying. "Now that may seem a little expensive, but the workmanship . . ."

"Don't tell me about the workmanship," the customer growled. "Christ, am I wearing dark glasses? What I want to know is whether you've got any more of them?"

"Why, no, sir. I don't think there's another," Gullakian said. "You see, this is imported, so it would be difficult to order another, but I'm sure your little boy would like the colors . . ."

"Suppose I've got two little boys?" the customer asked. "Suppose they were both wild about the colors? What the hell kind of a father would give a car like this to one of two little boys, and not the other?"

"They could take turns," Gullakian said.

"Maybe I don't want them to take turns. Maybe I don't want my kids yelling over whose turn it is . . ."

"I see, sir," Gullakian said. "Perhaps there's a similar car in

145

one of the other stores in town. Would you like to wait a moment while I ask our buyer?"

"All right. All right. But not similar. Identical. Better. Maybe there are two better ones someplace else . . ."

Gullakian hurried past Tom and Al, going for Finn, and in a moment the customer lounged over to watch them work.

"What the hell do you guys think you're doing?" he asked. "Sawing the spokes or . . . my god. Al. For Christ's sake: Al Pennington." He was smiling, open mouthed.

Al stood quickly. "Who?" he said. "Who? You must have the wrong man, mister."

"I do?" The customer was tall, gaunt, tired-eyed and young, with coarse hair, a day's growth of beard and the look of a man in permanent pain. He was carelessly, almost dirtily, dressed, in obviously expensive clothes. "Maybe I do, son. Maybe I have got the wrong man. You're shorter than old Pennington, and meaner looking."

"Okay," Al nodded, and turned away, walking quickly toward the stockroom.

"Do you know him?" Tom asked.

"No," said the stranger. "My man walked with a limp. Tell that bicycle salesman I'll be back to look at his cheap car. Gurnstein. Cyrus Suddbury Gurnstein. Tell him my name, and tell him not to sell it till he hears from me." And the man walked off. Tom, staring after him, was unaware that Miss Klamath had come up beside him until she spoke.

"Tom."

"Yes, Miss Klamath."

"What did that man say?"

"He . . . he said he'd be back about the little British car, Miss Klamath."

"What was he saying to Barker?"

"I guess . . . he thought Al was another salesman, or something."

"Pemberton," Miss Klamath said. "Didn't he say Pemberton?"

"I don't know, Miss Klamath, I wasn't listening," Tom said, and walked hastily away from her; when he was sure she wasn't watching, he hurried to Nickie's counter, where they could wonder together how upset Al might be.

16 Though payday, leaving day, was only for-
ty-eight hours off now, Al was disturbed. He
tried to think quickly, leaving the store alone,
hurrying, whether it might be best, under the circumstances, to double back to Seattle, which he knew
so well. But he had less than five dollars left; he'd have
to wait it out.

"Al."

The voice stopped him on the street. It was Gurnstein.

"Listen, you may not be Al Pennington, but I'm still Sudd
Gurnstein, damn your incognito hide."

"Okay, Sudd. Do you mind if I walk along rather quickly?
There'll be people coming out."

"I'll meet you two blocks up and one block left," Gurnstein
said. "Two minutes."

Al hesitated for a second; then he yielded. "Okay."

"You'll be there?"

"I'll be there, Sudd."

Gurnstein swung away to the left. Al kept straight for two
blocks. He was both excited and reluctant. He and Gurnstein
had been close at college; to talk to him would be just the sort
of terrible, pleasurable renewal of an idiom, an identity, a level
of feeling, which ought, because it would move him, to be
avoided; yet of the two dangers, being moved, or leaving an old
friend hurt and puzzled, the second might be greater.

He turned left.

They met again, and Sudd said: "I didn't spill to your boy
colleague, Al. 'My man was taller,' I said. 'He limped.'"

"Thanks."

147

"Let's get a drink."

"You wouldn't care to . . . just go that way, and forget it?"

"You'll feel better if we have a drink, Al, and I tell you just what a forgetful sonofabitch I am." They were quiet for a moment, looking at one another. Then Sudd said, quietly but with something like a break in his harsh voice: "Jesus, Al, you don't know how good it is to see you."

"Let's drink," Al said. They walked on Kearney. "You living here now, Sudd?"

"Not living anywhere."

"What are you doing?"

"Drifting, Al. But the man's not after me. The man still after you?"

"You know about that?"

"Before I forgot."

"What's wrong, Sudd?"

"Want to go to Mexico? I've got a car."

"Let's go in here."

They turned into a small, somewhat dingy bar, just past Pine Street, and settled into a booth.

"What's wrong, Sudd?"

"In a minute I'll start telling you, and you'll wish I'd stop."

"Okay."

"I heard about you, Al. Quite a bit. I heard it from the eff, and I heard it from the bee, and I heard it from the goddamn eye."

"What'd you hear?"

"That you took off. I tossed herrings to a seal named Usez all one Christ-forsaken afternoon. Different colored herrings. You pull it wrong? He wouldn't say much."

"Yes and no," Al said. "Say, I just took off . . . say, they don't want me for anything you'd think I ought to be turned in about. Is that enough?"

"You didn't have to say that," Gurnstein said. "I wouldn't give you to the effers if you raped J. Edgar's mother." There was a pause. Then Gurnstein said: "What's happened to our boys, Al? Damn few still left standing. I don't mean the class; most of those smug bastards are probably fine. I mean just . . . our boys. Remember the retooling party?"

"To celebrate when you got the court order, changing your name back again, from Greystone to Gurnstein?"

"When I became retooled. Jesus, was my old man sore. Old man Greystone."

"One of the great parties, Sudd. I'd forgotten there were such things. Imagine, a time when parties could have greatness."

"The guys at the party, Al. I couldn't name them all now. And those I could, I'd be happier if I couldn't. Remember Johnny Fisher?"

"Sure."

"So attractive. So brilliant. We used to worry he'd turn homo. You'll be enchanted to know he never did turn homo, Al. He thought of something infinitely more charming, all his own. Johnny's a phone booth man, now."

"Phone booth man?"

"Buys a paper when he gets the urge. Turns to the society page. Finds a picture of a bride he likes. Gets the number of the brand new household from information. Then, at four in the morning, he finds himself a lonely phone booth, in Penn Station or somewhere like that. Dials the number, assumes he's interrupting something. Stands there masturbating while a puzzled voice on the other end says breathlessly, 'Hello? Hello? Hello?' "

"How'd you find out, Sudd?"

"He called me up one night, after he'd done it. We were living in New York then. I was the only psychiatrist he knew. I told the poor bastard to wait there, I'd come in a cab and get him. He was gone. I never found him. That's what's happened to our boys, Al. We're crazy, every goddamn one of us."

"That's a professional opinion, Dr. Gurnstein?"

"Straight from the horse's ass, Dr. Pennington."

"If these are the years that the locusts have eaten," Al said, with a smile, "there must be some fairly sick locusts around." There was a pause. "Good God," Al said. "I am a doctor, aren't I?"

"Any adventures, Doctor?" Gurnstein said. "How's a knight of the road make out for quests these days?"

"Keep looking for windmills," Al said. "All they turn out to be is dragons."

"Nothing you want to tell me?"

"Maybe," Al said. He was tempted to talk a little to Gurn-

149

stein, but his friend seemed quite hollowed out with troubles of his own, whatever they might be. Quite abruptly he learned:

"Ever hear from your wife, Al?"

"No."

"This Usez told me that you'd left her."

"I'm glad to hear he has a name," Al said. "But that was . . .?"

Gurnstein nodded. "Years ago."

Al shrugged.

"Want to know whether I ever hear from my wife, Al?"

"Okay."

"Not unless you know a goddamn good medium, Doctor. She's dead."

"Sudd."

"Yeah. Sudd is right. Went cuckoo, crazy, bats, killed herself." Gurnstein reached for his highball glass, and Al caught it to keep it from spilling over.

He held on for a moment, holding the glass against Sudd's hand, till he saw the bony fingers control themselves and close around it.

"Do you remember her, Al? Alice Jackson? The happy girl, from Quincy?"

"Sure I remember her, Sudd. From Quincy."

"Born teacher, Al. Never could see how anybody could stand it, but she loved to teach. Just sheerly loved it."

"I guess some do."

"We came out here. Good teaching jobs. Good clinic for me to work in; plenty of nuts in the lovely suburbs of Los Angeles. Good climate for Alice's health, too, Al. A perfectly lovely climate for Alice's health."

"Easy, Sudd."

"Her folks live there. Retired. Money."

"Okay."

"Lovely old white haired, white-assed Protestant folks. Seems that when the local nuts decided it was loyalty time in the public schools, these parents felt it was their patriotic duty to call attention to their leftie daughter and her jewboy husband."

Al could only shake his head.

"You know what I'd done, for Christ's sake? Oh, I ought to have been boiled in Wildroot hair tonic, Al. I'd sent ten green, double-eagle American dollars to Henry Wallace. And what's more, I had a brother get his treacherous ass killed in the Spanish War. Why, they should have tarred me up, Al, and feathered me around some; it was real civil rightsie of them to let me off with hounding my wife to suicide."

"They had hearings?"

"She was practically the only witness," Sudd said. "There was a real Commie in the system; little jerk who taught history. He signed the oath. Oh, first man up. But not Alice. Jesus, you should have seen her fight, Al. I never loved anything so much . . . I never could love anything so much. Week after week, appeals, rehearings, star chambers; she didn't have anything to fight with, no strength, no health, no backing. Finally, no voice. Just guts. I'll never forget the last hearing. Some State Senator was there observing. So was I. She didn't have any voice left, Al; she could only shake her head or nod it, and try to croak the answers out; Al, she was so thin I could have put her in my pocket. I'd begged her to drop it. We had dough. We could have moved. No. No. There she sat. They weren't getting her for being a leftie, Al. They were getting her for marrying a man named Gurnstein. Our neighbors on the school board. 'Do you share your husband's faith, Mrs. Gurn . . .' 'Is it *steen* or *stine*, Mrs., um, Jackson?' " He paused, started to raise the glass to his mouth, forgot what he was doing and stared across the table. "Oh, Jesus, do you share my faith, Al?"

"Sure, Sudd."

"I fixed things good. They were yelling at her to answer them, and she'd already given them her voice, her health, everything she had. Them and their goddamn white-assed Protestant kids. The Senator says, 'Speak up there, woman.' I jumped up and went after him, yelling at them to shut up, recess the hearing, my wife wasn't well. Boy it made a ludicrous picture for the papers, with the two cops cracking me with their billies; only they retouched the billies out, so I just looked drunk."

"They do it to you good, Sudd, when they do it."

"I spent the night in jail. When I got let out in the morning, and got home, Alice was dead. She'd sent the kids to her mother's." Al quietly took the nearly empty glass out of Sudd's hand, and put his half full one in it. After a moment, Sudd looked

151

down at it, then raised it shakily to his mouth and drank. "Do you share my faith, Al?"

"Sure, Sudd."

"Let me tell you about the kids, and that'll be all. They made a big thing out of me being in jail, and Alice sending the kids to her mother before she . . . got out the gun. Aroused public opinion held that I might not be a suitable father for my kids, a jailboy jewbird; the senior Jacksons rather inclined towards the same delicate point of view. Anyway, they had possession. Jesus, Al, I was so . . . shellshocked, I guess . . . I wasn't sure but what they were right. My old man would have fought a thing like that, but he's dead, leaving the money-pots behind. I've got money, Al. Real big, inexhaustible goddamn money."

"I guess that's good."

"Yeah." He shook his head. "Fine. Well, I'm not going to wheel it into court. I've been thinking about it, and I don't think I'm going to court. Would you get your kids into that? Let some lecherous, white-haired Protestant judge ask them if they don't love their Lambie Granny better than their baddy daddy, who made commie mommie shoot herself? No. No, Al. So I'm allowed to go into Mainway's Toy Department, and spend my old man's money on presents, oh, all the presents I want to buy—and have them mailed. That's what I'm allowed. And visiting. I'm allowed to visit my kids sometimes, if I threaten a little bit, only Granny likes to be there, so she threatens a little bit, too . . . oh, Jesus, Al." His voice ran thin and stopped. Then he said wearily: "Do you share my faith, Al? Do you share my goddamn faith, Al? Do you sh . . ."

"Sure, Sudd," Al said. "Take it easy." He looked for the waiter to call for another drink. "Take it easy, Sudd."

"Believe in God," Sudd said. "That's my faith. Believe in Him as hard as you can. Then if He does exist, and you get to heaven as a reward, and get admitted to the Presence, maybe you'll get a chance to slip up and get Him, for all He's done, before the lousy angels can stop you."

What could Al say to this friend, this torn, this shredded Gurnstein? Quietly, trying to keep the pity out of his voice: "That's a pretty good faith, Sudd."

"Listen, I'm almost crazy enough not to knock myself off, on

152

a chance it might be right. You don't get to heaven if you pull the switch yourself, isn't that the way it goes?"

"That's the way it goes," Al said.

"You've got to be pretty nutty not to want to knock yourself off these days, huh, Al?"

"Pretty nutty."

"But imagine; maybe if you stick and join every single one of their churches, don't leave a thing to chance, pray, fast, worship . . . imagine, they might let you in. Imagine having your hands around that Celestial Neck? Imagine it? And boy, He Who Knows Everything would know what for. You wouldn't even have to explain it . . . you could hear all your friends in hell cheering, as they battered at the gates; you'd be kicking away the angels so fast the chicken lice jumped out of their wings . . . and He's sitting there dead, and the boys from hell come piling in with their torches to fire the joint." His voice was rising in a kind of bitter exhilaration. "There'd be a melting of harps, wouldn't there, Al?"

"The harps would melt."

"And the good white Protestant asses crackling as they roasted like the government-inspected pigs they are? And it wouldn't bother the boys from hell at all, that heat, they'd be used to it, all my friends, the niggerboys, jewboys, lefties—isn't that a faith, Al? Isn't that worth signing the big oath?"

"You had anything to eat recently, Sudd?"

"No."

"Remember doing any sleeping?"

"I sleep in my car, Al. I sleep with my car, what's wrong with you? Americans love their cars . . ."

"Let's go over to my place, Sudd. We've lost a lot of the boys. Let's not lose you." He got up.

"Go to hell."

"Come on, Sudd."

"Up uranium, physicist."

"A threat, Sudd?"

"Being funny, funny fellow."

"You're too well trained a man not to know that you're damn near over the edge, when you get that kind of funny. Come on."

"Appeal to professional pride, huh?"

"Competence, anyway."

"Screw you, Allerd . . . oh, all right. I'll come."

When he had put Gurnstein to bed, and heated the first can of soup for him, the man wept.

"Christ, I was hungry, Al," he admitted.

He ate through the chicken noodle soup; then he ate a can of oxtail. He had half a loaf of bread, biting it off in chunks, and halfway through a can of split pea soup he fell asleep.

He woke frequently during the night, though, and talked, quite lucidly for the most part and, towards morning, even calmly. He had been living in his car for two months, sleeping in it in parking lots, shaving in filling stations, spending his days driving aimlessly around or trying to shop for his two sons.

Once, when Gurnstein woke up, Al was sleeping lightly; he was out of bed almost as soon as Sudd was.

"Just going to the can," Gurnstein said. "I feel better, Al." He came back from the bathroom, got into bed, and started to read a magazine. "You sleep, boy, I'll be okay."

About two, Al woke up again to see Gurnstein cutting at the magazine with a jack-knife.

"What are you doing, prophet?" Al asked.

Gurnstein looked at him without smiling. "Trying to cast an intelligent ballot," he said.

"Who you voting for?"

"Miss Rheingold. This is the time of year when every red blooded young man casts his vote for Miss Rheingold." He stared at Al somberly. "I suppose you think I'm not red blooded? Well, I am. I've been bleeding quite a bit lately, and it's all red."

"I know you have, Sudd," Al said.

"All right." Suddenly Sudd relaxed and smiled. "I was trying to scare you," he said. "Here." He reached the magazine across the narrow room and Al took it. On the page of stamp sized color photographs of half a dozen girls, the hair had been neatly cut away from around each face. "You've got to participate in their myths, Al. That's the only way to understand them. I was really trying to vote. I thought I'd remove the hair from each girl, and if I could tell any one of them from any of the others, maybe I'd want to send in a vote for her. But they're all the same, Al.

154

What good's a vote, if there's no difference in the candidates?"

"You're more of a leftie than I am," Al said, able all at once to feel better about Sudd. "You still think it matters."

At about five Al woke again to see Sudd fully dressed, sitting on the bed watching him.

"I was waiting for you to wake up, Al," he said. "I feel much better now. I'm ready to go."

"Where?"

"Mexico, I guess. Maybe I'll like it better in Mexico."

"I hope so."

"Come with me."

"Can't, Sudd."

"I've got dough enough to last for seventy lifetimes."

"Thanks, I'd better stick to my own road," Al said.

"Wouldn't it be better to travel with a friend?"

"Much better."

"Is it because you think I'm over the edge?"

"No. No. It's just . . . it's the West Coast for me, Sudd. For too many reasons. And best alone."

"I'll be better away," Sudd said, gaunt in the gray light of false dawn. "Maybe I'll be all right away. You know it's funny, Al. I couldn't get with their myths, and sometimes, like in bringing up the kids, I really wanted to. I can't make my mind work like theirs. Are we such aliens? Not you, maybe, but me. You're more with them, Al, and more of them and you choose alienation. That's different. Even when we were kids, when alienation felt good, like a source of strength, I knew some day I'd want to overcome it. But I can't; not without really going over the edge. I know what you have to do, and I can't do it. I know," he continued sadly, the fury all spent now. "I know. You're eighteen. That's the key age in America and they give you a key. A car driving key and a car driving license, and you car-drive into the drive-in restaurant and the pretty little teen age hoppers hop you with dishes of whipped cream; you drive to the drive-in movie for three years, and the screen is full of whipped cream; when you're twenty-one, you drive to the drive-in bank, and the dollar they give you is good for a dollar's worth of whipped cream. And pretty soon the superhoppers hop you, and drive you away to Crazy. That's where the road maps lead, Al: *Crazy,*

155

population a hundred and eighty million. When they car drive you there, you're not alienated any more. Oh no. Because you change your name to Greystone, and you're whipped cream yourself." His chin dropped to his chest. "And if you can't do it, you're just whipped, Al. That's a professional opinion. Tell that clerk I won't be back for the pedal car." The great silhouette heaved itself up. "So long, Doctor."

"Luck, Sudd," Al said. "Have it good in Mexico."

"You're the only one of our boys still standing, Al," Sudd said. "I hope you can last." And he moved slowly to the door and out.

17 For a moment, as he returned to sleep, the will-muscles which held Al's sense of guilt firm relaxed enough so that he was on his way with Sudd to Mexico, to live easily in a warm place, with a friend.

To have been friendless, to have found his companionate affections, his conversational energies, his bone-deep curiosities about the minds of others, engaged only by people of different turns—men and boys met casually on jobs, like Tom and Finn—this had been as much a deprivation as being womanless. And so the power of wish gave him an hour's cease from it—a minute of dreaming the wish accomplished, and fifty-nine of dreamless sleep. Then, as sleep began to release its hold to the muscles of guilt once more, Johnny Fisher, shy, attractive, brilliant, asked Al for a dime to make a phone call and he woke alarmed.

It was payday; it was pulling out day. How curious, he thought, as he dressed, the rhythms of the lives we lead: the world of day's work, the world of personal present, the world of personal past, each succeeding the other daily, touching at the edges but seldom really impinging, three different realities. And now that he was ready to break the rhythm, abandon one reality, he almost felt as if he oughtn't to, though it had been established only two weeks. How much more difficult for men who held jobs for years, he thought; what a vast power of inertia American employment stability had going for it.

In the department, as the force prepared to receive the impact of another weekend crowd, on this second Saturday before Christmas, there was a quality of people bracing for ordeal; the week had been a strain, and there was a feeling that all of it would be repeated and intensified in getting through Saturday, with only Finn pleased about it, excited by the prospective crush, as he swung with Al and Tom from counter to counter, checking goods, urging the clerks to sell hard:

"Give 'em the old wringer," he'd cry. "Today you've got them where you want them. Time they fight their way to you, they've got a clerk, they'll buy anything twice. They ask for one, give them two. Promise delivery. Load them up. Put them through it. Squeeze till you hear 'em go bong, give 'em one more shake, and let the next one grab you. Sell hard, sell fast; it's going to be the day . . ."

This reassured only the clerks who didn't need it, like Gullakian; it frightened most of them and made them tenser. Sally it annoyed.

She had been dismayed to find herself apologized to, in mumbling fashion, by Finn on Tuesday morning; and since then, except for one brief interlude, she had been ignored. The interlude had occurred during a short lull on Thursday. Piqued, her confidence a little shaken by the puzzling turn things had taken, Sally had spotted Finn standing alone at the service desk, and wriggled past him, very whorey, saying: "Wonder what Santa has for little girls today?"

And gone back to wait on the cot for nearly five minutes before Finn came furtively in; when he did he looked jumpy, said nothing, tumbled her wordlessly without giving her time to build up to it, and said, immediately he was through:

"Ah, Sally girl, we mustn't. Sally, it's the devil that's in us," and tiptoed out again, leaving Sally to get herself together and reflect that this guilty little lust was hardly the ride she had thought the big man would take her for. After it, she turned resentful, waited now for Finn to take some sort of initiative, so that she could do herself the justice of refusing him; and was doubly irritated when he continued to avoid her counter or, when it was impossible, addressed his fatuosities about selling to Winnipeg.

158

It had been a heavy week, and it was a crushing morning. Within five minutes after the store doors opened downstairs, the aisles in the Toy Department were so jammed that one could only move in the same direction as the prevailing current; only with a sharp sword, Dolly Klamath thought, watching from the sanctuary island of the service desk, could she make progress against this current, cutting the waves in two at their waists, working slowly, jumping back each time from the pressurized spurt of blood.

To her the heavy week, dominated by Sally's awful laugh when she had listened by the shell on Monday, had been a week of evil, a week of sex. She watched the crowds, pushing tortuously past her, and every man seemed to be rubbing himself into the buttocks of the woman in front of him. There was an intimacy about the transactions, the customers with their privates pressed against the counters, reaching into holes in their clothing for money to pass, in frantic slow motion, across to the clerks whose hips pressed back at the customers while they took the money, only the glass width of the counter itself separating the actions. Something Dolly had overheard in the ladies' room had started this disturbing way of seeing, an awful thing which she could not escape, trapped in one of the little booths.

Betty Connaught, the pinched girl, had said it to Sally Malinkrodt: "God, I'm breaking down. I sit there, hunched over that damn little machine, watching the little needle go in and out of the pink cloth, and that smell of people rubbing together, and the noise, and I start to come. I can't help it. Six or seven times a day, involuntary orgasms. It's driving me nuts."

"Two more weeks, Betty," Sally had said with wicked cheerfulness. "Maybe it'll ask you to marry it."

The demonstrators barely had to demonstrate that morning; people were in too much of a hurry to buy, anything in a package, anything at a price, so Nickie told Al, hugging his arm delightedly as they pushed their way out to lunch.

"Fine."

"Al, you just don't know what this does for my ego, having you ask me out."

159

"Got paid this morning," Al said. "Want to blow my roll on a pretty face."

She squeezed the arm. "Wonder how long it takes to ice champagne?"

There wasn't much time; they had to wait for a table at a coffee shop kind of place, where the service would be quick once they were seated.

"I don't care if we're late," Nickie said. "Klamath can beat me all afternoon . . . oh, Al, I was beginning to think you thought I'd died."

"Take it easy," Al said. "I only asked you because Winnipeg said she had a date."

She put her mouth close to his ear. "Take it back," she whispered.

"No."

Softly, she heated the inside of his ear with her breath. "Take it back?"

He couldn't get his head away. "I take it back," he said, a little flustered. "Stop, Nickie. You're prettier than Winnipeg." She stopped. "From some angles."

They were given a table.

Mostly they joked. The only sober moment was when Nickie said: "Al, I dreamed about him last night."

"Him?"

"The baby."

"Why him, Nick? Her. Them. Maybe a miscarriage. Did you know that something over fifty percent of all first pregnancies miscarry?"

"They do?"

"I dreamed too. I dreamed about a classmate of mine, who probably wasn't too much wanted at home. The only thing he's wanted for now is locking up."

"All right, Al."

When they were through eating, and had gotten up to go, Nickie said: "Haven't I been good? Not a single question."

"Very good, Nickie," Al said. "Thanks."

They went back out onto the crowded street.

"I have something I've been wondering if I ought to tell you."

"Okay."

"Al, they . . . they wanted Tom to sort of spy on you. Right from the beginning. To find out about you. Not Mr. Finn; others."

Al nodded. "Okay," he said.

"Tom knows quite a lot, at least we think he does; he knows you drink at work. But he won't tell them."

"Thanks, Nickie. I won't ask what else he knows . . . I'd be tempted to correct it. You and Tom are . . . good people."

"He's very loyal, Al." A touch of excitement came into her voice. "Al, shall we try to find out what they know? If anything? We could mislead them . . ."

"Be double agents, Nickie? That's a rough career. No, I think you'll find it won't be . . . really necessary. Just forget whatever it is you've learned. Make the dough; get yourself in shape. Worry about Nickie; don't worry about Al." He was trying, cautiously, to say goodbye.

As they walked back to the store, as close as they'd ever been, Nickie holding his arm tightly against her side and humming to herself, he thought: this girl. This girl. She's a born virtuoso on the man. Give her another year and she'll play us like harps, plucking music from us, coaxing, striking, demanding, releasing . . . her laugh will run us in glissandi, her prayers strike chords we didn't know were there. And they aren't there, of course. We'll learn that when she passes us along to lesser artists. The music is in the player, not the instrument, and we'll never hear ourselves producing chords like that again. Addressing her silently he said: that he was glad he had known her, Nicholas Nimblebee, in the years of her early promise, and not later . . .

As they came to the door of the store, she said: "Al, just because I don't say it every time, I'm not forgetting that you're letting me intrude . . . and I can't tell you the way it renews me, just to be with you a little. You're my whiskey at work, my wonder drug."

"You won't depend on it too much?"

"I'm dying to become an addict, but I know I mustn't. I'll be good, Al. Just a little longer. If I can get through the job, and reach Christmas, I'll be fine."

"I'm not sure I'll make it all the way myself, Nick," Al said, reluctantly. "Don't be too disappointed if I don't show up . . . some morning."

161

The jam persisted until two; then, unexpectedly, it began to let up. "These early shoppers, they seem to be pretty much morning shoppers this year," Finn said.

By three, one could get around the floor once more. By four, it might have been a rather slow weekday.

"It's crazy," Finn said. "Where'd they go? What's happened to my afternoon?"

It did seem wrong; it threw the clerks off balance that the energy marshaled and hoarded to endure such a day should suddenly be superfluous. People began slouching off the floor, unaware of why they were suddenly feeling ill tempered, to take their breaks in silence.

At the service desk, Dolly relaxed for a moment. Then she arranged her hair, and started out. She caught Gullakian with his tie loosened and his shirt collar undone.

"Straighten up that tie," she snapped.

"Have a heart, Dolly."

She stared at him coldly until the tie was fastened.

Dolores Hughes was half sitting, against an open drawer.

"The day's not over yet, Miss Hughes," Dolly said. "You can lie down at home." The girl straightened up.

Then, at the electric train counter she saw Harris, wearing his thick, horn rimmed glasses under the engineer's cap. He was frantically trying to connect some wires in the switchboard; she smiled when she saw him jump backwards slightly. He had shocked himself. The sweat on his hands would have made it hurt a good deal. She ducked into the center of his counter, coming up behind him.

"Harris!"

He dropped the wires, and jumped around to face her; one of them, brushing against something in accidental contact, sent a train racing forward; he jumped around again and pulled it away.

"Harris."

He faced her.

"Mr. Finn has told you those glasses are not an acceptable part of your costume."

"Yes, Miss Klamath." He took them off. "It's just," he tried a weak smile. "I can't see to make connections without them."

162

"I'll take them," Dolly said, not responding to his smile. Hesitantly, he handed them to her. They were real pansy glasses, she thought. Just the kind they were so proud of. Thick horn frames.

She studied his face. She could see a weak try at charming her forming in it.

"You're not to wear these, Harris," she said, and broke them in half at the bridge.

An expression like a silent scream crossed his face, and his hand shot out convulsively towards her. Coolly she placed the glasses in it. Was he going to cry? Had he cried the first time one of them had thrown him down and hurt him in that place? That strange, painful place.

As he turned away, she felt like laughing, and she turned herself, ducked out, suddenly began to hurry off, her steps guided by a need to be somewhere quite specific, to do something, the nature of which would be clear when she reached it; she found herself, the laughter turned to fever, at the doll counter.

Thank God, Sally was gone. No customer or clerk watched. She slipped, hearing her own breathing, behind the counter. The drab, ecclesiastically dressed Winnipeg girl turned towards her in fear.

"Let me see your salesbook," Dolly hissed.

Trembling, the girl produced it.

"Open it. Flat. On the counter. Stand next to me," Dolly ordered. The girl complied, moving almost against her on the left. With her right hand Dolly reached across and seized the girl by the elbow, pulling her against herself, so that they appeared to be standing side by side, looking at the book.

"Can't read your slips," Dolly tried to say, hearing a gasp in her voice, while, with the left hand, hidden now, Dolly hoisted at the girl's dress behind and searched, unastonished at herself, whole, righteous, vindicated, alive, dizzily triumphant at the girl's terror.

Immediately, Dolly was done; tension gone out of her, relief flowing into her arms, sweat rolling under her clothes, hurrying away before the raped girl could really know what had happened to her.

But she'd know all right, Dolly exulted as she fled toward the service desk, she'd know. And never dare complain. And if she did, Dolly would say a friendly goose, just trying to keep good feeling, book was such a mess, friendlier way to discipline her than bawling out again, had to bawl her out so much, surely she didn't misunderstand, a friendly goose. And then, glancing nervously over, seeing the girl in a state of walking collapse and blonde Malinkrodt still not there, Dolly lunged for the drawer where she kept her purse and shopping bag, and almost screamed. Hadn't she, hadn't she brought it, oh, yes, yes, yes, there it was, in the bottom of the shopping bag, under a folded scarf, it was there, she found it, yes it was, a little quilted plastic case, eight inches long, lined with heat resistant stuff and closed with a zipper, found it and held it concealed against her side and hurried across the floor, dashing through the stockroom and into the ladies' room.

It was there that Nickie saw her, only a minute or two later, and came out to report, in an urgent, puzzled whisper to Al, calling him away from the group of clerks who sat grousing on the packing cases:

"Al, the strangest thing. I was going to the john. I opened one of the little booths, I didn't think there was anyone there; it wasn't locked. Miss Klamath's in there, Al. She looks . . . kind of drugged. She has the seat down and she's sitting on it with all her clothes straight . . . well, you know, not using it . . . and her eyes rolled crazily up at the ceiling; she didn't even notice me, Al, or lock the door. And she's sucking on a . . . she's feeding herself milk out of a nursing bottle, the kind you use for babies."

Sally's report came minutes later. "Al, something's happened to the kid from Winnipeg. I got back from my break, and she looked dreadful; half dead. When she saw me, she grabbed her purse and ran. I don't know where. Out of the store, I guess, she even forgot to get this out of her drawer," Sally held out a narrow, brown envelope. It was the week's pay.

"Crying?"

"Not exactly."

"Say anything at all?"

"No. She just looked terrified."

Finn came in: "Is something wrong, Miss . . . Sally?" he asked. She looked at him without answering, shrugged, turned and walked out, leaving Al holding Winnipeg's abandoned paycheck.

"Something seems to have happened to the girl from Winnipeg," Al said. "Sally said she just took off in a panic, and left her paycheck."

"Oh, dear God," Finn said, anguished. "Dear God. It's this crazy afternoon. Dolly has broken Harris's glasses, and M'nerney and I have had the devil's own time trying to calm him down. I'm going to have to pay out of my own pocket, to keep the store from hearing. Sally won't speak to me; that sewing machine girl's practically gibbering. The cowboy man has cursed M'nerney. Al, what's wrong with people? A little work and they go to pieces."

"I don't know," Al said. "Here. You'd better have this." He offered Finn the paycheck.

"Al," Finn said, hesitantly. "Maybe . . . would you take it to her? I'll get the address for you. And see if she won't tell you what it was happened to her?"

"Well, Hub, I'd planned to be . . . away this weekend," Al said.

"Al, boy, I'd go myself, but I wouldn't know what to say." The big man sounded miserable. "I wouldn't want to send M'nerney. Maybe . . . Dolly might . . ."

"I'll do it," Al said quickly. "I'll go tonight, and let you know on Monday."

18   He didn't manage to see the girl that night. He rang the bell marked with her name, in the lobby of the modest apartment house on Steiner Street, three times that evening. There was no response, and the windows in the apartment he calculated to be hers showed no light. Finally, he left a note in her mailbox: *"I have your pay for you. I'll be here again at ten tomorrow (Sunday) morning. Al Barker,"* and went on to Weary's where the juke box never played too loudly but never stopped.

In the morning, at ten, he rang her bell again, and this time the buzzer answered; he let himself in and walked upstairs. He found her dressed in a boxy, plaid suit, wearing a hat, with overcoat and purse beside her, seated on a lumpy looking couch; primly, she asked him to leave the door open into the hall.

"I'm ready to go to church," she said.

"What church is that?"

"Presbyterian."

"You're Scottish?"

"My great grandparents were."

He took out the pay envelope. "Here," he said. "You'd better count it. I rang your bell a couple of times last night; I guess you weren't in."

She accepted the envelope from him. "I heard you," she said. "I was . . . I'd gone to bed."

"Was it that you were afraid to open the door?" Al asked. "Or didn't want to?"

"I always go to bed early."

"If you were at all afraid, I'm sorry I alarmed you," Al said. She didn't answer.

"Why did you leave the store that way?" Al asked. "Could you tell me?"

"I don't lie, Mr. Barker. I was in bed last night."

"But . . . you might still have been afraid that it was somebody else?"

"I have to go to church," she said.

"I'd like to help if I can," Al said. "If someone's done something, or something's frightened you. Sally thought something had frightened you."

"Please tell Mrs. Rivers not to worry. She's been very kind."

"Can't you tell her yourself?"

"I can't return to the store," the girl said, tight lipped.

"Miss Robertson," Al said. "I didn't come to pry. This is kind of official. Mr. Finn asked me to come; perhaps there's something going on which he should know about, as head of the department. Miss Robertson, people at the store care about you. Sally is very anxious about you."

"It's nothing I can tell to a man," the girl said. "Or even to a woman."

"Could you tell a doctor about it?"

"I don't know a doctor here," she said. Suddenly there were tears in her eyes. "I don't even know one."

"Miss Robertson," Al said. "Perhaps it's hard to believe: I'm a doctor. I don't tell lies, either."

"You are?"

He nodded.

"But why . . . I have heard something . . . that's what they say about you, that you must have some profession. Are you truly a doctor, Mr. Barker?"

He nodded.

"I must know . . . I want to know if . . . oh, I'm so worried."

"What happened?"

"Miss . . . Miss . . ."

"Miss Klamath?" The girl nodded. "What did Miss Klamath do?"

"She said she wanted to look at my sales book . . ." the girl began. "And she, she . . . I can't say it."

167

"She touched you?"

The girl nodded. "In a private place?" Again the girl nodded.

Then she burst out: "In back." She lowered her eyes from his, and added, after a moment, in a flat voice: "It hurt."

"It must have been very unpleasant," Al said. "But . . . it doesn't still hurt, does it?"

Still avoiding his eyes, the girl shook her head.

"You're all right today, then," Al said. "You feel well? No real harm done, except the unpleasantness of it?"

Suddenly she rolled her face up towards his again; it was streaming with tears. "You don't understand. I was innocent. That's the worst part . . . I'm engaged. I'm going to be. When I can earn enough for a . . . a trousseau. I was going to earn enough and now, now I'm damaged goods . . ."

"You mean you think . . .? Miss Robertson. Wait a moment. Listen to me." Could she really be so confused? From the way she was sobbing, apparently she was. "Didn't your mother ever . . .?"

"She'd never talk about a thing like that. But, isn't . . .?"

To a wonderment he knew he mustn't show, Al found himself telling her, as to a little girl, what men and women did when they married. When he had finished, she seemed unutterably relieved.

"Oh, you must really be a doctor, aren't you?" She smiled for the first time.

He smiled back. "You mustn't say so at the store."

"How could I? I'll never go back to that place."

"Maybe that's best," Al said.

"But I . . . I want to. I don't know what to do."

"If you want to, go back."

"Oh, I wish I could," she said. "I wanted to work there so much. My . . . my friend. He's a mechanic. He's coming to the States in the spring, after the hockey season. I'd be entitled to a discount, you see, and have enough money to, to . . ."

"I understand," Al said. Then he added, slowly. "You know, I have an idea that if Miss Klamath knew that I know, and I undertook not to tell, I think she might not bother you again."

"She wouldn't dare, would she?" Now the girl turned fierce. "Would you do that; will you tell her?"

168

"If that will make you feel free to come back to your job," Al said. "And if you'll promise not to speak of this to Sally, or anyone." He saw now that Finn might be spared the knowledge of all this, if it worked out.

"I promise," the girl said.

"All right. I'll see Miss Klamath today. And after Christmas, if they keep you on in the store, I'm sure you could work under a different service manager."

Smiling now, the girl stood up, wiping at her face, righteous. "She's a vicious woman, Dr. Barker. You tell her I said so."

"No," said Al. "She's a sick woman. I'd rather tell her you forgive her."

There was a pause. Then the girl shook her head. "I don't think I can," she said. "But I'll pray for her."

"And try to forgive her?" Al said. "Try to feel pity for her, because she's sick."

"All right," the girl said. "All right."

He walked her to the church. It was a rather bright day, and not cold. He sat for a time in a small park called Buena Vista. He was going to make an enemy now, perhaps an able, certainly a ruthless one. He found himself enjoying the sense of risk. He walked for a while afterwards, found the address in a phone book, and crossed town to the section in which the Service Manager lived; about mid-afternoon, he phoned her from a drugstore.

"Miss Klamath?"

"Yes."

"This is Al Barker. I wonder if I could see you for a few minutes?"

"I don't receive male callers, Mr. Barker. And I don't discuss business on Sunday."

"It's not exactly business, Miss Klamath. I've just been to see Kay Robertson, the girl from Winnipeg. I . . . was asked to take her paycheck to her. She'd forgotten it."

There was a pause. Then she said: "I see. And I suppose she accused me of something. Being overstrict, perhaps? Was that it?"

"No, Miss Klamath. I had to tell her I was a doctor before she'd . . . make any accusation."

169

"I see," the woman said. There was another pause. "I see," she repeated.

"Wouldn't it be best if I came by?" Al asked. There was a rather long silence. She neither answered nor hung up. Then he thought he heard steps, walking away from the phone. He waited another minute.

"Miss Klamath? Miss Klamath?" Did a door close, somewhere within range of the connected phone's capacity to pick up sound?

He hung his own instrument up, somewhat alarmed, and went to her apartment house. He gave his name to the doorman who picked up the house phone to announce him. Putting it down, the man said:

"Sorry, sir. It's busy."

In a moment he tried again. "Phone's still busy, sir," he said. "Were you expected?"

"Yes, I was."

"Well," the man said. "She hasn't many callers, you know. I don't suppose I ever announced one before."

"Really?"

"Pretty girl, sir," the man said. "But cool. Never says hello, just nods. Glad to see she has a friend like yourself." He tried again. "Still busy."

"Why don't I just go up?" Al suggested. "What number?"

"All right," the man said. "Four-B, sir."

When he got to the fourth floor, using a self service elevator, Al found the door to 4-B open. He called her name; there was no answer. He walked in, closing the door behind him.

It was an immaculate apartment—a gleaming living room, a spotless bedroom opening off it, both empty. Opposite the open bedroom door was an alcove, with a swinging door at its end; on a small table in the alcove stood the phone cradle; the instrument was lying on the table beside it.

Al entered the alcove and pushed open the door.

There, in the kitchen, wearing a white nylon nurse's uniform, Dolly Klamath was standing at the stove, stirring a pan of milk and humming to herself.

"Miss Klamath," he said. Then, a little louder: "Miss Klamath."

"Oh," she interrupted her humming, turned, and smiled brightly at him. "Hello. It's Mr. Barker, isn't it? This will be ready in a minute." The voice was high pitched and merry, quite unlike her normal tones of speech. "How nice of you to come and see me."

"Hello, Miss Klamath," Al said.

"Just one more minute. There." She turned out the fire under the pan, and faced him brightly. "That's all done now. Oh, yes; it's important, though, not to let it boil. I think I can take a minute now. Just let me slip out of my apron, and let's sit in the living room."

"All right," Al said. She was undoing an apron of the same white nylon as the uniform.

"Sanitation can be fun," she said brightly. "If you have the right attitude. Don't you think?" She laughed. "What a nice surprise," she said going past him, and into the living room. "Is it still a nice day out? It was lovely when I went to mass."

"A very nice day," Al said.

"Did you go to mass?"

"No."

"Naughty boy," she shook an admonishing finger at him, still smiling the bright smile. "Oh, naughty." She sat in a straight chair. "I'm sorry I'm not dressed for company. But I like to wear these anyway. They feel so clean."

"Did you work in a hospital?"

"Now that you're here," she bounced up again, "you must let me show you the house. Come on." She beckoned to him. "This is my room."

She led the way into the bedroom.

"I had to have more closets built for my clothes. I love clothes, Mr. Barker. I guess all women do."

"I guess they do," Al said, as she threw open the door of the closet.

"There, you see?" The closet was full of dresses, expensive things, Al judged; party clothes. "I don't suppose you'd be much interested—I save so for these. The brown taffeta, isn't it sweet?" She reached in and took a satin padded hanger off the rack, on which was hung a richly simple, strapless cocktail gown. She held it up to herself, posing.

"Do you wear it often?" Al asked.

"I have wonderful gloves to go with it. Look." She hung the

171

dress up, smiling eerily at it, turned and half ran over to one of the three large dressers. "Look," she cried. "Do you like gloves? I have forty pairs." And she plunged her hands into the top drawer, and pulled out a huge double handful of unworn gloves, turning and holding them out to him with the most pleading look on her face that Al had ever seen on man or woman.

"Miss Klamath," Al said, slowly, "they're beautiful gloves. I know that no one with clothes like yours, and with such a beautiful, clean apartment could mean to do anything wicked."

She turned from him again, and her shoulders began to heave as she let the gloves fall slowly back into the drawer. He crossed the room and put his hands on the shoulders. Immediately she sprang forward, away from him.

"Don't touch me," she cried. "Don't you dare touch me."

"I'm sorry," Al said.

"What did you come here for?" She turned, facing him once more. "If you attack me, I'll scream. I'll scream so loud . . ."

"I won't attack you," Al said.

She stared at him for a long second. Then she crumpled forward onto the bed. "Attack me," she said, in a dead voice. She turned over, spreading her arms limply across the bed. "Attack me, if that's what you came here for. I won't scream. Do you want me to wear my pretty dress?" She half sat up. "Go out a minute, and I'll put on my pretty dress."

"Miss Klamath," Al said sharply. "Miss Klamath. I came to bring you a message. Kay Robertson asked me to come to tell you she's forgiven you."

For a moment the still form didn't move. Dolly Klamath stared at him.

"Kay Robertson, from Winnipeg. She's forgiven you. She asked me to tell you."

"What?" She stared.

"She forgives you. She forgives you. I left her at church. She asked me to say that she understands, that we're all under strain, that she doesn't hold you responsible and won't complain. She forgives you."

"Winnipeg forgives me?"

"Yes. Yes. It's all over," Al said.

Dolly Klamath shook her head slowly, in some sort of wonder-

172

ment and relief, and when she spoke again, her voice sounded somewhat familiar for the first time: "Will you excuse me a minute while I change my dress? I wasn't expecting you quite so soon."

Al went into the living room, closing the door behind him, and lit a cigarette. When he discovered there were no ashtrays, he put it out on his shoe and tossed it out the window. She came in briskly, wearing a store dress.

"Now, Mr. Barker," she said. "Sorry to have been unprepared. What . . . what you were referring to was a very weak and foolish thing, wasn't it? It was good of you to bring me Miss Robertson's message."

"Not at all," Al said.

"Only you and I know? And she, of course. She doesn't want to make trouble?"

"That's it," Al said. "She doesn't want to make trouble. That's what I've come to say."

Dolly said, crisp as ever: "That's very generous of her."

"She's rather a nice girl."

"Why didn't she come herself?"

"Would you have?"

"I suppose not. Would you please thank her for me, and say that I am deeply apologetic? That I very much regret my weakness, and feel that it is most generous of her to take a forgiving attitude? And say that, I realize I can make no amends but that I will try to avoid her in the store so as not to cause embarrassment."

"I'll tell her all of that," Al said.

"And now, Mr. Barker," and there were overtones of impending dismissal in her voice. "I want to tell you that I know there was a man in the store the other day who addressed you as Al Pemberton. I don't feel that there is any reason why I should give this information to . . . say Mr. M'nerney or Mr. Finn."

"I didn't come here to trade," Al said. "You must do what you think best about that. But my name is not and has never been Pemberton."

"What did you come here for, Mr. Barker? Oh yes, to bring me the message from little Winnipeg, of course. How did you get in?"

173

"What?"

"I'm sorry. I wasn't expecting you so soon, after your call. How did you get in?"

"The door was open," Al said.

"That's odd," Miss Klamath said. "I understood that the doorman was supposed to call when a visitor presented himself downstairs. Wasn't he there?"

"He tried to call," Al said. "The phone was busy."

"Nonsense. There've been no other . . . if he had called, you'd never have found me napping in the bedroom in that old uniform. No. I should have been quite prepared . . ." She had been sweeping the room with her eyes while she spoke; now something held them. "The phone is off the hook. Did you take it off? Why did you do that?"

"Miss Klamath," Al said. "What were you heating when I came in?"

"Heating?" She seemed genuinely puzzled.

"When I came in and found you in the kitchen, what were you cooking on the stove?"

"Why are you trying to confuse me?" she asked. "I haven't been in the kitchen since I washed the luncheon dishes, hours ago."

"Miss Klamath, would you think it terribly impertinent if I told you I was concerned for you?"

"How so, Mr. Barker?"

"May I ask . . . you honestly have no recollection of having been at the stove when I arrived? Of leaving the phone off the hook? Of showing me your gloves and dresses?"

"Why . . . you must be mistaken . . ."

"It seems to you that you were napping in the bedroom, or something of the sort, and had been since my phone call, when I came in?"

"Yes. Yes."

"And if it's you who are mistaken?"

"Why then . . ." She sat, frowning. "Then you'd be right to be concerned. Then I'd, I'd be concerned myself."

"Have you ever been aware of having had a memory lapse? At any time?"

"Can you show me that I've had one now?"

174

"Did you leave anything on top of the stove, when you finished the luncheon dishes?" Al asked; she shook her head. "Want to go look?"

"I guess I'd better," she said, reluctantly. She got up and crossed the room. She went into the alcove. He could hear the door swing open, and then a gasp. She came quickly back in, her face white. "There's a pan of milk there," she said, in a small frightened voice. Then she added slowly: "Yes, I think I may have had memory lapses before."

"Sit down."

She did.

"Very often?"

"Not until recently."

"I don't like to bring it up again but . . . do you, for example, remember the encounter with the girl yesterday?"

"Yes," she said. "Yes. And I remember breaking the man's glasses, just before that. I don't know why; something awful seems to have got into me." She paused. "I don't seem to know what happened afterwards," she said. "I think the next thing I remember is that I was out on the street, after work. Am I . . . something's the matter with me, isn't it? Isn't it, Mr. Barker?"

"I think you should go to a doctor," Al said. "Do you know of one you could go to?"

She shook her head.

"Just the convent, Mr. Barker. I was brought up in a convent. There's a hospital. I could ask to go there. I'm sure they'd take me there."

"I think you should arrange it right away," Al said.

"Should I really?"

"Can you phone them?"

"Not the convent," Dolly said, getting up. "And I'd rather . . . well, you see. I'd want to write to them. The convent; not the hospital. You see, I was going to be a nun. I think, I'm sure they'd let me come back. And make me well again."

"Perhaps you should stay away from the store until you hear."

"No. Oh, no, Mr. Barker. Oh, you don't know what it's like to be alone. I think I'll be all right at the store, now. I think it would be good for me to stay there until Christmas. I'd feel I was doing my duty, don't you see, and I wouldn't be alone?

175

Wouldn't that be better, Mr. Barker? Al. Everybody calls you Al, don't they? May I call you Al, privately, when we talk alone?"

"Of course."

"You're being so kind. These things have frightened me. All last week I was . . . I was wild. It's so good to talk about it. Did you ever have to live with something about yourself you couldn't talk about? It shouldn't happen to a person, should it? But now, now I've talked to you, I can talk to you, there's all the more reason I should come back to the store while I'm waiting to hear. I mean, if I feel myself, if I start worrying, or feeling wild. Or if you see or hear of me doing anything, or starting to, if you'll, if you'll just say: 'Dolly, there was a pan of milk on the stove. Dolly, there was a pan of milk on the stove . . .' "

"All right," Al said. "I won't try to decide for you. You do seem quite rational now."

"Yes. Yes, I am." It was getting dark outside.

"Would you like me to stay for a while, while you write to the convent, Dolly?"

"Would you, Al? That would be so nice. And eat supper with me. Then I could take a sedative and go to bed. And when I've gone to sleep, you could take the letter out and mail it. Would you do that for me, Al? I don't . . . it's been so long since anybody has been kind."

While she wrote her letter, he read some Chesterton essays from a volume in the bookshelf. It took her almost two hours.

"The Mother will be terribly pleased to hear from me, I think," Dolly said. "Even if the news isn't so good. I hope there's enough food. I eat very little and . . . don't men have terribly big appetites?"

"It varies from man to man," Al said. "I'm not really voracious."

They dined on delicatessen boiled ham, sliced very thin, undressed lettuce and a can of niblet corn; in the middle of the meal, Dolly blushed and got up. From a shelf she took down an enormous jar, half a gallon, of little green olives stuffed with pieces of pimento. "Do you like these?" she asked. "I'll bet I eat a jar like this a week."

"They're great," Al said. "Thank you."

After supper she wouldn't let him help her with the dishes. As he sat watching, she seemed almost gay, chattering about her

176

girlhood: "We really had fun at school," she said. "People don't think girls in convent schools have any fun, but I had a lovely time. And at vacation, I could go home and play keeping house for my father. Do you know, you're the only man I've ever fixed a meal for since?"

And finally, about nine, she mixed herself a sedative with hot milk, grimacing when she set the pan on the stove, the same pan. "Would you let me do something silly?" she asked. "I'm . . . when I was a little girl, well, a pretty big girl, because I used to do it when I was five or six . . . my father used to let me fix myself a bottle, just as if I were a baby. And I'd get in bed and sip the warm milk, and he'd read to me. It was so comforting after a hard day. It was, a sort of game we played. I was just a baby to him, you see? I don't know how old I was when we stopped the game . . . do you think it's terribly silly?"

Al shook his head. "It sounds quite human," he said.

"Sometimes when I've had a hard day now," she said. "I . . . I still fix myself a bottle to go to sleep with. Or just to sip, for comfort. Does it seem foolish?"

"We all have private means of comfort," Al said.

She poured the milk and sedative into a nursing bottle, and fitted a nipple over the top. Then she put it into a pan of heated water, and carried it out of the kitchen.

"Now," she said. "I'll get fixed for bed. And when I call you, will you read to me a little?" From the bookshelf she took out a big volume called A Child's Book of Saints and Martyrs. "Read me from this? Saint Theresa?"

"Sure," Al said. "Just call when you're ready."

And so he found himself at nine-thirty Sunday evening, by which time he had thought to be halfway to Los Angeles, sitting instead at the bedside of Dolly Klamath, terror of the clerks at Mainways, reading to her of martyrdom, as she snuggled under the covers in striped pajamas and her hard eyes closed in the sleep of girlhood.

When he was certain she was soundly asleep, he turned out the lights, put the book back in the bookshelf, took the letter, and quietly left the apartment. So that was the risk, that was the danger, that was his only conceivable adversary; he was almost disappointed. He had undertaken now, to be sure, to stay on until

177

Christmas, undertaken this to—he smiled as he walked towards home—what might very easily be the last two virgins left in the world, doctor to the simple one, father to the mad one. He sighed. He had, in the years of flight, known madness before.

19   —John, John Stag, the mad Osage.
—In what year was it? No answer. Where?
Tulsa. How had it happened? Wait a minute—:
—There was a day clerk at the No Questions Asked
Hotel in Tulsa, a sort of underworld employment
agent on the side, perhaps, though it was nothing like
a caper which he offered Al: "A job. A guard job. No ques-
tions but they want a smart man."
—"Guarding what?"
—"Some screwball Indian. Old man's fat with oil money; this
one's his son. Place used to be a private nursing home. Don't
know much about it. Want the address?"
—"Maybe," Al said.
—"Forty bucks a week. Room and meals. Sell you the address
for twenty, tell you who to see. Wait till you get the job, cost
you forty."
—"What makes you think I'll get it?" Al asked.
—"Need an educated man," the clerk said. "They don't stay."
—"We'll make it a week's salary, if I get the job . . . and want
it," Al said.
—At one time, Al learned, having been hired all too readily,
the stout, white suburban house had had a dozen patients and
a licensed staff. Now the place existed for a single patient, and
its three doctors were European psychiatrists, refugees; they took
shifts talking to John Stag and watching over him by day. Al's
duties would be to guard his room at night.

179

—"When the other patients' families complained," Hartmann, the man in charge, explained, "Mr. Stag the father bought the house. When the doctors would complain, he sent them away and hired us."

—John Stag had been a brilliant boy, Hartmann said, for Al must know this background; he would have to talk with Stag at night, when Stag wanted to talk.

—"There will be weeks when he will tease us," Hartmann said. "When he will say nothing but 'Ugh,' and 'Me hungry.' It can make you very mad."

—"I assume he can speak English well, then?"

—"He was Phi Beta and Kappa from Princeton," Hartmann said. John Stag had arrived at Princeton at the age of sixteen, handsome, charming and arrogant. His wealth, his poise and his brilliance entitled him to bids from the best clubs; he ignored them. He had brought along to college, paying their ways, another Osage boy and a Cherokee, so that he would have no reason to seek white companionship.

—A genius by any test of Hartmann's or his past, Stag had gained, first in college, then by travel, a remarkable knowledge of the geography of the American continent. His other passion had been military science, and the first of his bitter disappointments had come when, on completing college, he was disqualified for the R.O.T.C. commission he had worked so brilliantly towards: his psychiatric examination showed him to be unstable.

—Following that, John Stag and his companions had toured America intensively. They had visited, in particular, the Indian reservations, state by state; if there were a census of Indian men outside of the government bureaus, it would be in John Stag's amazing head.

—For three years, he had traveled, spent money, drunk whiskey, and fought. He fought white men, in bars, with the cold, skillful passion of one who hates his adversary. There were some serious injuries in the wake of Stag's travels; men had to be bought off. Finally, there were threats of criminal suit, and a great sum was spent to avert it; part of the settlement required was that John be put away.

—When Al met him, John Stag had become a little fat. "When he had Indian attendants, they would exercise," Hartmann said.

180

"All day, athletics, running in the halls, wrestling, shouting, fighting. I said nothing." But one afternoon, Stag and his band of Indian boys, his braves, playfully took Hartmann's assistants prisoner; they wanted laboratory alcohol.

—"Indians like-um firewater," Stag had roared, through the locked door of Hartmann's room. "Barter you white captives for firewater." Hartmann had refused. "Burn 'em at stake," Stag had cried, laughing wildly. "Bring Little-beard."

—Little-beard was their name for a Doctor called Freitag, who wore a goatee. For some reason they had especially despised poor Freitag (he had gone before Al's day).

—At the height of the afternoon of terror, they had held Freitag in the hall in front of Hartmann's room, which had no telephone, removing the goatee hair by hair. Finally Hartmann had managed to get out of the window of his room and work his way down a trellis; phoned Stag's father from next door to send in reinforcements of tough private cops.

—After the battle, Hartmann had insisted that the Indian attendants be dismissed. No pocket money was to be allowed John Stag for bribery. Hartmann's word was to be law; otherwise he would leave. Now the only other Indian allowed was the harmless, semi-eunuchized *mujerado,* a wasted Navajo whom Stag preferred to a woman.

—"I do not think he will be cured," Hartmann said. "This I tell the father. He does not believe. And somebody must watch the boy." When Al arrived, the boy was thirty-six.

—"I wonder if I can trust you?" Stag had said, when they met.

—"No," Al told him. "I'm paid by the other side."

—"Good," Stag had said. "Honesty is an Indian characteristic. When I meet it in a non-Indian, I like him. You know the little-boy term, honest Injun? I wonder if they still use it?"

—"I don't know," Al said.

—"Let him talk to you," Hartmann had urged. "It may help him," and gradually, because it was irrepressible, Stag had revealed to Al his great design. "No one believes me," Stag would say. "So it's safe to tell. Do you know, I think it might more readily be possible today than ever before?"

—"Why is that?"

—"Because of the Russians, of course. They have a particular

181

interest in the territorial and political ambitions of indigenous, exploited peoples. I suspect, Al, that if we are to win back the continent you stole, we may need Russian help."

—Al had smiled.

—"No, let me show you," Stag said. His room was a library of North American maps and texts and through the month that Al was with him, he revealed his intricate plan, battle by battle, campaign by campaign, fully worked out—logistical, tactical, and strategic—for the war. There was an enormous, semi-coded correspondence, at which Stag spent most of his days. When he talked about the coming war, it was almost as if he were describing history. ("But it excites him," Al objected. "No matter," Hartmann had said. "He likes you. Be his friend, and help.")

—"Have I told you about the Battle of Corvallis, Al?" Stag might say, unfolding a street map of that city. "A devastating new weapon. Smell. If there's anything American whites can't stand it's their own smell. To take advantage of their sanitation phobia—that would do it. Dynamite teams of two scouts each—thirty teams could do it, sixty men—infiltrate at dawn. Pry open the manholes, dynamite the sewers. Filth is spewed, covering the streets. And with the smell of garbage and excrement pinning the enemy to their houses more effectively than any artillery, we could attack and put the city to the torch without cover."

—And again: "We have already started training cells on the reservations. Fortunately, the Indian is still remarkably primitive. Only primitives make good soldiers. Look at the Arabians, after Mohammed. It takes men to whom life has always been a nuisance to die with that ferocious indifference. It takes men by whom cruelty has been daily given and received all their lives, as breath has been inhaled and expired, to achieve that glorious failure of sympathy for one's victims which makes a proper soldier. History is a chronicle of pain, Al . . ."

—"I guess I could do without history, then," Al said.

—"Ugh. Get-um bedpan," Stag would say. He hated disagreement.

—"You're not up to walking to the bathroom?"

—"Get-um bedpan, white man, or you have Indian rug to clean." ("Let him tell it all at once," Hartmann said. "Exhaust

182

the vision, not only details. Afterwards, reality." "What good will reality do him?" Al asked; but Hartmann was the doctor; Al urged John Stag to talk.)

—"Here in Alaska," Stag instructed him, "the war will start. Now. Look at the map: here is an airfield, with an army camp adjacent. Utterly isolated. A young Seneca who is with us spent his army time there; fine boy. Knows the place backwards. Pity he's not old enough for command."

—"Go on," Al said, reluctantly.

—"All right. Watch. This post is supplied only by plane. Every man there went in by plane. Every stick of equipment; and what equipment: small arms, ammunition, one and two man rocket launchers; cold weather rations; self-propelled artillery; fighter planes; snowmobiles; vast stores of explosives . . . everything. This first phase can be handled by six hundred men. Swarming in quietly, unobtrusively, by passenger car and truck up the Alcan Highway, joining lumbering crews, traveling by ship from Spokane as tourists, the cadre will be assembled here; and here and here. A mere six hundred braves. Fanatics. Fullbloods. Do you know how many fullbloods are left of fighting age in the United States? About twenty-five thousand. But that's two divisions, Al, and many have had military experience.

—"From the assembly points we would leave in twos and threes, by night, traveling overland to reach the Post. A week's journey, much of it on snowshoes. Real men could do it. Guard duty at this post is a joke; they walk long tours, and we have every tour spotted. The knives, Al, the silent knives—can you imagine the terror of American white soldiers, overtaken by knives? Having dispatched the guard, straight for the communications building. Look"—he unfolded a diagram of the camp. "Drawn from memory," he said, "but checked. Checked. It's accurate. With communications cut off, the operators in our hands and at the mercy of our torturers to keep the proper signals going, we would begin a quiet, systematic company-by-company slaughter of the sleeping men. Five hundred would take part, leaving the other hundred posted, or busy with the torture of officers. There are three thousand men on this post; that means each brave would be responsible for killing six. With the advantages of surprise, purposefulness in confusion, being well armed among sleeping men

183

—their rifles are locked up, Al, think of that!—we should be able to wipe out every man saving only those whose skills we'd need before dawn.

—"We have fliers, Al. I personally located nine good Indian pilots; six, at least, can be trusted. From this first base, which includes infantry supplies and equipment for a regiment, we could quickly arm and organize the Aleuts, the Alaskan Indians, the Kutchins. Preliminary work among them would have been done. Working swiftly, keeping the signal apparatus in a proper appearance of communication, avoiding towns until we were ready, we could take over the other isolated posts, the airfields, one by one. Every man an infantryman; no one in support. That's the way Indians fight. Living off the land. That way a thousand men are like ten thousand.

"And so we have control of the non-urban posts in Alaska within weeks. All liaison is by plane. Simple. Let them land, give them their trusted signals. Kill pilots and crew as they step out, having delivered us another prize. Planes and airfields. Bombers. Big bombs. And the United States still doesn't know it's at war. Thousands of men, millions in equipment, lost already in the secret Battle of Alaska, and the nation unaware. Meanwhile:

—"Cadres have prepared the Indian populations of the West Coast—about thirty-three and a half thousand. Five thousand of these are fullblooded braves. For under half a million dollars, they too have been armed with hunting rifles. And we would not scorn the halfbreeds at first, though they might have to steal their arms. With the Alaskan bases fully organized, manned chiefly by residents—there would be simultaneous blows struck —massive military blows, now, destructive of retaliatory power, against the Alaskan towns and harbors. Dynamite, cordite, explosives; those are the weapons; we could wipe the white man from Alaska overnight. How could they retaliate? By air? Ha. We are sleeping in snowbanks, hiding in hills, sniping at any white survivors we have not captured or enslaved. What are they to do? Organize landings? There is no objective to recapture.

—"And before they can organize landings, the West Coast blows begin—five thousand ruthless guerrillas, terrorists, saboteurs and their halfbreed cohorts. Army camps, fields, Naval in-

184

stallations, spreading confusion and fear. And now, launching the captured vessels from what remains of the Alaskan seaports, and destroying what we leave behind, we take advantage of the West Coast bewilderment and horror. We land in force from the Alaskan bases, in Washington and Oregon and overrun them. Simultaneously: uprisings, raids, all over the country. Where are the attacks coming from? Where is the enemy? How could they tell—for days, for weeks—as we strike, wherever there are Indians, whether the four hundred and sixty-four in Alabama or the sixty-three thousand in Oklahoma, striking against anything, killing wantonly, spreading into the cover of the woods and swamps. I have an excellent man among the Seminoles in Florida; with but three hundred braves available in Florida, he can operate from the Everglades in such a way as to pin down whole divisions. One bold raid to capture supplies and truck them into the swamps, and they would be set to operate for years. There are only seven hundred Indians—perhaps a hundred and fifty braves —in Iowa, but they could fire the cornfields. Ten thousand in North Dakota, with two thousand braves to fire the wheat. Rape and pillage, burning of crops, strikes against cities, dynamite, dynamite, dynamite. The country could be disrupted.

—"And now, with the civilian population immobolized by fear, and the Army disorganized by having several hundred simultaneous actions of undiscernible importance to try to control, with maniacal bombing raids by single planes at unexpected places—sometimes the tiniest towns, Al, the least important—with single pieces of heavy artillery rolled into curious positions and fired at targets of wanton opportunity, fired and fired until the ammunition runs out, then dynamited and abandoned to block roads; all the things we could do unsupported; might not the Russians come through with air support? At least with supplies into our West Coast ports. And would the U.S. dare to begin atom war against them? No. They'd drag in some British, some French, some Canadians, in the East; they'd try to isolate the war. There's where we'd have them. For with the Russian supplies, we could arm recruits; wouldn't they pour in from Canada, though, those hundred and fifty thousand Indians? But the secret, the real secret, Al, is Mexico.

—"Twenty-five million people, of mostly Indian blood. With

185

an official army and air force, in apparent alliance with the U.S., supplied by them even, of fifty-one thousand. With the securing of the continent west of the Rockies, we would bring to a head our preparations with Mexico and, behind them, the vast Indian potential of South America.

—"I have been in touch with men in Mexico, Al. This is more easily possible than you would believe. In Mexico, a remote village or two is reported burned. There is an appearance of disorders similar to those in the U.S. An appeal is made for troops, knowing a worried U.S. Congress will refuse. But it will give money and supplies; especially when martial law is declared and a strong man arises; your government likes strong men for other countries—if they appear friendly. This one would appear very friendly. Oh, very friendly, as he accepted the money, the supplies your Congress offered in lieu of troops, and tripled the size of his army.

—"And now the great feint, Al! A large force from the West Coast bastion is allowed to come under U.S. observation, moving out across Arizona. The finest units available are placed in defense positions to annihilate our attack. They face us. It appears that the day for decisive battle has come. And it has, Al, it has! In the greatest act of duplicity in history, as we engage their front in patrols and feints, across the Rio Grande pour the treacherous troops of Mexico to attack their rear. An enormous pincher, in Texas and Arizona, picking up reinforcements of Apaches and Navajos to man the captive tanks. Now the fanatical, pure blooded Mayan troops from Guatemala can be hurled into battle! Now the Canadian insurgents could wheel through the Northwest, the grain fields, and going up to meet them we would infest the plains, as the valiant guerillas of the Middle West and East continued their harassment, interdiction, terrorizing and attrition! Perhaps the Negroes would rise with them, the gang-fighters, delinquents. In two years, we consolidate the continent, from Canada to the Mississippi; finally, now manufacturing our own supplies, our own equipment, the great amphibious operation across the river, to the distraught East, on to the Atlantic, killing, disorganizing, meeting them in any sort of battle with our new strength, until the only whites left would be the slaves, the buggerboys, the houris and the scribes . . ."

—"And you, John?" Al said.

—"I would be King." And he had gone to sleep smiling.

—In the first few weeks John Stag had seemed happy with his maps and plans, his correspondence and his daily treatments. But the following evening, coming on duty, Al found him cramming letters into wastebaskets.

—"It's stupid, Al, isn't it?" Stag said. "A kind of masturbation, almost. It's all grandiose, insane, impossible."

—"I'd assumed that you thought that all along," Al said, gently.

—Stag shrugged. "Half," he said. "Half thought it. It was something to occupy me, Al. Something. What else is a man to do, as he watches his race die?"

—"I don't know, John," Al said. "Different men protest in different ways."

—Through the rest of the evening, Stag was morose and said little. Just past midnight, he went to bed, far earlier than usual. Al locked his door and settled on the cot in the hall outside it.

—Just at dawn something woke him; immediately, he registered that the door was open; he sat up on the bed on which he slept fully clothed. And at the end of the hall he could see Stag, naked except for underwear, crawling on all fours, something held between his teeth. He was going towards Hartmann's room; he planned—it must be—to wait outside the door, to get Hartmann in some way when the doctor came out, on his way to his morning bath.

—Al looked at his watch. Ten minutes before Hartmann rose. He stood up and called:

—"John, John, come back. I see you."

—Stag stopped crawling, and slowly stood up. Al started towards him and Stag turned. "What are you doing, John? Where are you going?"

—From between his teeth, Stag removed the tomahawk he had gripped by its shaft. "To kill Hartmann," he said, simply.

—"Get back," Al said. "I've got a blackjack, John. You know that."

—"But no gun," Stag said, smiling. "Hartmann would never allow you a gun. I might steal it."

—Al reached him. "Be sensible, John. Why do you want to kill Hartmann? He's a good enough man. He tries to help you."

187

—"Because it's all stupid, Al," Stag said. "Because I want to kill one white man and die. I want one scalp . . ."

—"Why not mine, John?" Al said.

—"I could have easily enough. But you're my friend. An Indian does not hurt his friend."

—"Come back to your room, John," Al said.

—"No."

—"Then I will have to shout and warn Hartmann."

—"I won't let you past," Stag said. "I won't hurt you, but I won't let you past. Go away, Al. Leave."

—"Give me the tomahawk," Al said.

—"No."

—"If we stand here," Al said. "We will hear his door open. And I'll shout."

—Stag smiled. "I had a key for my room, didn't I, Al? I have a key for his, too. I've had it for years." He turned, and started on.

—"Stop!" Stag ignored him. "Stop!" Al shouted again. "Dr. Hartmann!" Stag began to run. Al ran after him; he leapt onto Stag's back, crooking his arm around the Indian's neck. Stag threw him off, and was at Hartmann's door, the key in his hand. Dragging the blackjack from his pocket, Al swung at the hand. There was sickening sound. The key dropped.

—Stag turned. "You've broken my hand, Al," he said. "A white man will hurt his friend." His face was impassive. "Could you stand pain like this?"

—"No, John," Al cried. "No. Come back to your room."

—"Not until you break my other hand and take my tomahawk away," Stag said, extending it.

—It was at that moment that Hartmann's door opened and the little doctor stood there with a hypodermic in his hand.

—And Al had tried to say, "Forgive me, John," and been unable; had turned, dropping the blackjack, and fled from the white house, and left that city, a modern landfarer, able to stop no funeral guest to tell the tale.

20 On Monday morning, both Dolly and Winnipeg were at work; but Sally Malinkrodt was not.

"I understand it always happens," M'nerney told them in the stockroom. "People drop out after paydays in the Christmas season. I don't suppose the way Hub handled her helped any."

"How did Hub handle her?" Al asked.

"Well, I don't know. But I thought she seemed sore at him. He gets people sore."

There were ten shopping days left before Christmas.

School was out now, and Tom would work full days the whole week through. Though the shopping crowds were not as overwhelming as the one which had engulfed them Saturday morning, there was a fairly constant push. In the morning came fierce lady shoppers, often with small children; about eleven, the school kids would begin running through, wanting to play with everything, capable of impulsive shoplifting, especially of the goods which would fit easily into pockets. Afternoons were relatively quieter, though at about four-thirty there were often well dressed men in the department who made large and careful purchases, business men taking the last hour of the day away from their jobs, sometimes accompanied by secretaries, with lists of which clients had children, and very competent about arranging the details of charge and shipping.

Because of the increase in adolescent larceny, there was always

189

a store detective on duty, now, stationed on the floor—a fat, irascible, elderly man, a retired policeman of some sort, who became a crony of Santa Claus'. They shared breaks behind the dais. But in spite of the detective, Finn told Al on Tuesday morning, evidence of a rather serious theft had turned up on spot inventory, something over a hundred dollars' worth of goods missing from the various counters.

"It wouldn't seem to be shoplifting," Finn said. "It's all gone at once. Some of the things were too expensive for display— they'd come from behind the counters. One of the little sewing machines, a big doll, two music boxes at twenty dollars, and other things. I'm afraid it looks like one of the clerks; so don't say anything."

"I'm sorry to hear it," Al said. "Hope it turns out to be some kind of mistake."

Tuesday afternoon, he was directed by M'nerney to pass notices around the department. The notices were mimeographed, and headed:

????? HOW'S YOUR OPPORTUNITITE ?????

The text dealt with the somewhat complicated rules by which a raffle would be held Christmas week, with employees in departments with improved sales records given various kinds of mathematical advantage to win a !!!!! FREE CHRISTMAS TURKEY—A REAL YUMMYBIRD !!!!!

"I suppose Finn told you about the goods being stolen?" M'nerney said.

"Yes," Al said, accepting the stack of notices.

"Tells you everything, doesn't he?"

"He does talk to me a good deal," Al said. "I don't suppose it does any harm, does it?"

"He has only himself to blame for this kind of thing going on, this stealing," M'nerney said. "I don't mean to criticize you, but you can't run a department by playing favorites. People resent it, and somebody begins to steal."

"Perhaps you're right," Al said. "But I don't suppose a man like Finn is going to change his ways after all these years. And after all, he's not unsuccessful."

"You don't need that heavy selling approach of his any more,"

190

M'nerney said. "Clerks are what these people are and should be treated as—not salespeople. Customers buy for their own reasons, not because they're sold."

"What do you suppose the reasons are?" Al asked.

"It would take hours to explain it all, Barker."

"Maybe they just buy compulsively, for no reason," Al suggested, smiling.

"How idiotic," M'nerney said, and walked away.

Al began to make a circuit of the department, distributing a copy or two of the notice to the clerks at each counter. He handed one to Mrs. Kelsner, the bubbler, and another to the Yippee-Cowboy-Zoom-Spaceman. He came to dolls. Nickie was here now replacing Sally, the record demonstration no longer active.

"Hi," she said.

"Want you to sell hard and win this turkey," Al scowled at her. They both grinned. He winked at Winnipeg.

He went by the service desk: "Are you eligible, Miss Klamath?" He offered her a notice.

"I guess not, Mr. Barker," she said, softly. In the past two days, she had barely been out from behind the service desk; it was the wonder of the clerks, the unaccountable way she had eased.

In wheel goods he found Gullakian showing the little British pedal car to two polite children, a brown-eyed boy and girl, dressed alike in sandy tweeds.

"I'm afraid mother wouldn't allow it," the boy was saying.

"But it certainly is a stunning car, sir," said the little girl. Hand in hand they walked on.

"Cute, huh?" Gullakian said, accepting the notice. "Now Al, what would I do with a turkey?"

"There are those who would eat it," Al said. "I shudder to think what you might do to it."

"Ho, ho, ho," Gullakian laughed. "Did you give one of these to Dolores?"

"She's on her break, I guess."

"There's my little turkey," Gullakian said. "You know what I'd like to do, Al?" He seized a bike, and lifted it exuberantly off the floor. "I'd like to take her for a bicycle ride. Know what I'd do?"

"What?" Al asked.

191

"I'd throw the bicycle away," he swung it away as if he were going to pitch it into the snowbank, "and keep the seat under my pillow." He brought the leather saddle tenderly back against his cheek.

"Gullakian," Al said. "You have a mind the size and caliber of a gnat's navel."

"Ho, ho, ho," laughed Gullakian.

By Wednesday, discipline had so far broken down, as the clerks began to take advantage of Dolly's new laxity, that Finn himself started trying to enforce lunch hour and break limits.

"What's happened to her, Al?" he asked. "M'nerney won't take a hand and she's hiding behind that service desk every hour of the day."

"I wouldn't worry about it," Al said. He hadn't told Finn about his Sunday calls beyond saying that Winnipeg was all right now. "Do you want advice?"

"Sure, Al."

"There are eight more days till Christmas. Nine with Sunday. Things are pretty well set. Don't try to do anything, Hub. Sales record's okay, isn't it?"

"Fine. Fine. We're piling up a good season."

"Don't speak to Dolly, then, and stop trying to straighten things out yourself. It'll go to hell, but let it. After all, what they look at upstairs is the record, isn't it? Unless there's an incident. Tell M'nerney the discipline's his worry, and forget it."

"Al," Finn said. "This theft . . . it's an incident already if it doesn't clear up. We haven't a thing to go on. And Mac's a hindrance to me, not a help. He just encourages them to be lax."

"Pretty hearty opportunitite, that yummybird," Al said. "Try to take it easy, Hub. Anytime you get annoyed and lose your head, it helps M'nerney. Try to take it easy."

At ten minutes to six that afternoon, there were only two customers left in the department. The clerks who were not waiting on them began to clear their cash registers, at Mr. M'nerney's suggestion, and the lid blew off Finn's temper. He called M'nerney into the office and shouted at him so loudly that Tom and Al heard every word in the stockroom.

"Well, I know, Hub, but it'll put 'em in a good mood for tomorrow," M'nerney defended himself.

192

"It isn't the way I want my department run," Finn shouted. "And goddamn it, M'nerney, you keep undermining me with the personnel and we'll take it upstairs."

"All right, Hub," said the younger man. "All right."

"I'll check the registers tonight by myself, by God. You stay off the floor. I don't want to see your face out there."

"All right, all right," M'nerney said. A moment later he brought his grievance into the stockroom. "You men ready to go."

"Yes," Al said.

"I suppose you heard all that?"

"Afraid we did."

"That man is about through in this store," M'nerney said. "And there's a very example of why. No sense about when and where to speak his piece. He couldn't even think to close the door of the office. Not him. Just unloaded right where you could both hear. Now he's keeping me off the floor, though it will make everybody late, just because he knows the department likes me better than it does him."

"Is that the reason?" Al asked.

"He wouldn't any more dare take me upstairs than he'd jump out of the window," M'nerney said. There was a silence while he waited for their agreement.

"You never can tell when a man might jump out of a window," Al said quietly.

"All right, Barker," M'nerney said. "I'm trying to make the situation clear to you, since you seem to have some sort of influence around here. I don't know why. What I'm telling you is that Finn is through, and everybody knows it but him. I dealt for most of this merchandise; I study what the public wants, what the manufacturers are developing. All he knows how to take on are the old line Christmas goods, a few trick items and some overpriced stuff like that British car. Dolly did most of the hiring. What's he done?"

"A little selling?" Al asked.

"All right, Barker," M'nerney said. He cleared his throat. He walked in a nervous circle, frowning. Then he said, abruptly: "Barker, would you hand me one of those black boxes, from the top shelf?"

"A Kid-Mix-'Em Soda Fountain?" Al asked, smiling. He got up

193

to get the stepladder. "They have instructions for making straw-berry jam milkshakes, it says on the front. You must let me know how they are."

"I want to buy it for my niece," M'nerney said, stiffly. "Christ-mas is coming, you know."

"No," said Al. "Not Christmas."

"All right, Barker," M'nerney said, accepting the box and smil-ing tightly.

Christmas; so that's what was coming.

He was involved in life now until Christmas, Al conceded, lying in the room with two beds, in the dark, an open pint of whiskey on the floor within reach of his hand. That night he envied Dolly her more powerful sedatives.

To be involved with life until Christmas seemed appropriate, for, he thought:

Because it is an intricately sentimental country, life ends for people all over the United States, just after Christmas, and doesn't begin again until spring. We count our lives by Christmases and summers.

He began to review his years alone by Christmases and sum-mers:

—If he had left in August, how had the journey begun? Through the South, from Birmingham to St. Louis, where he had bought the discharge; then by long hops west and north to Cœur d'Alene; then to Nebraska and the sugar beet harvest.

—Next he had gone with another hand, who took him along for company, to the sheep ranch in Montana, Barbour's place, where he had worked with the sheep, and the first Christmas Eve had been a night of drinking in the bunkhouse, and fighting in which he had managed not to be involved, and they had waked up Christmas morning to heavy snow, heavy pancakes, heavy heads.

—He had stayed on with the sheep, rather liking the work with animals, something entirely unfamiliar to him, and gone out as a herder after shearing in the spring. For the first time in his life, then, he found himself almost totally alone for a long stretch of time, seeing only the man who drove a wagon out, every two weeks, to bring fresh meat; otherwise, the wagon-bed in which

194

Al lived was stocked with everything he needed. He tried, but without much satisfaction, to write some sort of journal of his life that summer, and, abandoning the project, acquired some degree of self-taught skill on an elaborate harmonica.

—Burned the discontinued journal in his final campfire in the late fall, and brought his sheep in; gave the harmonica to a lean boy with an odd, mountain feeling for its nasal tone; collected his pay and went back East as far as Ohio to thaw out. Thus began the Fool's Fall, the Addled Autumn, those first months following the anniversary of his leaving, beginning on the Sordid of September, through October Ooze, to the Nothingth of November and halfway through the Christmas month.

—The Fool's Fall because only a fool cannot find somehow an answer to the awful question, What Next? Was John Stag, was Dolly Klamath, any madder than Allerd-Alvin Pennington-Barker-Clark?

—For he had been Al Clark, resident in Columbus, in a furnished room, with several hundred dollars under the gray pillow, with no urge to go and none to stay, no exhaustion to rest from and no energy to start again; he went to the movies.

—He worked out an elaborate schedule of movie houses. There were eighteen. Though some had duplicating bills, he listed them all—first run, second run, third run, adults only, art houses—any dark place without light or shadow, save for the parody of life dancing on the great blank window at the end. Mondays, consulting the papers, making phone calls from a pocket hoard of dimes, working at it like a job, he would calculate all the showings of all the films available for the next three days, and on Thursdays, when most bills changed, he'd repeat the process. The best he could do, rising at noon, was to see an afternoon double feature and an evening one, eating between. But there weren't twenty-eight different movies playing in Columbus in the course of a given week—there were seldom as many as twenty. And so he would fill the gaps by sitting in bars, watching television, and thus the fall turned gradually alcoholic until, by the first snows, he was sodden and his eyes seemed permanently red.

—Woke one morning in December, seized the thread of self remaining between him and annihilation, determined he must

195

make a journey to see his children on Christmas, and conceived a crazy plan to make it so.

—Went back to sleep and slept two days. Woke up, left his room, and with the last but thirty dollars of his sheep-herding money, bought a musette bag, three fifths of whiskey and a spotted puppy, and started hitchhiking to Alabama, the whiskey in the bag, slung on his shoulder, the puppy under his arm.

—Since he had been Al Clark in Columbus, he called the puppy Lewis, and the journey, with the whiskey to provide the celebration, was The Celebrated Expedition of Lewis and Clark. He remembered a speech he had made to Lewis on the grass outside a small town in Kentucky, waiting for a ride. "Lewis," he had said, "you may think that it was only a plaid dress, but I tell you there was never another plaid dress like it. It was light blue, and blue green, and green yellow, and yellow black, and listen to me, sir: that was a crowded party, that party, and I'd been there two hours and hadn't even seen her until I was on my way out. You left the party through a bedroom, and there must have been fifteen people on the double bed, all talking at once.

—"Now visualize this, Lewis, I say put down that stick and visualize it, sir: she was sitting on the side away from the door, and I was at the door; fourteen people in the way, fourteen raised voices. I saw the dress first, there was never a plaid like that made in all of Scotland, and then I saw her eyes, looking mischief out of a quiet face as I stood in the doorway ready to go. And she said, softly and gaily, but I heard it as clearly as if we'd been alone in the room, 'What's your name?'

—"You will deny, with your practical mind, that this is possible, Lewis, but remember your experience is limited in these matters, and believe me when I say that I could only shake my head in answer to that question; she had made me forget my own name. That was my introduction to Frances."

—And again, on the similar grass, outside some similar town, waiting for another ride: "You have asked me about my introduction to Susan, my older child, and if you will stop smelling that stump and listen, I will try to answer you. I saw her first, as modern fathers do, through glass. And I can make my feelings clear, don't chew that piece of bark, it isn't clean, when I tell you that I had always been a man who thought the wailing of babies a most irritating sound; but as the nurse opened the door to the nursery in the hospital, to slip in and select my baby and hold her up for me to see, I heard a dozen babies crying, and I found myself thinking: 'Don't they sound sweet, like lambs at feeding time?' What do you think of that for fatheadedness, my thin-headed friend?"

"Oh, I have done the married bit, Lewis," he had said once at night, in a tourist room, but quietly, because the puppy was asleep. "I know the early cuteness and the odd minutes of later boredom, I have made the shopping lists that say choc. pud. for chocolate pudding, t.p. for toilet paper, done my miles in super-markets, noted the week arrive when, for the first time, no new pet names for one another spring to mind, tried to read when Frances was restless, been restless while she talked to some impossible friend, squirmed when old Pete Bowie dropped around to flirt with Frances, tried to avoid her eye when I danced close with Patsy Furnivell, spent weekends in a country shack with the Eddie Rameys, hanging around, me and Eddie, stalling in the cramped place with the blanket dividing it, hung from the rafters, stalling about going to bed, each of us trying to catch a glimpse of the other's wife undressing—this you tell me I'm well out of? Cuteness, boredom, restlessness, jealousy—Lewis, I tell you these and the companion irritations of fatherhood are all the splendor that a man can stand. Tell them that, Lewis, that I'd give everything to have those irritations back, tell them Lewis, when you see them . . ."

—For that was the plan. As he must have told two dozen drivers, he was taking the spotted puppy to his kids for Christmas, though he kept the details to himself.

—In Talladega, fifteen miles from where he had lived, he sat in a diner on the day before Christmas, drinking coffee and reviewing what his moves would be. There was more than time enough. He would take the bus to the town, a half hour's ride, check into a particular tourist camp on the far side. He would sleep there and leave a call for four a.m. on Christmas morning. Early, when the streets were empty, he would walk to his house and leave the puppy in the backyard, tied to a fence with a red and green ribbon, and near him a bone and a saucer of milk.

197

He would slip away, then, and about eight o'clock risk a walk on the street behind the house, his coat collar turned up and his hat pulled low, and watch, for a just a moment, Susan and Jerry playing with their new dog. And he would feel, because he knew the dog so well, that when his children talked to Lewis, they all but spoke to Al. He would walk very quickly, hardly stopping for the glance, and be gone and away before anyone could know.

—Fifteen miles away, in Talladega, the day before Christmas, sanity returned, and he knew again that sentimentality always conceals a cruelty, and that he must not do it; he spent Christmas Eve in a movie he had seen before, with Lewis asleep on his lap; gave the puppy to a man on the street who admired him next day, turned the other way, headed for New Orleans. It was the closest he had ever been to seeing Frances and the kids again.

—The next Christmas, he supposed, must have been in Arkansas, in the Ozarks, in a hamlet called Magellan, where he had helped, for a few months, teach elementary school . . .

Al drifted off to sleep. He woke, near midnight, in his clothes, and with perfect continuity, remembered:

—That Christmas, 1948, had been Las Vegas, where he didn't gamble. And that by the next Christmas he had seen the black headline which sent him West. Since then he had been on a long treadmill, up the Coast with the spring to Washington, slowly; back, gradually, to Southern California in the winter; Spokane, Portland, Seattle, Los Angeles, San Diego, and now San Francisco, his six cities; and the several Christmases on the long treadmill had been only other days in several aimless sets of three-six-fives.

He thought, as he finished undressing in the room, killed the bottle and got back in bed again, that the feelings he couldn't seem to prevent from forming for various people in the toy department, of which the latest was the mindless and rather gratifying antagonism he and M'nerney seemed to be developing, represented as large a variety of emotions as he had permitted himself since he had handed Lewis over to the drawling stranger half-a-dozen Christmases before.

It was always a wonder to Casper Usez that the Pennington

case was broken at all. From the degree of familiarity the fugitive seemed to have reached with Hannibal Finn, buyer for the department, where he was working as Al Barker, the man must have known that there had been a theft and that it was being investigated. He must, even, have had an idea that members of the managerial structure had considered him suspicious, for the boy whom it was intended should watch Barker, had subsequently transferred his allegiance; thus the suspicions were probably not entirely secret.

Why had the man, for once, failed to leave before such suspicions could accumulate? Even after the opening for the break was made and it had begun to develop, Pennington had plenty of time to move on. The events progressed with what, in retrospect, seemed such painful inefficiency that Usez felt that, had he somehow been able to watch them, he would have been certain that the hunted man would escape, long before things could actually close in.

On Wednesday, December sixteenth, at the end of the day, the assistant buyer, a man with the improbably contracted name of M'nerney, had handed to a store detective a shiny black box, containing something called a Kid-Mix-'Em soda fountain on which, M'nerney said, were Barker's fingerprints. He stated that there was reason to suspect that the man was a fugitive, and suggested that the prints be checked. The store detective, a retired traffic patrolman, had bungled handling the box.

On Thursday, the following day, M'nerney had had to ask his stockroom man to hand him a second fountain set. Barker-Pennington's reported remark ("Your niece must be hitting that butterscotch and soda pretty hard") indicated a kind of recognition that the move was some sort of stratagem which (by an act of sub-will?), the man apparently prevented his usually alert faculties from registering.

That Thursday, then, the store detective had wrapped the second box in tissue paper and had, after working hours, taken it to the closest police precinct. Another day was lost, making it Friday, before the box was transferred to a laboratory for the prints to be processed and photographed. On Saturday and Sunday, the regular lab man being off, nothing further was done

199

beyond checking to see that these prints did not match any in the local file.

Not until Monday, the twenty-first, were Pennington's fingerprints transmitted, in the routine manner, to the FBI Identification Division's central file. They reached I-D on Tuesday; fortunately, although the case papers had been set away under *Inactive*, there was still a flag on Pennington's permanent print card at Central.

On Wednesday morning, December twenty-third, the information had been placed on Usez' desk when he arrived for work: a man, positively identified as Pennington, had been located working in a toy department in San Francisco. If it had arrived a day later, on Thursday, Usez would have been away with his wife Betty, visiting her family in Virginia over Christmas. Nothing, most likely, would have been done immediately, since only Usez had any sense that the matter was urgent; so the man might still have got away.

As it was, Usez got onto the direct wire with the San Francisco office; it was found that the San Francisco police record was imperfect when an attempt was made to arrest Barker on the second day before Christmas at the wrong department store—a place called Perrini-Vetcho which didn't even have a toy department.

On the last day before Christmas agents began checking all department stores and all toy departments. Late in the afternoon, with local police cooperation suddenly improved due to fresh complaints, the correct store was located and, at four p.m., agents and police together missed their man at Mainways by half an hour.

It was not until 0:45 a.m., Christmas morning, as the result of a phone tip as to the address at which Barker could be found, that the arrest was actually made.

In view of all this, Usez could not help feeling that, at the end of the chase, his man had stopped running and was virtually waiting for him.

21 On Thursday evening of the week before Christmas, having finished his share of the seventh shopping day before Christmas, Al found himself hailed on the street by Sally Malinkrodt, drunk.

"Hey, Al," she called. "When's blowhard, blowsoft comin' out?"

"Finn?"

"Yeah, our funny Finny friend." She giggled.

"The store's open late tonight, Sally," Al said. "I don't imagine he'll be out until it closes."

"Yeah . . . what're you doin' out, then?"

"Tom wanted the overtime," Al said.

"Tom's a cutie," Sally mumbled. Beside her, on the street, was a large package, wrapped in brown paper. "Got something here for Finn," she said. "Very funny, Al. Joke."

"What's that, Sally?"

She threw her arms wide. " 'normous big doll, this big. Music box. Other stuff. Half what I stole."

"You stole it, Sally?"

She nodded extravagantly. "Finn gives me a pain. Hot an' cold. Not so hot and very cold. Can't treat me like some li'l' one-bang salesgirl."

"Sally, you want to tell me what this is all about?" Al asked. "Tell me the joke. I don't seem to be getting it."

"Ver' funny," Sally said. "I got half the stuff here. Other half at home. Easies' thing in the world to take it. Jus' wrap it up for myself, put it in my locker upstairs. Eighth floor. Yest'day, came in dressed like a customer. Got the stuff. Wrote myself a couple sales slip. Lugged it down to third floor, one batch, second floor other batch. Bought some other stuff. Said: 'Here, deliver these for me, too, please. All together.' 'Glad to, madam.' All 'rived today. Courtesy Mainways . . .'"

"Okay, Sally," Al said. "That's how you did it. Now about the joke on Mr. Finn?"

"Gonna give it to him. Tell him come on out my place, an' get the rest. Husban's home tonight, Jerk. Finn's second jerk. Watch the two feeble jerks 'pologizing to one another over me. Very funny. Isn't it funny, Al? Won't it be a good joke?"

"Sally," Al said, holding her arms at the elbows. "Honey, it's the saddest joke I ever heard. Don't do it."

"Why not? Thought you'd laugh. On'y man left in the worl' with a sense humor." She nearly fell against him. "Good old Al. On'y man . . ."

"Sally, you shouldn't want to do a thing like that to poor Finn."

"Gave me the ol' one-two," Sally said. "Wouldn't talk to me afterwards. Gave me the ol' one, ol' two, wouldn't give me the ol' three at all . . . no, sir. Just a little ol' shopgirl, doesn't get the ol' three. Some kinda facility, that's all. Not a real man, Al. Don't think there's any real men left."

"Finn's all right," Al said.

"You're not even a real man, Al."

"No," he agreed. "I like Finn, Sally. They're closing the lid on him; don't help push it down. It's no fault of yours or his, if things went badly."

"Isn't?"

"No."

"Joke . . . joke isn't funny, Al?"

"No, Sally. It's not funny. Come on. Let's put this stuff in a cab, and I'll take you home."

She shook her head. "Too drunk to go home," she said. "Got drunk. Jerk didn't like it; wouldn't say anything. Wouldn't throw me out. Threw myself out. 'Get out, drunken whore,' I told myself. 'Bring your lover back, an' I'll beat him black and blue,' I said. Jerk just sat there. I went out yelling, 'Please, please, gimme 'nother chance,' and 'No, no, not till you face me with him,' dragging my damn package after me . . ."

"Sally, would you like to come to my room and sober up for a while?" Al said. "It's not far."

"Can't do joke to Finn?"

"No."

"Little ol' Al," she said. "All right, little ol' Al. You take care Sally. Take care everybody else, might as well take care little ol' whore, too."

They got a cab and rode to Al's place, and he helped her stretch out on the bed Gurnstein had used.

"Get some sleep, Sally," he said. "I'll wake you in a couple of hours, and see that you get home."

"Turn out the light," she said. He did. "Don't suppose you'd care for a quick one, Al? 'm a kind of specialist in quick ones."

"Thanks," Al said. "You're a tempting woman, Sally, but I don't guess I'll yield. It would only be another disappointment for you."

"You want that Nickie, and won't let yourself."

"You're very wise," Al said.

"You're another jerk," Sally muttered. "What good's bein' wise? Jus' means you finally realize everyone's a jerk. Including self."

She went to sleep.

Al left to eat. At about nine he returned and woke her, gave her a shot of whiskey to revive on.

"What now?" Sally asked.

"I don't know, Sally. Home I guess, for you."

"What's at home?"

He shrugged.

"All right," she said, talking much more soberly now. "Like you to see him, Al. Poor bastard."

"Don't know that I want to," Al said. "I seem to know a good many poor bastards already. Let's get the . . . hot toys."

"Don't want them, Al. Haven't got any kids. Don't know any kids. You got any use for them?"

"I might try to return them," Al said. "I'm afraid it would be a little risky."

"Hate to throw them away," Sally said.

"Perhaps I could just leave these here in the room, when I go," Al said. "It'll be the day before Christmas. Maybe someone sent in to clean will know some kids and find them just in time."

203

"Everyone ought to know kids," Sally said. "How're you going to handle a hot teddy bear when it comes along, if you don't know any kids?" She giggled; then she said: "There's a sweet teddy bear in there. Want to know something awful?"

"Okay."

"I can't have them, Al. Used to think it was Jerk, wasn't man enough. But he's man enough. Even him. It's me. I'm not woman enough. What do you think of that? I told him he ought to divorce me, marry somebody who'd have kids. Know what he said? 'What for?' He doesn't want them; I can't have them. No sense getting divorced."

"I suppose not," Al said.

"No sense staying married, either. Why can't I do anything right, Al? Or anything wrong? Why can't I do anything, right or wrong? I wouldn't mind if everything I touched turned out awful; but it just won't turn out at all. Everything I touch goes to sleep. Why? Why can't I . . . I'm all right, Al. I'm pretty enough. I'm alive. I make sense, don't I?"

"Sure you do, Sally."

"What's wrong then? What goes wrong?"

"I don't know," Al said. "Maybe wanting to live just runs counter to the current of things now. Vitality frightens people. Intimacy frightens people. You and Finn . . . it's too bad you didn't get together. You're a fine pair of anachronisms; maybe you could have had a little anachronism who would have saved the world. A nice, upside down Prometheus to shove the fire back . . ."

"What are you talking about?"

"Nothing," Al said. "Nonsense. Let's go."

They went out and found a cab.

When they arrived at Sally's address, she said: "Al, would you come in and get the rest of the toys? For that maid, who's going to know those children?"

"I don't really want to come in much," Al said.

"Jerk won't bite you. I feel awful about having the toys, now that I'm sober, Al."

"All right. I'll take them away, Sally," he said.

She let herself into the building with a key, and into the ground floor apartment with another. In the vestibule she pointed to a second bundle, like the one they'd left at Al's.

"Sally?" a light, tired voice said.

"Maybe," she said, her voice suddenly a fair duplicate for weariness. "Who wants to know? Man Mountain Dean?"

"Did you bring him, Sally?" the voice asked, closer. A rather nice looking young man of middle height stepped into the hallway with them. "Are you Mr. Finn?"

"No," Al said. "My name's Barker. I'm just an acquaintance."

"How do you do?" the young man said unhappily. "I'm David Rivers."

"The man knows your name, jay-bird," Sally said, her normal energy as little apparent now as if the current had been switched off.

"I'm sure he does," Rivers said. "I'm sure you told everybody at your store, Sally."

"How do you do?" Al said.

"I have an idea," Sally said to her husband. "Why don't you poke him one? He's never exactly screwed me, but it isn't because I didn't ask him to."

"Please, Sally," Rivers said.

"I must go along," Al said. "If you'll excuse me."

"Please," Rivers said. "Wouldn't you like to stay and . . . have a drink with us?"

"Sure, stick around," Sally said. "We'll throw some pins up and listen to them drop."

"Please come in," Rivers begged. "Don't mind Sally. She's in a bad mood."

He couldn't refuse the man. He walked into the living room. It was clear, from the comfortable modern furniture, two good original paintings on the wall and a Matisse drawing, fresh flowers in the modern crystal vases, heavy carpeting, a bottle of fine Scotch on the coffee-table, clear that the Rivers were well off.

"I was reading," Rivers said, apparently determined to ignore Sally. "I read mostly nonfiction." He indicated a recent book on foreign policy. "Would you like some Scotch and water?"

"That would be very nice," Al said.

"I'm thinking of joining the World Federalists," Rivers said.

"He's been thinking of it for two years," Sally said. "We have many things under consideration here. World Federalists. What shoes to wear tomorrow. Whether to go out to dinner Christmas or eat at home. I tell you we're throbbing with activity?"

"Are you . . . in the World Federalists, Mr. Barker?" Rivers asked.

"I'm afraid not," Al said. "I think it would be fine if you joined, though."

"Do you?" Rivers had poured Scotch in a highball glass. "I'm afraid the ice has melted," he said. "Sally, would you get some ice?"

"No," Sally said.

"Oh. I'll get it then," Rivers said, unhappily. "I'll get it."

"It's all right," Al said. "I seldom use ice," but the man had already left the room.

"Don't give me that reproachful cow look, Al," Sally said. "What else can I do?"

"I don't know," Al said. "What else can he do?"

"Nothing," Sally said. "Nothing. Not a thing. No thing at all."

Rivers returned with ice in a bowl. "We haven't an ice bucket any longer," he said. "We had a silver one my mother gave us. Sally put the garbage out in it, and one day someone took it."

"I should have put myself out in it," Sally said. "Maybe someone would have taken me. Doesn't he look like M'nerney, Al?"

"Not especially," Al said, although he did, a little.

"Who's M'nerney?" Rivers asked.

"Another man who hasn't screwed me," Sally said. "That makes two."

"Please, Sally," Rivers said.

"What would he do without the word please?" Sally asked, viciously kicking first one shoe across the room and then the other.

"What are you doing?" Rivers asked.

"I'm going to take all my clothes off and burn them in the middle of the rug. How will that be?"

"Typical," Rivers said.

"Nothing I could do would surprise you, would it?" Sally asked.

"Nothing unpleasant."

Sally threw back her head and shrieked, sustaining it for almost a minute.

"Yes, that was unpleasant," Rivers said, nodding wearily. "So it didn't surprise me." He finally dropped two ice cubes into Al's drink. "It may have surprised the Parkers upstairs. If it did, they'll phone."

"That looks fine," Al said. He crossed to the coffee table and picked up the glass.

Now they were all three sitting.

"Don't you think Jerk would be happier if he turned fairy?" Sally asked, in a conversational tone. "So many of the boys are doing it now."

"What would you do if I did?" Rivers asked.

"What do I do now?" Sally countered sweetly. "It would be much easier for you, dear. You see, you'd be the one underneath, lying still."

"Please don't, Sally," Rivers said. "Please don't."

"Why don't you throw your glass at me, for Christ's sake?"

"Would it really help?" Rivers asked, raising his glass and looking at it. "Mr. Barker, Sally thinks we should be divorced, but it's a step I'm very reluctant to take . . ."

"What he means," Sally said, "is that he's got the moola, and he's got the grounds, and I can't even pin a cruelty rap on him as long as he won't throw that damn glass."

"That's right," Rivers said, setting the glass down.

"I was going to show that I could make it as a working girl, Al," Sally said, suddenly moody. "Support myself. Apparently that's not the kind of stuff I've got."

"I'm sorry," Al said, drinking off his whiskey, and getting up. "Would you excuse me? I'll take care of the toys, Sally."

"Toys?" Rivers asked.

"Some toys I stole," Sally said, dispiritedly.

"Sally please," Rivers said. "Do you never stop lying?"

The phone rang.

"The Parkers," Rivers said, looking helplessly at his wife. "Would you . . .?"

"All right, I'll get it," Sally said, slightly contrite, getting up. "Good night, Al. Come back some time when you feel like having a nice quiet evening."

"Good night," Al said. "Good night, Mr. Rivers."

Rivers sighed, nodded, sat down and picked up his book. "Nice to meet you," he said.

". . . no," Sally was saying, into the phone, as Al picked up the bundle of toys and let himself out. "No, everything's just as fine as always. Jerk's reading, I'm screaming, and our guest's been driven away . . ."

And that was marriage, Al thought. The honorable solution. The pact against loneliness. The combination of strengths. There were a man and woman for you—educated, well off, handsome, intelligent and with good taste. What he had known must have been some different institution.

He walked down, carrying the bundle of toys, towards the waterfront. He came to a playground, left the toys there on a bench. Then he walked on to the street which ran along the bay, turned right and started home. He thought of them sitting there, no point in staying married, no point in divorcing. Rivers conscientiously reading up on foreign policy, Sally smoking, drinking, perhaps turning on the television set eventually to annoy him when she ran out of things to say or do; for the set would never stop saying and doing, and perhaps they would finish the evening mutely watching it until first one and, finally, the other, was ready to go to his or her separate room.

22   "My dears—
"The United States of America has had a
strange, foreshortened history." (So began the
second of Pennington-Barker's San Francisco letters
written, as Usez thought, to the world.) "The continent one-third of whose land mass it occupies began
with conventional enough oceans of time between discovery and colonization; there followed, after the regular hundreds of years, exploitation and assertion of independence.

"And then, unprecedentedly, the cells of progress began to mul-
tiply too rapidly; there were too many inventions, there was too
much communication, there were too many resources, too much
wealth, too much responsibility. And in consequence the United
States, within one hundred and seventy-five years of its estab-
lishment, had already completed much of the cycle which, for
the great nations of the past, had spread over six and seven
centuries: it had had pioneering and expansion; early wars of
survival, later wars of aggrandizement; arrival as a world power,
and domination; a cultural first flowering and a golden age; after
only a century and three quarters, in what ought to have been
late childhood, it had, incredibly, run all the ages of national
experience, run them so rapidly that hardly any of the cultural
achievement could hope to stick, no national characteristics could
form without being destroyed a decade later. Already it is en-
tering its decadence.

"But there is something still more curious: a decadent nation

209

can be a comfortable place for its people to live; the United States is not. For the impulse to decadence has grown in the hearts of its citizens long before the puritan impulses of pioneer morality have been eradicated. And this sets up, in the nation, a condition precisely analogous to acute neurosis in the individual: shame and desire in fundamental and insoluble conflict produce tensions, outbursts, frustrations, crimes, anxieties, fears —these are the moods of the age—denied, concealed, repressed, but obvious to any man waking at dawn for a cold, gray look at his times: homosexuality, the bellwether symptom of decadence throughout history, burgeons but is not flaunted, as in the past; it is persecuted, and most of its practitioners are not arrogant and entertaining but rather live in terror of discovery. Official bodies make stern laws and hysterical investigations, trying to promote a return to the simple virtues of national childhood, so that in a nation in which fifty years ago there was no such thing as political crime, it now becomes the only crime there is. Scientists, producing marvels of technology and destruction daily, produce simultaneously marvels of agonizing in newspaper interviews and works of testimony and confession, apologizing for their own fearful creations. Business men, manufacturers, laborers, perform their tasks by rote, neither feeling nor wishing to feel a sense of goal, numbed in their off duty hours by martinis, by bourbon, or by beer, seeking further numbness through furtive sexual forays among their female counterparts. Creative men are less and less productive, having less and less idea what to write, what to paint, what to compose. Today's great or indispensable man can look forward only to being tomorrow's villain and the next day's fool.

"Perhaps the continent can look for leadership from Canada, still in its years of innocence, under a less and less restrictive royalty, emerging slowly as a nation should; or from Mexico, where the aboriginal peoples of the continent are gradually, after four hundred and fifty years, growing once more towards a conscious and distinctive national life. But the United States seems, by now, to have used up its citizens' energy—the only national resource worth calculating—in too short and bright a flash; it will leave an odd little chapter in the book of the world as a country which, having reached zenith as a prodigy, must now, instead of enjoying the comforts and splendors of decline, finish its course as a place of curious unhappiness, history's first neurotic nation."

"But," Casper Usez said, face to face with his man at last in their first and only confrontation, and holding this document in his hand. This was after the excitements and the arrest, when the Lieutenant (for Pennington could not, of course, lose that rank until the court martial stripped it from him), was being held for arraignment. "But doesn't the intellectual criminal, like the saint, always think his times are out of joint?"

23 "I don't know," Pennington said. "I know very little about what the intellectual criminal and the saint always think."

Usez had finished his detailed questioning, the tracing of routes, the search for accomplices; the man had been fairly cooperative. He had, it is true, stubbornly refused to locate certain of the places he had stayed, saying that people would be turned up whom there was no point in questioning. Usez, having satisfied himself that the Bureau's chief concerns—espionage and organized subversive activity—were not involved, was disposed to allow these minor concealments.

"Couldn't we have a talk?" he asked. He put aside the shorthand book in which he had been pretending to make notes. Actually, there was a recording device concealed in the wall of the Interrogation Room to collect accurate evidence; such a gesture as building, through hours of questioning and patient pretense, to a place where laying aside a dummy notebook would make a seeming point of confidence was so habitual a part of Usez' interviewing technique that he hardly even considered it a trick.

What follows is a transcription from the tape, with which Usez closed his file:

P: A talk? Something in the Russian tradition, you mean? Raskolnikov and . . . Ivan Nemesisovitch?

U: I don't think I'd fit the nemesis role too well. It would be more fun for both of us if I'd been relentlessly clever, wouldn't

212

it? But I'm afraid it would be more accurate for you to think of me as a rather plodding bureaucratic investigator who has had the solution to a perplexing case handed to him by dumb luck—and who is still perplexed.

P: You're a very disarming man. It's hard to believe that anything perplexes you.

U: It's true, though. I have a very unbecoming impulse to argue with you.

P: Unbecoming?

U: To an official.

P: Argue about what?

U: Well, I wonder if you'd agree to the statement I made— that the intellectual criminal and the saint always see their times as out of joint?

P: I don't think you're trying to argue at all. I think you're just offering me a tricky choice between declaring myself a criminal and declaring myself a saint. I don't feel like either one.

U: But you do have (*Offered prisoner document last quoted —C.U.*) a strong sense that life in this country, in this century, has decayed?

P: And if I do, that makes me saint or criminal? Which is to say—insane or antisocial? That is, you feel that a reasonable man couldn't take such a view?

U: I do, you know. As I read history, the tendency of the romantic in any given generation is to believe that things have never been worse . . .

P: Oh, yes. The Macaulay nonsense about a man's familiarity with the past preventing him from feeling morose about the present.

U: You think it's nonsense?

P: Of course it's nonsense, Usez. It's the present in which one lives; if a man thinks his present unhappy, and the past better, isn't he an optimist? Doesn't he see history as establishing the possibility of improvement?

U: Suppose he's unhappy, but thinks the past was even worse?

P: I doubt that he can, Usez. But unless he's an optimist, he'll probably feel that the past was no better, that the human condition remains pretty much unchanged. But isn't it possible that a man may think the past not relevant because not really know-

213

able; that he may think it was happy for happy men and gloomy for gloomy ones; and that to refer to it is nonsense, after all, since it is one of those vague scriptures which can be quoted endlessly and pointlessly, to prove whatever case you like?

U: But your own present has seemed to you unhappy?

P: Yes. I'm glad enough if others feel differently.

U: Wouldn't you prefer to feel differently?

P: To some men unhappiness is a burden. To others, it seems a kind of privilege.

U: To members of the tribe of Socrates?

P: Now you're trying to make me claim to be a sage.

U: I confess I'm trying to fit you into a rationale that I can understand. I would like to think that you have acted consistently . . .

P: What inconsistency do you see?

U: Let's say it was a decent impulse which made you run in the first place, one I can understand without necessarily approving. But what kept you running? Why didn't you reach a point much sooner where, if you felt you deserved punishment, you stopped, waited for arrest, let society administer it?

P: The irony was a little too neat, I guess. Society wanted to punish me for the impulse of decency, just as it wanted to cuddle me for the crime.

U: No man runs seven years from an irony.

P: But you know nothing of punishment, Usez, or you would know that in all these years, Society has punished me by pursuing me. As a pursued man, I have been kept in poverty and insecurity; as a kid I knew poverty, Usez, and I hated it. I grew to be a man who loved comforts, and good food and being settled; I was a man who dreamed of building certain sorts of homes, and owning certain sorts of cars; I was a man who wanted the respect of his profession, the earnings of his work as well as its joys. And in prison I would have been only a man separated from the possibility of attaining those things by a few more years, and not a man cut off from them at all.

U: But . . .

P: No. Wait. Perhaps you're going to have your rationale. You wanted me to claim sainthood; don't you see how much easier it would have been, to have that kind of goal? To have thought there was something worth the sacrifice? Or to have given up my life for an art, or for wisdom, or even for a crime? It's pointlessness that's the real punishment, Usez. That's a goal, isn't it, to cap your rationale? To have sought pointlessness, in order to atone, in order to deserve the inevitable comfort of one's death . . .

U: But why should your punishment have lasted all these years?

P: Must guilt be logical, more so than other emotions? Or . . . (*smiled—C.U.*) maybe I've been able to pick up a little guilt transfusion along the way.

U: Like what?

P: Ever hit anyone with a blackjack?

U: No. I hit a man on the head with a lamp, once, a boy I was trying to arrest. He wouldn't come along.

P: How did you feel about it?

U: Lousy.

P: Are you sure? Altogether lousy? There was no little throb of joy or power? Just for a second, before remorse began?

U: Not that I can remember.

P: I can remember, Usez. I can remember a moment like that. When the crunch of bone breaking produced a pulse of gratification, before revulsion flooded it out . . .

U: Where was that?

P: (*Shook his head—C.U.*) But it can add years to your running time, Usez, a thing like that. I don't think you have to be a criminal or a saint . . .

U: I take those back, Pennington. I don't want you to think I'm trying to have the same kind of fun with you that the Sunday supplement boys are going to be having for the next twenty years . . .

P: What do you mean?

U: You'll be a great feature, I'm afraid. In the public mind you're already a kind of supercriminal mad genius.

P: I don't seem to see why.

U: First the toys. That makes you a thief, a slightly crazy one. Then the confusion about what actually happened at the store . . .

P: Yes. I was afraid of that.

215

U: And finally, of course, the killings. You must admit, it's hard to believe that what appeared to happen actually did.

P: I don't find it difficult.

U: You knew the woman.

P: But how am I connected? Even in tabloid logic?

U: Well, in the lead they sum up the case as provable in court: desertions, theft, assaults; then they postulate subornation of an adolescent witness, possible blackmail of an adult one (*Pennington laughed—C.U.*); you begin to look capable of anything . . .

P: And that witness business removes the alibi?

U: For the writer's purpose, at least. And now he's ready to begin on you and the woman: you had visited there at least once. You were seen talking intimately several times at the store. He works up to Christmas eve. She was dressed as if she were expecting someone. She tried to find out how to phone you; she even told the operator she thought you were at the door . . .

P: You boys working pretty hard on that angle, Usez?

U: Of course not. But the papers are.

P: I see (*A pause—C.U.*) What about . . . what about the papers back East?

U: I'm afraid the whole country's interested.

P: I see. I don't think . . . she'll believe it.

U: She? Mrs. Pennington? (*Decided to withhold information about wife's reaction—C.U.*)

P: (*Nodded—C.U.*) Frances. The kids. You must have seen them, didn't you?

U: I admired your wife.

P: Someone else's wife by now, I'm sure.

U: A man named Bowie.

P: Nice man. What about the kids, Usez? Were they pretty nice kids?

U: I thought they were fine. You know I wasn't going to ask . . .

P: What?

U: About your family. It's what my wife, Betty, would want to know. How you justify leaving them?

P: What should I have done? Taken them along? Tried to provide for them out of a fugitive's odd job earnings? I know

216

what poverty does to kids, Usez. I know what it does to adult relationships, and what that does to kids too. Not for my family, Usez. Especially not when . . . you admired Frances?

U: Any man would.

P: That's it, Usez. (*Sadly—C.U.*) Penelope wasn't in it with Frances, at the post. There were so many agile halfbacks around, waiting to fall on the ball if I ever fumbled. I knew it was just a matter of leaving something to see them through for a few months . . .

U: It came to almost five thousand dollars, with the insurance and selling the car.

P: I'm glad it was Bowie. I always liked Peter. How long did it take him?

U: Just under a year.

P: Your wife wouldn't think that was better, ten or twelve anxious months and a new marriage, than years of discomfort and insecurity with an unhappy man?

U: I don't know.

P: I'm sure they won't believe it, Usez.

U: I hope not, Lieutenant.

P: Lieutenant? That's right. Doctor, Lieutenant, Supercriminal, Saint, Sage. (*Shook his head—C.U.*) Have you chosen one now, Usez?

U: I'm not your lawyer, Pennington. If I were, the choice would be easy; I'd pick—well, in your terms, Saint. Therefore insane. The charges they can prove—especially if they make the assault rap stick, and I think they can—they carry a lot of time. California time, after we're done with you at Leavenworth.

P: It seems a curiously elaborate lie. Maybe I'll like jail.

U: You won't, though. You think now that you'll declare yourself out for good by being locked away. That you'll finally achieve this loveless, living suicide, alone with your sense of guilt, which you claim to deserve. You're wrong, Lieutenant. In jail you'll still be surrounded. To live is to be surrounded; to die is to be alone.

P: (*Reluctantly—C.U.*) Perhaps you're right.

U: (*Disappointed, perhaps, to have scored so easily—C.U.*) No argument?

P: (*Shrugged—C.U.*)

217

U: We must have more to say to each other.

P: What?

U: I still don't understand what kept you going . . .

P: I've told you.

U: Have you?"

P: If you think about it.

U: Then perhaps it's the whole thing. Why was the initial motivation so powerful? You weren't a mystic; you were a scientist. You weren't more than normally rebellious; by the time you left college, you wanted pretty much what other Americans want—position, a family, prosperity . . .

P: All right, then. When the rascal meets Nemmie Nemesis, he gets to ask questions, too. Isn't that the way it goes? (*His tone was wearily obliging—C.U.*)

U: Whatever questions you like.

P: You believe in the structure of law, in the police branch which upholds it?

U: I had legal training before I joined the Bureau.

P: And, as any earnest man for the structure which includes his work, you love law?

U: I think I do.

P: You're trained for it, for enforcing it, and nothing else? You believe in the whole structure, ideally, practically, with all its imperfections, and in the social and governmental systems it supports? Not only here and now, but in history and in foreign countries?

U: I do.

P: Okay. Suppose tomorrow the big boys, the great men of your field, called you in and said: "Usez, we're putting you onto something. A big secret project. Biggest thing ever tried. The best men in the country will work night and day to crack this one; we can't tell you what it is, but here's a lovely, challenging piece for you to work up. It'll take all your training and all your love. Anything you need, ask for. Now get going." Be pretty exhilarating, wouldn't it?

U: I'm afraid I know where you're going.

P: (*With a certain sardonic exhilaration—C.U.*) Sure you do. Sure you do, Usez. You'd work like hell on your piece; you'd do the job of your life. You'd reach the point where you knew

218

the thing must be coming together. And then one morning, you'd switch on the radio, and hear some gleeful ass say: "At last, ladies and gentlemen, it's been done. All the best lawyers and judges and investigators and sociologists, working in unprecedented concert and with millions in government funds, have developed a mechanical legal brain, able to instruct our agents in enemy lands in the method of committing any crime without violating laws, able to plan rape and pillage, friends; arson, murder and the mutilation of generations yet unborn without the possibility of detection, fellow citizens. Oh, boy, nothing can touch our rats, now, and it'll take the enemy years to catch up, folks. Years. It's anarchy at last!" Where would you be, Usez?

U: (*Reluctantly—C.U.*) Right where you're sitting, Al. Betty Usez would be a lonely girl tonight.

P: She'd be eating lonely oysters, wouldn't she, Casper baby? You bet your beagle nose she would.

(It was the closest to a malicious thing Pennington-Barker was ever reported to have said or done; and even so, Usez found himself quite unable to take offense.

(In the following weeks he studied the transcription carefully, playing it back over and over, until finally he believed he understood everything the man had meant.

(But in print, he felt it read uncharacteristically; and because his file on Allerd Pennington was, in a sense, the man's true history, as distinct from the lurid newspaper accounts, Usez' final decision was to delete the last half dozen exchanges from the written transcript, and to expunge from the tape the sound of Pennington's voice saying the words.)

PART THREE

24 On the day before Christmas, the final shopping day, business started brisk. Somewhat to Al's surprise it was not so much jammed as hurried. Harassed people, mostly apologetic, would fly into the department, scoop up as many things as they could carry without bothering to inspect them much, pay and run for the escalators. It was a feverish sort of shopping, full of anxieties for the clerks.

"By noon," Finn said. "They won't even bother coming in any longer. They'll be doing their shopping at drugstores and cigar stands. Last day's never a good one for department stores."

Though it was a tense time, the final flush took only a toll of one: Betty, the sewing machine girl, ran the needle through her finger and had to be taken to the nurse.

"We'll have only a few customers this afternoon," Finn said, "looking for small things. I'm letting Gullakian off. Going to handle wheel goods myself, though there'll be nothing doing there."

"Really?"

"He's going to play the fiddle," Finn said. "The store has a little glee club, goes around the last afternoon singing carols. Gullakian's going to play with them."

Just before lunch, Gullakian himself confirmed the news. "I want you guys to listen to my concert now," he said. "We're going to be here at two forty-five."

"We'll be here," said Tom.

"God, what a morning," Gullakian said. "I almost preferred the jams. People are so nervous today."

223

"Christmas scares them," Al said. "Those great, blinking, inhuman trees, ready to fall on them tomorrow and eat them up."

As Finn had promised, the last tense dash of customers had abated by noon. By twelve thirty, they began to feel that they had made it. At one fifteen, returning from a final lunch with Nickie, Al found the relaxation universal. Whatever scattered sales there were were made carelessly, almost lackadaisically. Clerks who shared counters and hadn't spoken in the past week could be seen chattering together. Dolores Hughes, whose coldness to Gullakian had been a chief theme of departmental gossip, made a public ceremony out of kissing him for luck as he went off to join the glee club. Even Winnipeg, when Al delivered Nickie to the doll counter, told a tentatively risqué joke, something about a dog and a fire hydrant.

Nickie was fine, Al thought. "You've made it, girl," he said, as Winnipeg drifted back to her station.

"I'm awfully proud of myself, Al."

"You're blooming."

"I feel wonderful. Al, got any plans for tonight? I've been turning down dates, in case you didn't."

"Hope you didn't turn them all down," Al said.

"Oh, Al."

"I think I'll be leaving San Francisco tonight."

"I won't see you again. Not even for a drink, after work?"

He shook his head.

"Oh, Al. That's the only thing that spoils it, spoils having made it."

"Stop, Nickie. Go out dancing, have a lovely time. Think of me once or twice during the evening, if you really like; and feel deliciously melancholy and sad. That'll make it even better."

"Oh . . ."

"Come on."

"Damn you, Al Barker. All right. I'll be deliciously sad, if that's how you say I'll be."

"Good girl, Nickie," Al said, and he left her at the counter.

He went to the service desk. Dolly was away. He stood there waiting for her, tempted to congratulate himself. Everyone had made it: for Finn, there was no incident more serious than the thefts, and that would be forgiven in view of the fine sales record. All the clerks were money ahead with no major casualties. And he, King Al, had defied his anxiety as never before, and was still free.

Dolly came up.

"Hello, Miss Klamath," he said.

She glanced around. "Hello, Al," she whispered. "Hasn't it been a strange morning? I'm afraid . . . I'm afraid I was unpleasant to that girl who hurt herself on the sewing machine."

"Don't worry about it," Al said. "Have you heard from the Convent?"

She shook her head. She seemed a little jumpy.

"The Christmas mails are always slow," Al said. "I'm sure you'll hear soon."

"The store is letting me have next week off," Dolly said. "I thought if I didn't hear, I'd go up there and talk to them."

"That's very sensible," Al said. "I think we're going to have a nice, relaxed afternoon."

"Oh, I hope so," Dolly said. "Mr. Finn is in the office drinking with that store detective. It . . . I wish they weren't."

Almost the moment Al reached the stockroom, Finn swept in, flushed and shouting: "Got some Christmas for you in the office, Al my boy. Come along, no argument."

Al followed him in. On the desk were a fifth of blended whiskey and some paper cups.

The store detective, who was sitting there, also somewhat flushed, looked up and said: "You're Barker, are you? This is Barker, Finn?"

"This is my boy," Finn said. "Have a drink, Al."

"He's all right," the detective muttered. "He's clean, he's clean. Your assistant is a fool."

"M'nerney?" Finn said, pouring one for Al, and drinking his own off. "No hard feelings, Henry. Don't say a word now; it's Christmas and let's have a merry one."

"Merry Christmas," Al said, toasting them.

"And now," Finn announced. "Now I'm going to sell that pedal car. You shall watch a real salesman at work, gentlemen."

"That would be quite a piece of selling," Al said. "Considering there are no customers left."

They stepped out of the office, Henry the detective following.

225

"Will you be needing this in your work, Hub?" Henry asked, showing that he had the bottle under his jacket.

"I've another," Finn stage-whispered. "Down in the little corner behind Santa. So you can leave it there for Al and his lady friend," and Finn, grinning, waved his hand in the direction of Mrs. Kelsner who, perhaps alone in the department, hadn't let up but was steadily blowing her stream of bubbles without looking to right or left.

Halfway across the floor Mr. Finn, Al and Henry were stopped by Dolly Klamath. "Mr. Finn," she said. "I tried to take a bottle of liquor away from the man in Yippee Cowboy suits. He wouldn't give it up; he says it's Mr. M'nerney's."

"Why, Dolly girl," Finn said. "Don't you fret about it. Who'd ever have thought Mac had it in him, eh? Come on now, smile. It's merry Christmas time." And he tried to put his arm around her.

Dolly jumped away. "I won't be responsible, Mr. Finn," she said primly.

"We must see that the ladies get some Christmas cheer, Al," Finn whispered, as they moved on. "Oh, I wish Sally were here, eh boy?"

"Do you?" Al said. They reached wheel goods.

"Who'll buy my pedal car?" Finn shouted; he really was pretty drunk. Recrossing the floor towards the stockroom, Al realized that so were many others. He supposed that, if he weren't careful, he might easily get drunk himself; when he reached the stockroom, he got his own thermos of whiskey out and poured its contents into the sink in the men's room. Then he stood in the doorway for a time, watching the hilarity develop:

Harris, looking happy, seemed to have a friend with him at the electric train counter, for he had put aside his cap and was demonstrating how to make the trains run backward to a slim, elegantly dressed young man whose horn rimmed glasses matched Harris' own.

Betty Connaught, the sewing machine girl, her finger neatly bandaged, had abandoned her demonstration and was giggling with Dolores Hughes at the music box counter, as the two girls teased a grinning Tom.

M'nerney and the Zoom-Spaceman-Yippee-Cowboy clerk now

had their their bottle openly on the counter, and were urging the ballet student to execute a kick over it.

Nickie and Winnipeg were dressing a toy dog in a doll's dress. Al went out to Mrs. Kelsner.

"I should think you could relax now, ma'am," he said. "Nobody else is taking the work very seriously any longer." Even the few customers who hurried in seemed to catch the general mood of feckless exhilaration which followed as tension drained away; they would slow their shopper's pace, smile as if caught in a harmless folly, and drift bemused about the department, fingering and chatting.

"Is there drinking going on?" Mrs. Kelsner asked.

Al nodded. "You can pour yourself one in Finn's office," he said. "The boss has another bottle up behind Santa Claus. He'll never miss it."

"Well, just one perhaps," said Mrs. Kelsner, merrily. He walked her to the office and watched her pour a drink and toss it off. "And now," she said, "I must get back to my bubbling."

Al returned to the stockroom. Suddenly he found himself wondering where the elves were; let off, perhaps, since there were hardly any children to see Santa today. If they were off, he thought then very likely Evans was drinking, too.

He shook his head. He sat by himself among the Kid Sister Sewing Machines, reluctant to go back onto the floor where people might be offended if he ducked their liquor. He listened as the happy clack of voices, clerks' voices, now, rose to match the volume of the insistent *Jingle Bells*. It would be just the right time to leave, he thought, and he had put his jacket on to do so when *Jingle Bells* was switched off.

There were sounds of exaggerated shushing and he could hear Finn's voice, suddenly, from all the way across the floor, shouting:

"Quiet now. They're going to sing for us."

Al understood that Gullakian and the Glee Club had arrived.

He walked to the stockroom doorway to watch. The group was on the other side, Santa's side. Clerks were leaving their counters to gather around. Al walked on out as far as the service desk.

In a space near the hobbies counter, a small electric organ had been wheeled into place. A girl in choir vestment was sitting at it. Standing beside her was Gullakian, with a violin, and behind them in a semi-circle were a dozen choristers.

Standing in front were the clerks from the toy department, and among them, strange clerks, a traveling audience from other parts of the store. Two or three bottles could be seen passing carelessly around.

"Let's all sing *Deck the Halls*," the girl at the organ commanded merrily.

"*Deck the Halls, Deck the Halls* everybody," Finn cried.

"*Deck the Halls*," boomed a still louder voice. Al looked over; it was Evans, erect in his Santa costume, wavering slightly as he stood before his throne.

"They've made the old man drunk," said a voice at Al's elbow. It was Dolly.

"Too bad," Al said. "That's too bad."

There was a rousing if ragged chorus of *Deck the Halls with Boughs of Holly*, the clerks trying to outsing the Glee Club, followed by applause, shouting and laughter. Next everybody sang *Hark, the Herald Angels Sing*, even more exuberantly, and when it was finished, the organist had to get up and wave her hands to get them quiet.

"Now," she said, when the clerks were finally attending her. "Now Mr. Harold Gullakian, of your own department, will play that lovely Christmas ballad, *Silent Night*." She sat again, and struck a chord. She glanced at Gullakian. He fitted the violin beneath his chin and nodded. She struck the chord once more, very softly, and Gullakian began to play.

Rather to Al's surprise, he played with considerable restraint, keeping his tone simple, almost harsh, cutting the notes cleanly, avoiding the slurs which could so easily have turned the old piece to corn; when he had played a chorus through, the girl at the organ took the melody from him, and Gullakian played a descant, improvising quite beautifully; only on the third chorus was taste abandoned, as the Glee Club took over the melody, humming, and Gullakian played a rather sloppy soprano lead.

When he finished, one of the girls from another department cried out, before the applause could start:

"Sing it again, Harold, like you did before."

"He sang it for us," another sighed, smugly. "Harold sang it."

"Sing it, sing it, Harold," cried the toy department girls, and the clapping was wild. Gullakian looked bashfully at his shoes. "Oh, sing it, Harold."

He looked up with a tentative, little-boy smile, and said: "I'm not really much of a singer, but if . . ."

"*First Noel, First Noel*," boomed Evens, from his throne.

"Shut up," the girls shrieked. "Shut up, Santa Claus. Harold's going to sing."

Gullakian glanced at the organist for his chord, got it, spread his hands for silence, half-closed his eyes, and crooned into the microphone:

"Si-i-lunn nigh, Ho-wo-ly nigh, . . ."

"No," Evens roared out, and began to boom:

"Thu-uh fi-rist No-o-el . . ."

"Make Santa Claus be quiet," the girls cried. "Be quiet, Santa Claus. Oh, sing it, Harold."

"Allll uzz come, alllll uzz brigh'. . . ."

Out from behind the shell staggered the bleary store detective to lead Evens away.

"He's arresting Santa Claus," someone giggled, and there was a loud laugh. Gullakian was holding out his hands; he started again:

"Si-uh-lunn nigh, Ho-wi-ly nigh . . ."

"Ohhhh," the girls moaned, as he sang. "Oh, sing it, Harold." He sang.

A fat girl was weeping as he finished: "It was so beautiful," she sobbed, surging towards him. Dolores Hughes, there first, plastered her body against Gullakian's and began to kiss his face. Another girl tried to push between them.

"Harold," screamed a girl, tearing angrily at Dolores' dress; the sleeve ripped, and Gullakian was knocked to his knees by a swam of black-clad girls.

The organist played loud chords.

"Let's all sing, *God Rest Ye Merry, Gentlemen*," she screamed. "Come on, everybody."

"Please," cried Gullakian, struggling up. "Please. *God Rest Ye Merry*."

229

Suddenly, Al noticed, Evans was on his throne again.

"Now," he shouted. *The First Noel. The First Noel.*

Ignoring both him and the girls, who were demanding that Gullakian sing again, the organist swung full-volume into *God Rest Ye Merry, Gentlemen,* and the male clerks, drunk and competitive, outsang Santa Claus and outshouted the salesgirls. Al, edging towards the old man on the dais, wondering where the detective was, saw that Evans kept trying to sing against them all.

As the chorus was finishing, a stray child, a little girl, wandered up the ramp. The male clerks, victorious, applauded themselves; Gullakian, clutched now only by Dolores, grinned and brushed at his hair with a free hand; Evans, still singing, tried to push the child away. She eluded him, cuddled against one of Santa's legs, her cheek against the tight red cloth of the costumed thigh. Evans reached down, seized her about the waist, and swung her into the air.

In the diminishing noise, Al shouted and leapt forward, dashing through the wheel goods department.

"Let the little children come to me and suffer," cried old Evans, in a terrible voice, creating instant silence; he stared furiously at the clerks, holding the struggling child above his head at arm's length.

Al hurdled the low fence, leapt onto the dais behind Evans, and sprang to the seat of the throne to bring himself to the old man's height. As he pivoted frontwards, he saw Finn running towards them with the detective beside him, and Tom. Directly in front, Evans' back bulged. Sure now that Santa Claus meant to hurl the child into the mob, Al jumped straight out, grasping the small body out of the great hands. Gathering it against himself as he fell, he rolled to land beneath her, sending Santa sprawling with an accidental kick.

There was a huge groan from Evans, shouts from the men, screams from the women, and a wail from the child. The mother came running up the ramp.

"That man," she was screaming, pointing at Al. "Get my baby away from him. Help," and she bumped wildly into the store detective who was coming up from the other side.

Al set the little girl on her feet. She was crying, but seemed unhurt. The whole toy department was closing towards him. He saw, as he stood there a moment above their shouts, Finn trying to extricate himself from the wrecked wicker sides of the little British pedal car, over which he must have tripped as he tried to reach them. He saw Tom clutching the mother, trying to explain. He saw M'nerney, pushing his way, drunken but officious, into the surging throng. Al moved.

Straight down, hurdling the fence again in the other direction, threading quickly through an opening in the crowd, pushing Harris out of the way, Al went at a run towards the escalator.

The last thing he saw of the toy department was Mrs. Kelsner, still erect, still serenely blowing bubbles, at the stockroom end.

25 At nine o'clock Christmas Eve, the maid interrupted Nickie's dressing to say that there was a phone call for her.

"Who is it?" Nickie asked. Deeply confused about Al, for there were twenty versions of what he had done before he ran out, she had decided to go to the dance she was invited to, and to try to put him and the whole, frantic, toy department interlude out of her mind.

"It's a Mr. Vanderbeck, ma'am, Mr. Tom Vanderbeck."

"Tom?" Nickie said. "All right." There was an extension in her room. Half dressed, she sat on the bed and picked it up. "Hello, Tom. Merry Christmas."

"Nickie. You know where Al lives?"

"Yes."

"Listen. Mr. Finn's here. He's been with the police all evening. They checked the address Al gave the store and it was false. And Mr. Finn wants to know . . ."

"I wouldn't tell him in a million years," Nickie said.

"No, wait, Nickie. You don't understand. We want to warn Al; that kid was hurt somehow, and they say that if he didn't do it, he'll have to be a witness against Santa Claus. But that isn't all, Nickie. There are FBI men, too. And they want Al for something else, we don't know what. And Mr. Finn is going to lose his job, but he wants to try to warn Al, and he says it's such a mess . . . anyway, so Al can decide whether to get out of town."

"Where are you?" Nickie asked.

"At my house," Tom said. "Mr. Finn drove out here. He thought I'd know, and he didn't want to use the phone . . ."

"They might have followed him," Nickie said. "Where is your house, Tom?"

He gave her the address.

"I'll drive by," Nickie said. "I'll get you, Tom. Tell Mr. Finn to leave and go a different way, so that if there's anyone following, they'll follow him."

"All right," Tom said. "Hurry."

She pulled her dress on, snapped a look at herself in the mirror, put on lipstick and ran downstairs. Her father was sitting in his dress clothes in the living room, waiting for her mother; they were going to a different party.

"Daddy," Nickie said. "Daddy. What are you giving me for Christmas? Tomorrow?"

"Surprise, darling," her father said, getting up. "My, you look nice."

"There's kind of an emergency," Nickie said. "It it's money . . ."

"Well, it is money, among other things, sweetheart," he said, chuckling. "You know, I heard about you working. I haven't let on but I knew you were at Mainways all along."

"You did?"

"I found out," he said. "And I just decided my little working girl ought to have a Christmas bonus, thought I'd match those paychecks you got at Mainways, for being such a good little saleswoman, eh?" He put his arm around her.

"Daddy, that's darling of you. Could I have it now? Please?"

"Something mysterious," he chuckled again. "What an independent baby."

"Please?"

"You want it tonight?"

"Yes," she said. "Right away."

"A hundred and ninety dollars? To take to the Taylor's party?"

"It's for something I have to do first," she said. "Please don't take time to argue . . ."

"All right, dear," he said. "All right. Doesn't do me any good to argue anyway, does it, with such an independent baby?" He took out his wallet. "Here's four fifties," he said. "Have a good time, whatever it is."

233

"Daddy, you're a sweetheart too," she said; she had a violent urge to insist that he acknowledge she was out of nursery school. Instead, she took the money, smiling a sweet, false smile, and hugged him. As she ran for her coat, she called back: "If Dick comes before you leave, tell him I'll try to be at the Taylors' later and explain everything then."

She grabbed her coat, and ran out to her convertible which was parked in front of the house; got the key in, reminded herself to drive cautiously so as not to attract attention, then forgot and drove very fast to Tom's house.

Tom and Finn were waiting.

"Nobody followed me, Nickie," Finn said. "I'm sure of it."

"He wanted to come with us to see Al," Tom explained. Both of them got into Nickie's car.

"I'll leave mine out here," Finn said.

Nickie started up. "Maybe Al's gone already," she said.

"I hope so," Tom said. "I hope he's miles away."

But when they got to Gerke Street, there was a light in Al's window.

26 During the long week between Christmas and New Year's, Frances Braden (Pennington) Bowie bought every edition of every newspaper available. Her first reaction, to a phone call from Casper Usez informing her of the circumstances of the arrest as he had heard it from San Francisco, was simple disbelief.

"It's a mix-up. A mistake. A different man," she told her husband. Then, as the newspaper accounts began to confirm it, she began to accept: "Oh, God, Pete, this makes me feel awful."

As the later details developed, however, her feeling turned to a curious kind of relief. She had lived a long time with the notion that as fine a man as she might ever know had been married to her, had found her inadequate, had left her in part because of some failure of understanding of her own; now, as the newspaper accounts made him out a sex criminal, implicated him in stranger and stranger crimes, she could shudder at the thought that it was only luck that his crack-up had been delayed until after their life together was over.

"The poor old bastard," Pete would say, when she handed him a new story.

And Frances could reply: "God, Pete. A maniac. I'm glad we told the kids he died."

They kept the papers away from the children as much as they could without making too much of a point of it.

"I've told them it's a different family," Pete said. "No relation.

235

That first name's a pretty rough coincidence for them to swallow, but they seem to believe me."

"Oh, Pete. What goes wrong with human beings? Or was it me? I used to think that Al was practically God himself."

"Honey," Pete said. "There's nothing been proved. It's just circumstantial stuff. . . ."

"Pete." She was a little annoyed. "He knew that woman, didn't he? And there'd never been any other men . . . poor little thing. And she even said he was there. On the phone. And it was so crazy and horrible . . . who else could have done it?"

"Listen, would you like me to fly out there? See if I can find out what really happened?"

No, it was sweet, but she didn't want him to. She wanted to stop reading the papers. She wanted to forget it. When Usez phoned again, to say that he was ready to leave for California, for the interview, she asked him not to say that he had been in touch with her, and told him what she intended to do. She had told Pete of the decision that same morning. It was New Year's Day.

"Pete, I'm willing now."

"Willing?"

"To have the kids' name changed. You were right. They'd better be Bowies, I think. Susan even suggested it herself."

"What about Jerry?"

"He worries me even more," Frances said. "He tells the boys at school that the Mad Monk of Telegraph Hill is his uncle, and they'd better watch out . . ."

"We'll get them changed," Pete said. "I'll get a lawyer on it. I suppose we'll have to notify Al."

"I'll write him myself, when the time comes."

"Do you think he'll mind?"

"A man so crazy?" Frances asked. "I doubt he'll even notice."

"Poor old son of a bitch," Pete said.

27 The knock on the door was not unexpected. He had been packed for hours. He had unwrapped the remaining toys which Sally had stolen, and sat them across the room from him on the bed for whoever might find them. But he had found himself unable to leave.

Something had him, he didn't know exactly what—some feeling, compulsion, or perhaps no more than a need to know the resolutions of the day.

He had sat musing, sober, even hungry, aware of his own irrationality but indifferent to it, speaking occasionally to the toys of marriages and wars. He had finally decided to give himself —or them, or whatever this was—until ten to make a sign. At ten, if nothing had happened, he would leave the toys, take his things, go to Weary's and phone first Tom, then Dolly. And if all were well, if there were really no more need for him, he promised himself that he would eat and find the highway south.

At nine-thirty the knock came.

"Come in," he said. The door opened. It was Tom, stepping aside solemnly to hold the door for Nickie, flushed and stunning in a party gown, followed by a rumpled Finn.

"Al," Nickie said. "The police . . ."

"The Federals," Finn said. "The Federals are looking for you."

"Close the door, Tom," Al said. "Come in."

Tom closed the door.

"Al, the toys," Finn cried suddenly, seeing them. "Al, you were the thief?"

237

"No," Al said. "The thief returned them to me. I was a little afraid to bring them back."

"Who was it, Al?" Finn said.

Al shook his head.

"Was it . . . Sally?"

"I'm afraid it was," Al said.

"I don't understand that girl," Finn said unhappily, sitting on the bed across the room.

"May I sit here, Al?" Nickie asked, moving towards him. Al moved over for her. Tom stood by the door.

Finn said: "I thought maybe I should try to see her and . . . explain. But after this . . ." He picked up a doll, and looked at it. Almost unconsciously, it seemed, he moved it against his shoulder and slapped its back; it burped.

"Don't try to see her," Al said.

"I've no job any more," Finn said. "There's to be charges brought against the store, you know . . ."

"About the child?"

Finn nodded.

"I'm sorry," Al said. "They won't give you another chance?"

"Not when they learn that it was I gave the old man the whiskey," Finn said. "That'll be the end of me at Mainways, and most likely anywhere else in San Francisco."

"Tell them I gave him the whiskey," Al said.

"That's nothing to what they're trying to pin on you already, Al boy," Finn said. "M'nerney had the bright idea that it was really you injured the kid. That's what the mother thought. And nobody really saw; you see, if it was Santa Claus, it'll hurt every store in town. If it was you, well, M'nerney turned you in a week ago . . . so then the story would be that we were keeping you on because it was our patriotic duty. To keep you where you could be found."

"Would that get you out?" Al asked.

"Mostly it would get M'nerney in."

"If I ever get my hands on that M'nerney," Tom said.

"So you'd better be going, Al," Finn said. "If there's anything serious the Federals want you for . . ."

"You know," Al said, getting up. "I don't know that I'd want to leave M'nerney that story. Not when there's a better one.

Like this: Suppose the cops arrive, Hub, and here we are. You and I. I wouldn't want Tom and Nickie to stay for this." He paused, thinking. "No, we'll need Tom to call them. We'll send Nickie along, then, and Tom will call them, and say: 'Honest, patriotic Hub Finn, at the risk of his life, is holding madman Barker for the police at his room at 46 Gerke Street, first floor, don't ring as bell doesn't work.' Sound good?"

"Al!" Finn protested.

"Don't interrupt. I'll be the one who gave Evans the whiskey; look, I'll even be the toy-thief. Neither of those means much beside the government charges. But I won't be the child-assaulter; the old man will have to take that. I've kids of my own . . . or had once; and this will make the papers. Evans is honest enough, I imagine, sober . . . where is he?"

"Dolly took him to her house," Finn said. "He was pretty shaken up."

"Good," Al said. "Dolly will speak for me too. With both of them and Tom, I don't think M'nerney'll have much of a case to make."

"Al," Finn said. "You're going too fast for me."

"All right, I'll slow down," Al said. "I stay. Right here. Tom phones in the tip. They come. You're holding me, you've persuaded me to stay and face it . . . here we are. I gave the old man liquor; he hurt the kid. I'm arrested. You're the hero. M'nerney cracks his charming knuckles. How about that, Hub? Won't that do it?"

"Why would you want to, Al?" Finn said. "How could I let you?"

"No sensible reason, Hub," Al said. "Say I'm tired of running. Say it means nothing to me and a lot to you. Say it's too late anyway, because if I run now, M'nerney's story goes and I'm an assaulter of children, a sex criminal . . . they apparently know who I am, now, the Federals." There was a pause. Still thinking, he sat down again; it seemed tight enough—Dolly's word would carry weight, and Evans would have to confirm.

"Who do they know you are?" Nickie asked.

"What do they want you for?" Finn asked.

"Can you tell us now?" Tom moved from the door to sit by Mr. Finn.

Suddenly Al relaxed; he felt himself smiling and a kind of peace came into his limbs. "Sure I can tell you," he said. "And I will. If it takes from now to Christmas."

"Wait, Al," Nickie said suddenly. "Wait. There's a car outside, a convertible. It's a fast one. I have two hundred dollars. You could make it, Al. You could be in Mexico or Canada by morning; they'll be watching for you, but if I were driving till we got out of the city, I know they'd let us through. My father's awfully well known—and there are dozens of parties we might be going to on the Peninsula. There's nothing yet to connect you with me. And I . . . could get a bus back; unless you wanted me to ride along."

"God, Nickie," Al said. "You're all the girl there could possibly be, aren't you? It would be wonderful, and if I could say yes at all, I'd surely want to have you—ride along. We could even find a friend of mine with more money in Mexico. Isn't that neat? But . . . I feel that this is the halt that I can call myself, Nickie; and I'm addict enough of the sensation of free will to want to do it . . ."

"It means a lot to me, Al," Finn said, quietly. "I can't pretend it doesn't."

"Everyone should get what he wants for Christmas," Al said. He turned his eyes to Tom. "What would you like, Tom? A few straight answers to simple questions?"

Tom nodded. Then he reached into his pocket and took out a small looseleaf notebook. He opened the clasps and handed Al a sheet. Al read it, smiled, and returned it to him. "Good job, Athlete," he said. "Buckle on your glee pads and your zest protector, and let's fill it in. First, strike out Barker and leave Pennington. Gurnstein didn't convince you, did he?"

Tom shook his head.

"Pennington's a Carolina name," Al said. "But I was born in Pennsylvania. At my birth there was one sign and one portent." He smiled: "At the moment of delivery, my brother, aged ten months, was heard to say his first word. According to my father, who was sitting with him in another room, the word was 'all,' suggesting Allerd, my mother's family name which became my first. Actually, my brother and I always felt the word must have been 'balls.'"

240

"Where's your brother?" Nickie asked.

"He flew in Italy," Al said. "And stayed on after the war. What are the things you'd like to know?"

"Did you go to Harvard?" Tom asked.

He nodded.

"What did you study?"

"That's the key question, isn't it?" Al asked. "I studied physics, there."

Tom bit his lip, and nodded. "You were a scientist in the Army," he said. "You did secret research."

"You've got it, Athlete," Al said. "I graduated in 1940. I got married. I entered the Army. I even started basic training. Then, unexpectedly, I was transferred to a government-paid paradise. From K.P. to a direct commission. From a trainee in the barracks to a cottage on a little post with my wife. Both our kids were born there."

"On the post," Nickie murmured.

"It was a peculiar post, not Oak Ridge, Tennessee, but one connected with it . . ."

"An atom scientist?" Finn asked. "Is that it?"

Al nodded. "Can you believe that we had no idea what we were working on? I had a friend named Eddie Ramey, a chemist; he thought it was a death ray; and there was a physicist named Peter Bowie, who was closer, who had it figured for a kind of energy transmission. I was the innocent. I thought the Army had us working a big pure research problem . . ." he let it trail off.

Nickie, Finn and Tom were silent, waiting for him to start again. "I guess the scene you're interested in took place in a day-room," he said. "The morning that we found out. We learned what we'd been doing at the same time that the whole world learned what had been done. Eddie Ramey and I and a couple of sergeants, sitting around the radio, drinking coffee, and the word came from Japan: they'd dropped an atom bomb. I don't think Eddie, the chemist, knew even then—probably not for a few minutes—that that had been our project. But I knew. I knew almost before the announcer said it—I think I had the feeling of responsibility almost as he said the words: 'new bomb, a thousand times more powerful . . .,' before he even said 'atomic.'

241

Responsibility and desolation . . . oh, wait," he said. For suddenly he half-remembered something.

Again they waited. Whatever it was Al remembered eluded him again, and he sighed and went on: "I felt sick, I didn't want to look at Eddie. He was still intent on the radio, with the others. I didn't want them to look at me. I didn't want to hear one of them say, 'Hey, this is what we did.' I don't think I'd have cared if I never heard another human voice again saying anything, as long as I lived. I went out without their noticing, and got in my car. I drove to the gate; I had a special kind of pass to let me out. I drove a hundred miles. I came to a city. I got out, found a branch post office, and mailed the car keys to Frances. I thought she'd need that car; it was a little blue Pontiac coupe. Good car.

"Then I went to the bus station and bought a ticket to St. Louis."

"Why St. Louis, Al?" Tom asked.

He shook his head; then it came back and he smiled. "I thought it sounded like a stupid place to go, and I was supposed to be smart. If they were looking for me for desertion, they wouldn't look there . . . some such process of unreasoning. What I didn't think about until much later was that I wasn't just an ordinary deserter . . . that they'd think I might have known some secrets. Funny; I don't. Not any more than any competent physicist. Or maybe a detail or two, nothing important.

"I bought some clothes in St. Louis. Gave my uniform to a guy in a colored bar who said his wife could dye it. Since then I've been . . . Al, Al Barker, the wandering gentile, I guess."

"Al, I don't think I understand," Finn said. "Were you . . . disloyal?"

"To my very bones," Al said. "Not as a spy or a communist. But I had hoped and conspired, as scientists used to do, to overthrow governments by force, the force of reason. I was loyal to science, and it was a higher loyalty than loyalty to country. A scientist didn't work for his country, I thought; he worked for knowledge. I once thought . . . I thought a scientist worked for knowledge as an artist works for art. But the artist's goal was partly individual; he worked for his art and for himself. And

242

the scientist worked . . . for knowledge and for the next man along.

"When I saw what happened when science worked for nothing more than nationalities, I remember thinking: 'Science is dead, now,' and I had no loyalty left for anything."

"But . . . your wife and family?" Nickie asked.

"Think what I'd helped to turn the world into for them."

"Did you just . . . abandon them?"

"As long as I stayed and worked at the only work I knew, I was betraying them and all wives and all children," Al said.

"But hadn't you been happy?"

"Very happy."

"And have you been happy since?"

"Happy to have resigned?" Al asked. "Happy to be free of relationships, free of work, free of commitment, free of the things that make happiness?" He shook his head. "Happiness was something I neither wanted nor deserved," he said.

"You don't want it?"

"Nickie, Nickie," Al said. "Where on earth did we ever get this petty notion that happiness is any kind of fit goal for a grown man's life?"

"And . . . you don't think much of love, either?" she asked, looking unhappily down at her bright black shoes, the hem of the sparkling dress raised above her slender ankles.

"I think a great deal of love, Nickie," Al said, standing up. "Not as a goal of living, perhaps, but as everything else but. I believe in love and I believe in hate. And if I believed in God, I would pray never to know either one of them again."

"Again? Are you in love now?" Nickie asked, raising her eyes to him.

"Of course, Nickie. Who could help but be? Sit still. Don't get up. Though it's a worthless gift, you must have what you seem to want for Christmas, too, Nickie, and so I hereby, in the presence of witnesses, declare you to be my last remaining love."

"Al." She started to rise.

"I love you, Nickie. I've said it now; it's yours. Don't answer me. It's not as fine a present as you deserve, not the big love kit with kisses and songs and fun, but it's the best model I can afford. And now perhaps it would be good for you to take it home, because I had to charge it and my funds are pretty low."

Now she was standing. "But . . . you really meant it, Al?"

"Of course."

She moved closer to him. "Will you kiss me before I go?"

He took her hands. "I'm afraid a kiss could be the kind of trigger that would shoot us both to Mexico," he said. "Let's make it Merry Christmas, Nickie."

A tear sparkled briefly in a corner of one eye and then rolled rather quickly down her cheek. "All right. Merry Christmas, Al." Then: "The first time you saw me I was sick. The last I'm crying. Don't think of me as a mess."

"My dear," Al said. "I shall try, very earnestly, not to think of you at all. And, after a year or so, I'll succeed."

Nickie turned to go. Tom moved after her uncertainly.

"See her to the car," Al said. "And then make that phone call."

"I don't want to do it, Al," Tom said.

"Please do it for me, Athlete," Al said. "And don't forget to say Hub Finn is holding me."

"All right. I'm coming back, though." And Tom followed Nickie out.

In Dolly Klamath's immaculate, two-room apartment, Santa Claus was dead.

Dolly had hustled Evans out, into a cab, out of the hubbub of the store and home with her. She might have taken him to his own room but she thought he would probably need nursing and she had, in the bathroom at home, a cabinet full of hospital supplies. If a doctor should be needed, he could quite conveniently be called to Dolly's place.

Dazed, the old man had allowed her to push him along, wordlessly, into the elevator, down to the main floor, out the entrance. He had sat in the cab loosely, his blue eyes quite vacant and his head lolled back. Only the costume, the beard, the pasted-on white eyebrows, seemed alive; the man beneath them was missing; she could barely hear him breathe.

At her apartment house, the doorman helped her get Evans upstairs and stretch him on the couch. When the man had gone, Dolly partially undressed Evans, loosening the red tunic, pulling off the shiny boots, stripping him efficiently to his underwear. He was in pretty bad shape, she judged; the heart was erratic and weak. She considered whether to call a doctor. She must act now for the store, perhaps for the final time. If he dies now, she thought, or on Christmas day, it will make the newspaper stories that much worse. But if he dies the day after Christmas, the wretched old hulk won't be Mainways' Santa Claus; he'll simply be an out-of-work actor, involved in some sort of drunken carelessness, and dead in spite of the best efforts of a responsible person from the store. She wondered if the whole thing couldn't, if she did her part, be kept private—the mother settled with quietly, the child calmed, Santa out of sight. It really was the last thing she would do for the store, and she would do it well; even if he should die in spite of her care, she thought, covering him with a blanket, no one could know of it until after Christmas, for she would guard the body herself, braving it out for twenty-four hours if necessary, keeping them all away.

She went downstairs and gave the doorman a ten dollar bill.

"Poor Santa gave out, did he?" the man asked.

"He's quite all right," Dolly said coldly.

"Hope it won't keep you from going out tonight," the man said. "I mean it being Christmas eve and all . . ." His affability diminished under her stare. "I mean I thought the gentleman who came to see you last week, that Mr. Barker, he seemed . . . very nice . . ."

"Forget about any gentleman coming to see me. And forget about Santa Claus," Dolly said, handing him the bill. "Please forget all about it. Do you understand?"

"You mean in case anybody . . .?"

"Oh, don't be so stupid," Dolly said. "Have you been drinking? Aren't you supposed to be wearing a cap?"

She turned angrily away.

"I didn't mean no harm, ma'am," the man called after her. "Merry Christmas. He was a nice fella . . ."

She didn't reply.

She rode upstairs again, and locked herself in with Santa Claus. The doorman worried her a little. She didn't want him saying that Evans was sick when they'd brought him up. But then, if the doorman had been drinking, perhaps he wouldn't remember very well; she realized he'd be disappearing into a bar, soon enough; there wouldn't then be anyone on duty to know what had gone on Christmas Eve. And why, indeed, should she suppose that questions would be asked?

She wasn't hungry, but she went into the kitchen and ate some olives. Then she went into the bedroom and put on her nurse's uniform.

In the other room, she heard the old man groan. She went in to him.

"Lie still," she said. "Close your eyes. You're to rest." She tucked the blanket under him tightly, to prevent his moving his arms. Then she watched him for half an hour; he seemed to be more or less asleep.

After a time she went back to the bedroom and started examining her clothes.

The old man hung on for three more hours. Then the phone rang. The sudden bell alarmed them both.

Dolly ran in from the bedroom, feeling obscurely as if she'd been caught at something. It was as if the bell signaled the springing of some sort of trap.

As she arrived, she saw the old body, also responding, heave itself towards the sound. She ran to the couch, placed her hands flat on the chest, and leaned with all her weight, "Don't," she said. "Don't."

The awful bell rang again. Under her hands the body gave a second great heave, and rolled at her; she sprang away from it.

The bell rang.

Thrashing, Evans' body hit the floor. She clutched her neck. "Stop it," she whispered, afraid to touch it. Then she yelled: "Stop. Be quiet. How can I answer?"

The bell rang. The arms flung about, the legs, the mouth began to groan.

"Oh, stop, stop . . ." She took a step towards the body. If the bell rang again she would scream. She kicked out her foot, full strength, at the chest above the heart, feeling the sharp toe of her shoe move between ribs. Abruptly, the thrashing stopped.

The bell rang. She sobbed.

Now, controlling herself somehow, she picked it up. It was an elf, inquiring for Evans.

"Santa Claus is perfectly fine, Zinnia," she managed to say; then, as the elf pressed her, she exploded: "You just keep your little fingers away from the dial, Zinnia. Every time this phone bell rings it disturbs him. If you want to help Santa Claus, you'd better not try calling here again. You can find out from the store . . ." All this feeling certain that the old man was dead.

She hung up and knelt by the body. It was hardly necessary to feel for the pulse, but she did. Then she screamed.

Hearing the dreadful sound she made restored her for a moment, and she stood up quickly. She pushed the heels of her hands into her eyes, and said to herself: "Pan of milk, pan of milk, pan of milk . . ." Then she ran to the telephone, keeping her back to Santa Claus' body, and picked up the receiver.

"I want to call Al," she said aloud, but not into the instrument. It took a minute for her to realize that she had no number for him.

She dialed *Information.*

"I want the number for Al Barker," she told the girl.

"Do you have an address?"

"No."

"There might be several names like that, honey . . . just a moment," the girl said. Then: "You're in luck. I have an Alfred C. Barker, Dairy Products—would you care to write the number down?"

"That's not the one," Dolly said, tensely. "This . . . this might be a new listing. It's just a man, not a dairy . . ."

"Just a man?" the operator said, chuckling. "Christmas Eve date? We'll find him . . ."

Dolly didn't answer.

"Gee, I'm sorry, I haven't got any Al Barker."

"You've got to have," Dolly said. "You've got to have."

"What tough luck," the girl said. "On Christmas. He stand you up?"

"No," Dolly said, hearing her voice go up half an octave. "No. Not at all. Why, I think that's him at the door now. Yes, it must be. Yes. Thank you anyway . . . don't bother looking . . ."

"Merry Christmas, then," the girl was saying. "Merry Christmas," but Dolly had laid down the receiver. She ran to the front **door.**

"Wait," she cried gaily, through the silent door. "You can't come in yet."

Then she ran to the bedroom. Singing a little song, suddenly remembered from her girlhood, she threw open the closet door. She seized the taffeta dress from the hanger, and whirled around the room with it. Then she stripped off all her clothes, and, for the first time, pulled it over her head. For a moment, the silk was cool and exciting on her flushed and naked skin, then it began to chill her.

She ran to the bathroom. There was a label, *Strychnine,* in the medicine cabinet, a packet she had taken from the hospital years before. From the secret place in the laundry basket, where she had hidden them from herself, she took a nursing bottle and a little box with new nipples in it.

Still singing, but more quietly, she crossed through the living room, her eyes raised to the spotless white ceiling, and went into the kitchen. She heated milk in a pan at the stove, and added the poison to it. With the tip of her finger, and the tip of her tongue, she tasted it; it was bitter. She added quite a lot of sugar.

When it was warm she filled the bottle and put the nipple on it. Then she returned to the living room. She let herself down on the floor beside Santa Claus, pressing her bare back against him, putting the great arms around herself, curling her legs into her stomach, covered herself with a blanket, and began, contentedly, to suckle.

Tom returned.. "They'll be here in a few minutes," he said. Al smiled at him.

"It's . . . Christmas now," Tom said.

"Good," said Al. "Have you heard all you want to hear?"

Tom hesitated. Then: "What . . . what kept you going, Al? Why didn't you stop before? Why are you really stopping now?"

"What kept me going?" Al asked. "I think I know now. Think about me that morning by the radio, Tom. Can you imagine what it was I had to run from?"

There was a pause. Then, suddenly, Tom said in a slightly shocked voice: "You were glad."

Al nodded. "That's it. Just for a fraction of a second. As one is secretly, shamefully gladdened for the first instant when the news comes that war has started. For an instant, there, I was glad, before desolation set in; for an instant, I felt myself in exultation, willing the death of the world." He sat down. "I hadn't let myself remember till tonight," he said. "About why I'm stopping finally, Tom, I don't believe I know yet. Let's both think about that."

Finn was nervous. "Those Federal men and cops, I hope they won't be rough," he said.

"Why should they?" Al asked, smiling. "They're getting what they want for Christmas, too."

"And you'll be in jail."

"Sure, for a while," Al said, feeling a kind of confidence he hadn't felt in years, as he set himself to talk away the older man's fears. "What's there to worry about, Hub? Simple desertion isn't much. And the toy rap for Sally . . . what can that amount to? It isn't as if there were rapes and murders going on. There are no bizarre circumstances to make this routine deserter, this petty thief, more interesting. And as long as we can meet M'nerney on the assault story, with Dolly and Santa Claus to back us up, nothing much has happened, has it?"

"Sure," Finn said. "You're right, Al. You've got everything under control, and it's Christmas at last."

Al sighed. "Maybe I can even see my kids when I get out. It won't be bad to sit quietly in jail, out of sight for a year, Hub, will it? If the bomb still hasn't fallen, I can even imagine I might want to come out and make some other kind of try."

"I wish you believed in God," Finn said.

"I wish I did."

"I wish you'd gone with Nickie," Tom said.

"That would have been a great romantic example to set you, Athlete. Come on. Let's wait for them out front."

It was ten past twelve. He led the way into the hall, and out the front door of the building. They stood together on the stoop.

"That big Christmas tree on Union Square," Al said. "I thought maybe we could see the lights from here."

And so he was caught at last. He had tried to run and, weary of running, rested; and resting, been unable to reject forever and ended by accepting them all: his love for Nickie, his pity for

249

Finn, his responsibility to Tom, his fascination and compassion for the horror of Dolly, the impulse to oppose M'nerney—the need to take his stand. These things had held him, involved him, chased and trapped him, deprived him of his freedom to live alone with guilt—the hound of earth had caught him. No man, no matter what his time, his country, his condition, training, heredity or philosophy, forever escapes that hound, his own humanity.

Together the three stood at the top of the steps, gazing into the blue and frostless California night.

"*Sursum corda*," Al said, not quite drily. After that they stood quietly, listening and looking.

Listening for sirens, and the footsteps of policemen. Looking for what?

An enemy plane? A brighter than ordinary star? Perhaps. Or perhaps, shoppers among the soiled goods in the eternal clearance sale of the world, just looking.

A Note about the Author

Vance Bourjaily turned to nonfiction for the first time in his most recent book, *The Unnatural Enemy* (1963). Mr. Bourjaily's novels are *The End of My Life* (1947), *The Hound of Earth* (1955), *The Violated* (1958) and *Confessions of a Spent Youth* (1960). For the past several years, Mr. Bourjaily has been associated with The Writers' Workshop at The State University of Iowa in Iowa City.

79
83
85
89